EFFORTLESS
with
YOU

EFFORTLESS
with
YOU

A NOVEL
LIZZY CHARLES

Effortless With You by Lizzy Charles
Summary: The story of a girl who desperately needs an attitude adjustment, and the boy who gives it to her.

Editor: Mandy Schoen
Publisher: Swoon Romance YA
Cover designer: Victoria Faye

How to Date a Nerd sample copyright © Cassie Mae
The Funeral Singer sample copyright © Linda Budzinkski

ISBN 978-0615876252

Praise for

EFFORTLESS *with* YOU

"A definite MUST READ! *Effortless With You* left me smiling like a doofus and hugging my Kindle." – Cassie Mae, bestselling author of *Reasons I Fell For the Funny Fat Friend*

"Every emotion in *Effortless With You* was beautifully crafted ... the chemistry palpable. Even hours after reading, I'm still swooning. Fantastic debut!" – Theresa Paolo, author of *(Never) Again.*

"Lizzy Charles does an exceptional job pulling the reader in and making them feel what Lucy is feeling. She knows how to make a sixteen year old girl believable. Reminding you of your teenage years. I cannot praise or recommend this book enough." – Sub Club Books, 5 star review

"*Effortless With You* is a flirty yet deep romance filled with great comedy, tough struggles, and an ending that is sure to warm your heart!" – The YA Bookworm, 5 star review

"It will leave you breathless and craving more." – Le Book Squirrel, 5 star review

To my mother and daughters.

CHAPTER ONE

I can't resist the water's temptation after a sticky hour of tanning under the scorching sun. I slip into the empty pool and sink to its bottom. The water's cool thrill rolls through my hair. Misshaped forms blur along the pool's edge, feet dangling in the pool. Large bubbles escape my lips. I watch them float to the surface before I follow.

It's surreal to be here, hanging out without fear of attack.

I dunk my head in the water one last time, pulling my towel around my shoulders. I'm almost comfortable in a bikini, but don't want people thinking I'm trying to put myself out there. Snatching a magazine from my bag, I stretch out on my lounger. Fitting in with Marissa's pool routine is easy.

Marissa stretches out next to me, one leg long, the other bent up. This is her new tanning pose that makes her belly look flatter. I can't really tell the difference, and she's a size two anyway. She flips her blond hair and casually adjusts her top. A hot guy must be approaching.

I peer over *Cosmo*. Correction. It is *the* guy.

Justin Marshall.

Justin pulls his hands through his dark hair with a smile. He laughs, rubbing his chiseled jawline with its always-there, five o'clock shadow. He's every girl's dream. Well, every girl but me.

Everyone stops Justin on his way around the pool. Guys hold up high fives and girls offer giggling waves. It takes him over five minutes to walk forty feet. It looks like a nightmare to me, but he certainly seems to enjoy it. He deals with everyone like a prince, flashing his white smile and chuckling. He pulls his hands through his hair again, an obvious maneuver to make his shoulder muscles pop.

He's totally into himself. That much is clear.

I try to hide my sour expression as Justin nears. Marissa will kill me if I scare him away. I duck behind my magazine. Although I hate his ego, I'm not immune to his washboard abs. I refuse to let my lingering eyes betray me.

"Justin, hey!" Marissa calls as she tosses her bangs out of her eyes. "How's your dad's campaign going? It's going to be such a gift to Minnesota when he's our governor."

Eww. A little too much sugar on that, Marissa.

"Yeah, that's the hope." Justin's signature chuckle rolls from his lips.

Marissa giggles. "So, are you going to Watson's party tonight?"

His hand returns to his head, fingers tracing through his hair, creating the perfect tousle of curls. God, he just can't get enough. He leans in, placing his foot onto her lounger. "Hmm, well, it's the place to be tonight, right?" He offers a crooked smile, pouring charm all over her.

"Of course it is. I'll be there," Marissa says in a low, sultry voice. She sucks in her stomach, leaning toward him with perfectly batted eyelashes. She's skipped to stage three of flirting. We developed the stages this year over winter break while I crashed at her place. There's no way I could spend that much time at home.

"Well then, you can count me in." Justin nods at me and I return it slightly as I focus on the magazine's wrinkled water stains. Move on, dude.

A laugh escapes him as he pulls his leg off of Marissa's lounger, strutting to his next group of admirers.

Good. Be gone.

Marissa squeals to herself and I hold in my sigh. I feel a bit sorry for her. Justin going to the party has nothing to do with her being there. He's already dating the most perfect girl in school. Not that that matters to Marissa. If anything, it encourages her.

Justin climbs up the back of the lifeguard stand, planting a kiss on the cheek of a beautiful blond. She laughs as she pretends to shove him off before she climbs down. He steps aside as her replacement climbs up, wrapping his hand around the blond's before finding a table in the shade. "Ugh. What does he see in Jennifer?" Marissa turns over to her stomach, pulling her sunglasses down, watching Justin and Jennifer. Jennifer rises as he tilts his head down. Their foreheads touch and then they exchange a brief kiss.

"Well, she's the student body president. And there's that whole head-cheerleader thing …" Sarcasm is safer than honesty.

"But that's not enough to keep a guy going for a whole year. They just don't seem right together, you know?"

Jennifer tilts her head back as Justin launches a grape into her mouth. Marissa's right. They don't seem right. They're perfect.

"Gag me now." Marissa pinches my leg, demanding my attention. "She acts like she owns him. He needs someone less controlling, less high maintenance."

"Like?" I tease. Marissa claims they kissed once, back in middle school. But I can't picture them in a dark closet together. Doesn't compute.

"Me, of course." She answers too seriously. "This summer, I'm going to show Justin just how much he's missing. Come August, he's mine."

I cringe. Marissa always gets what she wants.

Justin wraps his arms around Jennifer in a bear hug.

My heart twists. Whatever plan Marissa has concocted is sure to ruin them. But really, should I care?

I plaster a smile on my face. "You two would be great together." Exactly what she wants to hear. I owe her at least that much.

Marissa saved me from social suicide. She fixed everything for me, from teaching me how to make a ponytail fancy with an extra bump to strict instruction on eyebrow shaping.

"Lucy, Lucy!" Marissa pulls the magazine out from under my nose. "I'm gonna wear my new capris with that cute canary tunic. You wear that green sundress I picked out for you. That way we can coordinate in all the photos." She opens her hobo bag and pulls out her Nikon, taking a quick shot of me before I can protest. Then she hands the camera over. I click away as she pushes out her lips for the shot.

The green sundress? I wasn't totally in love with the puke color but Marissa insisted it settled perfectly over my hips and butt. Marissa's a fashion expert. She pulled me out of the janitor's closet last year. It was easier to eat lunch there than have food thrown at me in the cafeteria. And safer. The seniors never found me there. But Marissa did. She turned my life around. I trusted her. I still do. With Marissa, people actually talk to me. They have no idea I was *that freshman girl* the seniors hated. I could breathe again.

"You know that green dress will drive Zach totally wild. It makes your butt look hot!"

My stomach flutters and my lips curl into a goofy grin. Zach. My new boyfriend. Okay, true. I'll totally wear the dress.

Zach's an outgoing, uncomplicated jock who's an amazing kisser. My stomach's still doing flips after my first kiss and however many more we fit in during the last forty-three minutes of the new *Scarn* movie. The smell of his cologne clings to my shirt at home. I can't bring myself to wash it.

Marissa pokes me, "Oh, sweet. His name makes you blush."

A super girly giggle escapes my lips. "Did I tell you we're going to dinner before the party?" I try to sound mature as I check my phone. Almost time to get ready.

Marissa squeals. "No! Oh my God. How could you

keep this from me? Where are you going? What will you talk about?"

"Romano's." Zach loves Italian.

"Oh, perfect. Sit in the back corner. That's where the most romantic lighting is."

I nod, imagining Zach and me in the *Lady and the Tramp* spaghetti scene as I grab my bag from under my lounger.

"Where're ya going?" she asks, rechecking the time on her phone.

"He's picking me up here. I'm getting ready in the locker room."

Marissa nods, picking up on my subtext. "Good plan. Avoid your mom. God that must be so tough …"

I bite the inside of my cheek. The day Mom met Zach she took him on a tour of her therapy garden where she educated him in the art of compost. She actually put garbage and worms in his hands. When we left, he didn't waste any time saying "Your mom's a freak." I can't argue with that.

"Hold on a sec." Marissa opens her bag, digging around and pulling out her new Coach clutch. She empties the contents and tosses me the clutch. "You've got to use this. It needs to go on a hot date."

"Thanks. This will be awesome." I lean down and give her a hug. Sweet!

"No problem. This is actually great. Now I have time to set my hair in curlers before the party. Tonight's going to be amazing." She stands and glances at Justin, lifting her eyebrows mischievously. "Watch out, Justin Marshall. Here I come."

I say nothing. She waves her hands while pushing me forward. "Get moving, woman. We've got men to impress.

See you tonight," she says in a cute voice that carries well over water. She walks with a precise sway, a light bounce which sets every part of her bikini into hypnotic motion. Guys' heads follow her the entire way.

Marissa, a master in the art of attraction.

***

The country club's locker room makes me nervous. I shimmy off the wet-suit bottoms over my hips. My hand automatically avoids the dark purple scar that rests below. The locker handles mock me. It's like they share secrets with the gym ones back at school. I was never safe after basketball practice.

I slip on some blue lace underwear and take my time getting ready, avoiding the locker handles with each move. I focus on adhering to Marissa's sparkle makeup advice as I think about Zach's biceps and his laugh. My tummy flips and I feel queasy, but I've heard that's normal for a first, fancy dinner date. Right? Right.

I fight to get into my skin-tight dark jeans, which I pair with a white, racer back tank with random clear sequin embellishments. The color pop? My red, open-toed heels. God bless Marissa for making me buy them.

My fingers twirl my auburn hair. Hopefully, it'll dry in waves. I tug on my tank top, adjusting it over my curves. My shape's not perfect but, like Marissa says, I have "something to work with."

With the right jeans, my butt's not awful but my boobs are too big. I hate them. Marissa's certain I'd look thinner without them. She convinced me to ask my parents for a breast reduction as a sweet-sixteen present. Mom nearly died when I asked. In fact, she yelled so much I thought she would.

I shake my head, trying to rid myself of the memory. That was not a fun fight. Mom will never understand that being curvy is no longer fashionable. Instead, she rants about culture and societal flaws. When I asked about the reduction, she started in on the MTV Music Awards and I foolishly rolled my eyes. All of my magazines ended up in the fireplace that night. They were "poisoning my body image." So I rebelled, buying three-year subscriptions of *People* and *US Weekly*.

Take that, Mom.

I adjust my jeans and add a black belt, hoping Zach will like it. My cell phone flashes five past six. Fashionably five minutes late, as recommended in the latest *Elle* magazine. The Minnesota humidity makes my hair frizz the moment I step out of the locker room. Why do I even try? I search for Zach's truck, hoping he won't notice my funky hair.

But it's not there. He must be caught in traffic. I sit on the bench and wait.

And I wait.

A long time.

My cell displays six thirty-seven. Maybe work is keeping him? The Fireside Bowling Alley often has a dinner rush. I check my phone, but no calls. I text him.

Me: I'm sure Fireside is busy. Take your time.

I really can wait. I have nowhere to go until the party.

I close my eyes and tilt my head back, enjoying the cooler evening sun on my face and praying it will calm my frizz. I hold my cell, waiting for it to vibrate with his response. As the minutes pass, I toy with the idea that maybe he forgot …

But he planned this. He wouldn't do that.

A light laugh interrupts me. My eyes jolt open and I gasp. I hate how easily I startle.

"Sorry, Lady," says a deep, smooth voice behind me. "I didn't mean to scare you. You just look so funny all dressed up but relaxing in the sun."

"Oh, it's okay." Great. I pull at the bottom of my white tank. I look funny.

He clears his throat, waiting for me to do the social thing. Interact.

Not in the mood. Not now. The dent in my phone demands study. If I turn the phone upside down, the dent looks like a cow. I shift, making sure my back faces the voice. Maybe the guy'll take a hint? My bench creaks with newly added weight.

Nope.

"So?" he says.

I force myself to glance up. My throat closes. Marissa would freak.

Justin stares back with that fake smile. "Who are you waiting for?"

"My boyfriend, Zach Filman." Confidence, yes.

Justin nods. "Oh, Zach." He looks at his watch and snickers. "I bet he's late, huh?" His eyebrow flicks up with his smile.

"No. I'm a bit early."

"You're lying." He moves closer to me.

Shaking my head, I focus on the lined pavement. The lines aren't parallel at all. I really suck at lying, but the most popular guy in school doesn't need to know my boyfriend's late.

"Well, then," he continues. "I'll just wait here with you. You don't mind."

I do.

He taps his finger on the bench's armrest. "Shouldn't be long now." His voice is thick with sarcasm which he pairs with his flashy, stupid smile. Justin may be gorgeous, but he is super annoying. He clears his throat. "Might as well get to know one another. I'm Justin Marshall."

No kidding.

"I'm Lucy." He doesn't need to know my last name.

"Well, Lucy." He pulls out his phone. "It's six fifty-two. When're you going on that date?"

"For real?" The heat from the sun must've fried my brain-to-mouth filter.

He claps his hands together, leaning back, enjoying my outburst. "Well, I'm bored. Jennifer doesn't get off for another twenty minutes. I need a little fun."

"Well, in that case, I'm pleased to entertain you." Sarcasm rolls thick off my tongue.

"Wonderful." His hands fold behind his head and his muscles twitch. But I'm steady, not a flinch and not even close to his regularly received swoon.

"So, where're you love birds going?" he continues.

"Romano's."

"Right, Italian food. How romantic. Very original, Zach."

Blood rushes to my face. I don't care if it is the typical place. This is my first fancy, romantic date and it's going to be perfect. I glare back, replying with silence.

"Okay, okay." He throws his hands up. "It's a good place. Great food, actually."

I ignore him, glancing back at my phone. An hour late. Maybe he got in an accident?

"Can I ask you two questions?" Justin prods.

"No." My filter's gone now. He's beyond irritating. Just because everyone worships him doesn't mean he gets to know everyone's business. Of course, he ignores my answer.

"First, why are you being picked up for a date here?"

I answer without thinking. "Zach thinks my mom's weird." My tongue thickens, making it hard to speak. Crap, shouldn't have said that.

"Oh? Should that matter if he's dating you? I mean, shouldn't he want to get to know her if he's dating you?"

He looks at me with a soft expression, like the ones people use on injured puppies on those emergency vet shows.

I press my lips together. He doesn't know my mom. This time he accepts my silence.

"Secondly, don't you think you deserve someone who respects you enough to either show up on time or at least call and let you know why he's late?"

Whoa, who is he to give me relationship advice?

"You've got to be kidding, right?"

"No. I'm dead serious. You deserve better."

"You don't even know me."

"No, but I know Zach."

"So do I. He's my boyfriend." I refuse to look at him, instead watching a group of ants pour out of a crack in the pavement. "You know you're a real jerk, right?" I add.

Justin lets out a long whistle. "Wow. I haven't been called a jerk since I was, like, eight?"

I don't care how hot he is. Why Marissa wants him blows my mind.

He pulls out his phone. "Let me show you something." He dials and flashes me his outgoing call: Zach F.

No. This is not happening.

I launch at his phone but he's too quick. He jumps off the bench and I eat pavement.

"It doesn't matter. He isn't going to answ—" I say as I scramble up off the ground.

"Hello?" a familiar voice booms. Speaker phone. Crap.

"Hey, Zach! It's Justin."

"Hey, man. What's up?" My gut relaxes. Zach's okay.

"Not much. Just waiting to pick up Jennifer." Justin paces, circling the bench and me.

"Right on, man!" Zach is always so positive. His attitude is contagious. I can't help but smile when I'm around him.

"What are you up to?"

"Disc golf with Tater."

My chest squeezes. How can Zach be playing a game with his cousin Tater? An I-Told-You-So expression sits in triumph on Justin's face.

Stupid face.

"Sweet. Awesome day for a game."

"I know, huh?"

Justin drags his shoe through some sand.

"Will I see you at the party tonight?"

"Hell, yeah!"

Maybe he didn't forget? He knows we're going to the party together. He must have gotten the times mixed up. Assumed he had time to play disc first.

"Sweet. I'll see you there. Got to run, Jen's done. We've got a great date night planned before the party and all …"

No, Justin, don't do this. I want to die.

"Oh shit, dude. I was supposed to pick up that Lucy chick for a date too." Zach laughs.

Three skipped heartbeats.

Zach forgot.

He forgot about me.

My nose begins to itch. Tears are inevitable. But I won't cry in front of Justin. I focus on my cuticles, trying to hold off tears while Zach's voice continues to boom from the phone. Justin finishes circling the bench, now standing next to me. So I can hear everything Zach says.

"Eh, she'll understand. It's a gorgeous day. I mean, who can remember a date when disc golf calls?"

"Well, good luck with that." Justin taps my shoulder. I want to break his fingers.

"Right on, man." *Beep.*

My eyes are heavy, probably now red and puffy too. I take a deep breath, trying to hold off the emotional impact of the moment. Justin's moved in front of me, waiting for my reaction. He's so rude. I glare daggers into his green eyes. Hate him.

My phone finally vibrates.

Zach: hey sorry work's crazy. Meet u at party L8R.

My gut twists inside out. Zach lied. He forgot about me and lied. Why did he ask me out if he didn't like me? I grab my bag. I need to get away from Justin before I break down.

"Let me guess," Justin says, "he lied?"

Prying ass.

13

A ruthless fire burns inside me, made especially for him.

"Can I ask you something?" I don't wait for an answer. "Why are you so unbearably rude?"

"Listen," he begins, "you deserved to know."

"No. That wasn't your place. Do you think you're like a god or something? 'You deserved to know.' Total bull. Don't I deserve to be treated with respect?" I pause for effect. His eyes widen and he opens his mouth to speak, but he doesn't have a word to deliver. "Right. You dish out Hallmark wisdom but don't follow it yourself. Don't be a hypocrite."

The tears are rolling down my cheeks but I don't care anymore. Now I want him to see it. Staring into his green eyes, I search to see if he understands what he's done. But his eyes are blank. Not even a hint of remorse. The pool gate jingles and Jennifer steps out. I quickly distance myself from the bench and start the walk of rejection back home.

I don't look back. I never want to see Justin Marshall again.

CHAPTER TWO

I am forgettable.

Of course I am. I'm not actually popular. At most, thanks to Marissa, I am someone who blends into the crowd. No. After that hellish year on the basketball court, I'm lucky to even be in the crowd. Of course Zach forgot about our date. Who can really blame him? He acts larger than life. Why would he remember a girl who barely has a life?

I fling myself onto my bed, pulling my purple pillow over my face. Marissa does a good job of helping me disguise my worthlessness but Zach saw through me, whether it was a conscious decision or not.

I am forgettable.

My phone vibrates.

Marissa: How's the hot date? Kissing yet?

My stomach falls through my feet. What do I tell her? I type "Didn't happen." No. Too pathetic. I delete it but my phone vibrates again.

Marissa: NM. Just texted Zach. Sucks about his work. Too bad.

Me: Yup. Oh well … next time.

Marissa: Yup, like tonight! See you L8R. Remember: green dress.

The party. I forgot. There's no way I'm going now. I can't fake happy around Marissa and Zach tonight. And, worse, pretend I have dignity around Justin. I reach under my bed and pull out a granola bar, a jar of peanut butter, and some crackers. My stash for when I want to avoid eating dinner with my family. I'd quit the family dinner when each meal became a lecture about "The choices you are making in life." It's nice to have Marissa to talk to. She totally understands how overbearing Mom is.

I dip a granola bar into the Skippy. There's no way I can stand being around Mom and Dad tonight. And even my little brother Eric, I can't handle my toes being obstacles in his car races. I've been through enough already.

Knock, knock. My door. I bang my head against the wall. "What?" I drag myself across the room to flip the lock, not even bothering to open the door for them.

Creak. Mom and Dad stand as an undivided front. Shit. They must've mailed the report cards a day early. This isn't going to be pretty. Faking indifference, I sit on my bed and gnaw on the granola bar. Mom and Dad file in, standing awkwardly in the middle of the room. I'd removed my desk chair when I realized it was an invitation to sit.

They've learned to stop trying to make themselves comfortable.

Dad starts the confrontation. "What is this?" He holds out my report card.

"Report card." I shrug.

"No." Mom takes the report card and hands it to me. "What is this?"

"An A, two B's, and three C's. So what?"

"C's?" Mom stares back at me, her face red.

"Yes, C's." I dip the granola bar back in the Skippy. "No big deal, Mom. C's get degrees."

Mom grabs a stack of papers off the top of the desk. The drawers are askew, not the way I'd left them. "Lucinda, this C will never get you a degree. What happened to your beautiful writing?" She tosses me the paper. My final *Pride and Prejudice* essay glares back at me with a large "C-" circled in the upper-right corner.

"It was a boring novel." Not true; I didn't read it. "Lots of students get C's."

"Lucy," Dad's voice is lower than normal, "if you got these C's by studying and doing your best—"

Mom interrupts. "You didn't even try. You always have a choice to try."

"—then we would be proud of a C. But you didn't," Dad finishes.

"Great. So you aren't proud of your own daughter? Wow, I've got amazing parents." I love twisting their words around.

Dad sucks in his breath. "No. That's not what I said."

Mom plops down on my bed, her voice more controlled. "What he's saying is last semester you got all

A's and one B. You've never had a C in your life. You can't expect us to believe that suddenly the academic standards have risen."

For real? They're so unrealistic. Some things are more important than grades. Like friends.

"We assumed your homework was done when we didn't see you doing it," says Dad. "That was our mistake."

"The old Lucy would have finished it." Mom says softly, almost talking to herself … *The old Lucy.* It's not like I disappeared or something.

"I tried." I tried hard to fit what homework I could into my busy schedule with Marissa.

"Lucy, this is unacceptable." Dad's voice is as calm as mine. It's creepy.

"First you quit basketball and now you're slacking in school. What's happening to you?" Mom's voice hits those horrid high notes. An occasional sob sneaks in.

"Mom, you promised never to mention basketball again. Why would you do that? Are you trying to make this worse?"

"No, honey. I just know basketball makes you happy."

"No, it doesn't. Trust me."

She had no idea what I'd been through. What those jealous seniors did to me because I took a starting position on the team as a freshman. Nothing was worth putting up with their torture on and off the court. Not even something I loved. I never told Mom or Dad what was going on because they were so proud. Their freshman daughter, lead point guard and All State Champion. Mom would've gone ballistic if she knew all the lockers I'd been slammed into or heard the names they got everyone in school to call me.

No, I couldn't have told her. I couldn't risk her snapping and slipping away again, back into her world of depression. It wasn't worth it then and certainly isn't worth it now.

Mom reaches out for me, but I refuse her touch. "That's not true, Lucy. Think of the years you spent dragging your father out to the hoop. And then you hit your sophomore year and suddenly quit? How can I just let that go?" Mom buries her head on Dad's shoulder.

"Okay," Dad puts his hands between us, "we've had this argument too many times already. We aren't going to figure this out tonight. Lucy, you're grounded until we figure out what to do with you."

Crap.

"What? No way. Not tonight. It's Watson's party, *the party*. I need to be there!" Why am I saying this? I don't want to go at all.

"I'm sorry. You did this to yourself. You won't be going." Dad rests his hand on Mom's back, leading her from the room. Mom just shakes her head.

I wait for them to start down the stairs before I slam the door shut, the crack above my door inching a bit deeper. Boom, the vents in the house shake. Mom and Dad don't know who I am, who I'm not and what I've been through. I text Marissa.

Me: Got grounded. Report card.

My phone rings immediately. "What? You've got to be kidding me. You did explain it was Watson's party, right?"

"It's useless. Bad report card," I mutter.

"Oh please. They're archaic. My report card came today too. My parents just say try harder next time. No big deal."

"I know."

"Well, you're going to this party, whether they like it or not." She pauses for a moment. "Sneak out. Seriously. They'll never know. Sneak out around ten while they watch the news. Put that great tree by your window to use." Marissa loves the oak tree by my window; the perfect escape route or boyfriend entrance. Not that it's any use to me now.

"I don't know." If my parents find out, I'll be doomed to live the life of an imprisoned princess. But unlike an animated princess, no prince will waste his time rescuing me.

"They won't even know. I'll help you sneak back in by midnight. You did say they were night owls, right? They'd never suspect you sneaking out while they're awake."

She has a point. Most kids sneak out while their parents sleep. My parents never check on me before they go to bed anymore. I'd bite their heads off if they did. My pulse quickens. This may actually work.

But, wait. Did I want to go to the party?

I scan my blank walls where basketball posters used to hang. My shelves are clean of trophies now too. Nothing remains. My own solitary confinement. The party holds better prospects.

"Alright, I'm in."

Marissa squeals and her words shift into a higher gear. "Yes! This is so exciting. I'm jealous; I wish my parents were lame so I could sneak out sometimes. I can't wait! I'll pick you up at the gas station down the block from your place. Five minutes past ten."

"I'll be there." Lucy, secret agent.

Marissa drops her voice. "And Lucy, don't be late."

***

I hate heights.

My hands tremble as I sit on the ledge of the open window, the humidity of the summer night pouring in. The tree limbs look much thinner and the ground much farther away than ever before. My legs dangle and then rest on the tree branch below, my feet exploring its thickness. I grab the branch above and pull up, lifting my weight off the window ledge.

My wrists strain as my toes struggle to guide me along the lower branch to the trunk. Closing my eyes, I steady my breathing, like I'm going to shoot a free throw. I keep my eyes closed, allowing my hands and feet to guide the way.

Snap.

My eyes fly open and I lunge forward, grabbing the trunk as the branch above gives way. I hug the trunk tight, getting scraped on the arm as the branch plunges to the ground. I hold my breath.

There's no way Mom and Dad missed that.

The living-room window opens and Dad's head pops out. Light filters out of the window over the grass below. Thankfully, it doesn't shine up. Dad scans the ground and glances up the tree. I hold completely still, smashing myself against the trunk. Let this puke green dress be enough camouflage, please.

"Yup. Must've been that raccoon again, Sarah. There is a nice-sized branch down." His head disappears inside the window for a moment, then pops back out, surveying the yard. "Nope. You're right, Sarah, time to buy a trap."

I let out a sigh of relief. I can't believe he didn't see me.

He closes the window and the living-room light disappears behind the shade.

I exhale slowly. Holy crap, that was close. My eyes take some time readjusting to the thickening darkness. Testing each branch, I navigate down the tree. My fingers struggle for hold on the flaking bark. I jump, landing hard on my feet. The impact vibrates up my legs. I bite my lip hard, holding in a yelp of pain.

This party better be worth it. But anything's better than here, right?

CHAPTER THREE

Watson's enormous brick house is surreal. The landscaping is gorgeous. Mom would spend hours here examining the gardening that frames Watson's brick mansion. A small lit archway stands before a brick path, bordered with small garden lights. As we walk down the pathway and to the backyard, my mind refocuses on Zach and Justin. The brief exhilaration of sneaking out distracted me from my worthlessness.

What should I say to Zach? Call him out? No, it wouldn't be worth it. I'll stick with avoidance. He didn't want to see me anyway. And Justin? Well, hopefully he's had enough fun for today.

White-uniformed servers effortlessly maneuver through the packed crowd on the dance floor while DJ Rain spins music in a booth near a brightly lit tiki bar. Pink and green lights highlight the edge of an eclipse pool disguised as a pond with large boulders. People shout at one another over the music.

Marissa doesn't seem fazed at all. She walks right into the crowd, grabbing a glass of pop off a waiter's tray, as well as some sushi-roll thing. She looks back at me, urging me to follow. I catch up to her and she hands me her camera. "Are you ready for phase one of project M and J?" *Crap.* It never occurred to me that I would be involved in this scheme.

I follow her over to the tiki bar where she tosses her pop in a bush and asks for a frozen daiquiri. She takes a sip. "This is good." She leans in, winking at the cute blue-eyed bartender. "It'd be better with some rum though, just like at home. But it's still good."

Marissa turns around, flips her blond hair and leans casually against the bar. She scans the crowd. I know she's looking for Justin. My palms grow sweaty, hoping whatever part I have in this plan involves distance.

"Now, Lucy." She sounds like an elementary-school teacher. "When Justin comes over, I want you to take some photos of us. Pretend you're me, grabbing some lifestyle moments." She waits for me to nod before continuing. "I'll wink at you when I think the shots are right and what I'm looking for. Once you take the pictures, you can go find your Zach and have a nice time." She pats me on my back before she turns back to the bartender. I feel like a dog. I ignore the pat.

Instead I focus on Justin. I don't want to see him even more than I don't want to see Zach. Zach had forgotten but Justin was knowingly cruel. What if he mentions our conversation to Marissa? She'll be furious I didn't tell her we talked. I turn the camera back and forth in my hand, playing with the dials. There's no way he'll pass up the chance to share.

"Justin, come over here," Marissa calls. I take a slow, deep breath. "I've got something to ask you." Marissa's hair stings my cheek as she flips it over her shoulder. She giggles. Her game is on.

"Marissa." Justin sounds unenthused but she doesn't seem to notice. Marissa leans in and gives him a long hug. Justin pats her back a bit before distancing himself. He asks the bartender for a bottle of water before turning his attention back to Marissa. "What's up?"

"What do you think of new uniforms for the basketball team? I've got an *in* with Midwest Jersey through my uncle and he told me he has a great new design you'd love." She lightly brushes his arm. When he looks down at his arm, she kicks her leg back, jamming me in the calf. Photo time. My calf throbs where her stiletto jabbed me. That'll bruise.

I take a deep breath. I can't believe I have to face Justin so soon. Time to harness my loathing energy and turn it into fake energy. Spinning around, I pop the camera up to my face and step out in front of them. Justin looks too perfect in a white Batman shirt and dark jeans, hair curling in the humidity. But his teeth do glow stupidly in the black lights. I'll focus on that.

"Hi, guys." I say in the most chipper voice I can find. Justin locks eyes with me. I immediately shift my focus to the led screen. "Do you mind if I take some photos while you talk? It's for a summer photography project."

"Oh, sure. Whatever." Marissa rolls her eyes at Justin. Great, now I'm even lamer. She turns back to him, talking more about new basketball jerseys. Justin lifts his right eyebrow at me. He shrugs, turning back to Marissa as she demands his attention. He seems indifferent.

He doesn't even care about this afternoon. No remorse.

I click away. Marissa's taught me to stand on my tiptoes to get a downward angle so she doesn't end up with a double chin. Whenever Marissa winks, I push the button. She leans in, whispering something in his ear. He pulls back gently, laughing. Another wink and I shoot as she turns her body, making it look like Justin is cornering her into the bar. She leans in again briefly for the photo. I have to hand it to Marissa; she's good.

Marissa looks back at me. "So, are you done yet? We're having a real conversation here."

"Yup. Thanks for helping me out."

She waves me off in response. Further proof of my loser status. I cringe. Marissa can be a bit clueless how she treats me sometimes. Once she gets her mind set, she'll always play the game to come out on top. I should expect it by now. I know she doesn't mean to make me feel like dirt. But I can handle it. It's way better than being called a dumpster slut. Marissa's easy to handle compared to my past.

Marissa's enormous camera stretches my purse. Disappearing into the crowd, I'm relieved yet oddly unsatisfied with my encounter with Justin. I have more to say to him.

No, I have more to yell at him.

The intensity of my emotions surprises and scares me. I'm usually able to keep my thoughts from turning into words, screening them from the real world. No one breeches this wall except Mom and, occasionally, Dad.

Proof Justin's an invasive nightmare.

Everyone else bows at his feet. I just want to stomp on them.

As I push my way through the crowd, ironically, I become more aware I'm alone. I can't remember the last time I walked around a party without Marissa at my side. Free, I look around, deciding what to do.

Too bad I don't want to do anything at all.

Scanning the crowd, I spot Zach playing volleyball in the pool. That eliminates that activity. There is a bench slightly off the dance floor. I can pull off sitting there, a dance break.

I pull out the camera, viewing the shots. Marissa's practice posing sessions have really paid off. It looks like Justin is hitting on Marissa. One shot even looks like Justin was leaning in for a kiss, pinning Marissa against the bar.

She is an evil genius.

I scan through, deleting a few of the unflattering jaw shots of Marissa. One photo stops me. Marissa stares at Justin, her hand on his shoulder and another playing with her hair. Justin doesn't notice her, his green eyes focus on the camera. Were they pleading? I delete it. Weird camera angle.

"How'd they turn out?" I jerk. That voice has become too familiar.

"Really, come back for more?" I gaze up, determined to face him.

Justin smiles. How can this be fun for him? My pulse quickens. I want to punch him.

He sits next to me, snatching Marissa's camera out of my hand and scrolling through the photos. I watch his thumb, ready to pounce if it nears the delete button.

Marissa would kill me.

"Wow. These are pretty incriminating. Awesome job." He hands the camera back.

I shrug. "Thanks."

"Does she realize there's no chance?"

"That may only encourage her." No point in trying to cover for Marissa. She'd say the same thing.

"That's what I thought." He leans back, putting his arms behind his head. His biceps flex and I look away. I don't need my hormones taking over.

"What?" he asks.

"You tell me."

He rolls his eyes. "Listen. I'm sorry. You were right. I was a jerk." Momentarily, I'm dazed. His apology doesn't seem real. I lift my eyebrow; there has to be more.

I'm right.

"But I'm not sorry about Zach." He turns to me. "Speaking of which …" Justin nods toward the crowd. Zach is walking toward us.

"Yo, Zach. How'd that game of disc turn out?"

"Tater got schooled!" Zach sits down between us, soaking wet. The side of my dress absorbs the water off his body. He puts his arm around me. My stomach makes a little flip.

He still likes me?

Zach turns to me. "Sorry again about dinner tonight. Work got busy and I lost a bet to Tater. I was so pissed that I completely blanked." He nudges me and flashes his corner smile. "They say I've got a tendency to get overheated."

I've heard that. Last season he threw all the lacrosse sticks across the field after they lost to Jefferson Academy.

"So," Zach gives my shoulder a squeeze, "I calmed down with a game of disc."

He leans in, kissing me on the cheek. "Forgive me?" My heart flutters as my emotions swing on a pendulum. His story could totally be legit, and he fessed up to blanking. The way his hand is wrapped around my waist just feels right. I'm not ready to let that go over a messed up date.

"Yeah, of course. No big deal." I shrug, wanting to appear like the cool, relaxed, girlfriend.

Justin throws up his hands behind Zach, defeated.

Zach looks back at him. "What, man?" his voice darkens.

"Nothing, really." Justin stands up, wisely removing himself. "I just remembered I promised Jennifer I'd dance tonight." He nods toward the dance floor where Jennifer stands eyeing him. "I might as well get it over with." He looks down at me. "See ya later."

Zach shrugs in response. I have the sense they weren't as close as they'd acted on the phone. Zach and I sit next to one another for a moment in silence. My mind races, trying to find something to ask him. "So, how's the pool?" is all I manage.

He looks at me blankly before a huge smile spreads across his face. He effortlessly leans over and sweeps me off the bench. "You're about to find out."

Faking a scream, I kick off my heels before Zach throws me in the water. Thankfully, it's warm. A thundering splash booms next to me. I swim to the surface and a large arm pulls me into a hug. It feels nice to be held so close. Zach looks down at me, his brown eyes filled with excitement. That look always makes me smile. He turns away from me briefly and whistles to Tater and Pete, his teammates. Both nod and storm the dance floor where they grab their girlfriends and obediently toss them in, too.

I instantly bond with the other girlfriends. Without words we turn on our guys, creating a wall of splashes with our feet. Zach breaks through the water wall, pulling me toward him. He kisses me before he yells, "Water fight."

Zach and I team up and attack Tater and his girlfriend. The force Zach makes with slamming his arm into the water is overwhelming. Giant waves slosh up in my face. I can't open my eyes. Water shoots up my nose and down my throat. It burns. Choking, I swim to the side.

The night's cooler air makes me shiver. Zach doesn't seem to be losing interest in the fight at all. The brunette swims up to the steps. "This can go on forever. I guarantee you," she says before climbing out. She's dated Tater for over a year, so I assume she knows what she's talking about. I follow her. The hair on my arms stands straight up. I wring as much water out of my dress as I can. Goosebumps pattern my skin.

I walk back to the bench and pick up my heels and purse. I sit down, pulling out my phone. Eleven forty-eight. *Crap*. Eleven missed calls. *Double crap*.

I jolt up, scanning the crowd, hoping Marissa will stand out in her yellow top. My eyes catch a flash of yellow, but it isn't Marissa's dress. My heart stops.

It's Mom's yellow gardening hat.

CHAPTER FOUR

This isn't happening. Not here. No.

Mom stands in the middle of the dance floor dressed in floral pajamas with that stupid floppy hat to cover her bedhead. Our eyes meet and the air thickens. She stomps across the floor. The look she gives me pierces my skin. I shoot up, walking the other direction. Maybe she'll follow before everyone notices?

"Lucinda Zwindler. Stop Now."

Crap. It really is happening. Everyone stares.

Bracing myself, I turn around. The space around Mom clears. She hasn't even bothered to put on a bra. I swallow a mouthful of spit that I'd made, an unconscious attempt at drowning myself.

"What do you think you're doing here? Didn't we tell you that you were grounded? C's, Lucinda, C's!" She grabs my arm. "Answer me!" Her face trembles.

I don't want to be like her. I try to stay calm. In control. I take a slow breath before responding. "It's only a C, Mom. Relax. I came for a few hours. I was just grabbing my stuff to head home." Marissa pops through the crowd; I nod to her. "We were just leaving."

"You." Mom points at Marissa. "This was your idea."

Everyone turns, their attention on Marissa. "Oh, no, Mrs. Zwindler. I tried to talk Lucy out of it. I swear."

Mom lets out a harsh laugh. "No. This is right up your alley, conniving and disrespectful. Totally *Marissa.*" Mom hits her high-octave notes.

Marissa forces a sob, grabbing the guy's arm next to her and putting her head against his chest. I doubt she even knows his name. People swarm around her, touching her back. I sigh. Marissa is the center of attention; she'll be just fine.

Mom's breathing is heavy, her face swollen and out of proportion. Boiling point. Her grip tightens. Pain.

"Mom. Let go." I look down at my arm. "Please, Mom. Let's just go home."

She follows my gaze and her fingers quickly uncurl. Her red handprint remains, blazing around my bicep. *Whoa.* She's never done that before. I search her face. Her mouth is slightly open, her eyes wet.

"Excuse me," she says as she passes me and pushes the gate open. I stand alone for a few moments, trying to collect myself before following her. I hear a girl mutter that I should never go home. Others just shake their heads and whisper.

But I follow her. I have to know if she is alright.

I find Mom sitting in the driver's seat of her green

Toyota Avalon. Her head is down on the steering wheel. I don't know what to say. Yes, I snuck out. Did that warrant being embarrassed and hurt in front of everyone? No. Maybe a nasty voicemail message or, at worse, just showing up and quietly telling me it was time to go.

Her social illiteracy will be the death of me.

The car purrs to life. Good, she hasn't shut down. We've avoided a total collapse. I can't deal with that tonight. I never want to deal with that again.

My first memory is of Mom. I wandered into our living room and picked up her bowl of dried noodles off the floor. I was probably three years old. She stared, dead eyes, as I approached her at her permanent station on the couch. I handed it to her and she patted my head before looking back up at the ceiling.

"Lucy, baby. Mommy's resting. Let's play outside," Dad said as his hand covered mine, leading me away from Mom.

Mom was always resting.

***

I awake to the inevitable tap on my door. "Lucinda," Dad says sternly. "It's time to talk. Downstairs in five." I groan, rolling over and looking at the clock. Seven twenty-six a.m. Can't this wait until at least nine? "Now." Dad answers my thoughts. Apparently not.

I grab my favorite pair of sweats and brush my teeth first. I'm at least going to be comfortable. Mom waits at the bottom of the stairs, her steaming cup of coffee in hand. I refuse to look her in the eye. She turns, walking into the living room. I follow.

I've grown to hate our living room. Being there belittles me; it's like my time-out spot, the place I go to receive my punishments. I'd sit in the blue checkered chair while my parents had the honor of dealing the final blow—usually not being able to go out with Marissa that night, a temporary grounding situation, or, so far the worst, having my car privileges revoked after skipping class to hang out at a college cafe. That was a mistake, definitely not worth the latte.

I haven't driven for two months.

I plop down on the chair, pulling my feet up under me. Mom hates it when we have feet on the living-room furniture. Her eyebrow twitches. She doesn't say anything. If nothing else, I at least have this small victory.

Mom takes a deep breath. I brace. "Lucinda Jane," she says. I flinch. I hate my middle name—it's boring. "We've never been so disappointed in you."

This is no new news to me. I want to say *Great, so now I'm your biggest disappointment in life,* but I stop myself, remembering my revelation before falling asleep. I'm not going to give them the advantage of knowing my thoughts. I'm going to be in control. Instead of talking, I meet Mom's eyes with a steady, serious gaze. She doesn't flinch. Excellent. I rock at staring contests.

Dad crosses between us, cutting off our eye contact. "Lucy, we have given you opportunities to redeem yourself." Really? Being grounded nearly every other day hardly seems like an opportunity.

"You no longer have our trust. It will be a long road to regain it," Mom adds, already pacing back and forth. My silence is creeping her out. Dad doesn't seem to notice. He probably thinks I care about what they have to say. But I have Mom moving. This may work after all.

"Your mother and I stayed up all night discussing what we should do with you …" he trails off, taking a deep breath before dealing the blow. He looks to Mom.

Mom walks up to me, putting her hand on the wingbacks of my chair. "We're monitoring your phone. Everywhere you go, we'll know."

"What?" I jump up from the chair. "That's a total invasion of my privacy." Forget the silent approach. They may as well have shackled my wrists.

Mom leans in. Shivers run up my back. "You don't deserve privacy," she whispers.

"It's a basic human right."

"Not when you're sixteen. Your business is our business."

"Like you would even understand my business." That was pretty lame, but it was the best I had. She won't get the last word.

Dad interjects, "Lucy, I called this morning and it's already set up." He takes out his phone and pulls up a family-locator application. I see my name next to a purple dot. The location says "Home."

My brain works at warp speed to try to beat this. I can just hide my phone wherever I say I'll be and then go elsewhere. Easy solution. I can still "hang out at the pool" when I'm really on a date with Zach. But wait, I won't be able to go on a date with Zach. There is no way I can get out of the house anyway. I'm surely grounded. My parents are so stupid. I lift my eyebrow, "Why waste money doing that when I'm going to be stuck here anyway?"

"That's actually something else we talked about," Dad replies. Mom sits down on the couch, her lips tight. She's obviously not a big fan of what Dad is going to say. "You're not grounded. That punishment clearly hasn't been working for you."

What? Seriously? Sweet!

Dad reaches over and holds Mom's hand. "*We* figure it only encourages you more."

We. I roll my eyes. Yeah right.

"Keep in mind that we'll be checking in on your location whenever we want."

"Oh, that's right. How can I forget? You don't have a real job."

I'm surprised when it's Dad, not Mom, who pounces. "Don't say that. You know what your mother's gardening blog means for this family. It's providing your college education." His words sting.

"Lucy, please stop being a snot," Mom says.

"Immature much, Mom?"

"Okay. Okay." Dad stops us before we can get going again. "Just let us know who you will be with and where you will be."

"Fine." I stand up to leave. This conversation is over.

"Sit back down. There's more we think you'll enjoy." The way the words smoothly roll off of Mom's tongue makes my skin crawl. I slam my body back down onto the chair, hoping it breaks a spring.

Mom takes the lead. "Now, just because you aren't grounded doesn't mean you'll spend all your time at the pool with Marissa."

My heart sinks and my jaw drops with it. No pool? What's the point of summer if I can't be at the pool? I glare at Mom. She really is evil.

"Your father spoke with a business associate this

morning about you. We got you a job."

"What?"

"Honey, we decided that since you want to make your own decisions and desire the independence of an adult, you wouldn't mind going to work at all," Mom says all too sweetly.

Dad rises. "I completely agree with your mother. In an ideal world, yes, you would have this as your last summer off. But you've shown us you want more responsibility so we're giving it to you."

I can't believe it. My entire summer at the pool with Marissa just disappeared. Mom and Dad would know my hours. How can I sneak away to go on dates with Zach? He'd actually have to come here to pick me up. How mortifying.

"Don't you want to know what you're doing?" Mom asks.

"Yes, why thank you. I would love that, Mom."

"Painting."

I think of an art class. I'm kind of decent with art. Would I be assisting in a preschool?

"The outside of houses," she adds.

A memory of our old house being painted flashes through my mind. Middle-aged men sweating high up on ladders or scaffolding while hauling huge gallons of paint back and forth. Ten-hour days. No way.

"Are you kidding? Isn't that dangerous?"

"Only if you don't follow the rules," she says.

Dad remains silent, sitting on the couch.

"Dad? Really? What if I fall? How am I supposed to carry those paint buckets?"

He takes a deep breath before rubbing his chin. He

obviously isn't comfortable with this proposal. There's no way he helped come up with this. "Well," he sighs. "You'll just have to be careful and creative. They aren't as heavy as they look."

"Why couldn't you have just gotten me a job at the public library?" I start to cry. I can't believe this. Not only is my summer ruined with a job, it just happens to be a super dangerous and physically impossible one. I stand up to leave. They don't try to stop me.

"Mom, Dad. What if I get hurt?" I picture a ladder being swept away under my feet and falling three stories to my death.

"You're a smart girl, Lucy, you'll be fine," Mom replies.

"Crawling around on roofs? Hanging off the sides of houses? Lifting huge tubs of paint?" I squeak as my voice cracks.

Mom's face softens a bit. "You'll be fine," she repeats.

"Can I leave now?"

"Yes," says Dad, still sitting on the couch with his hand held to his cheek. He looks worried. At least one of my parents doesn't thrive off of being evil.

I turn around to walk up the stairs. Dad calls after me, "One of the workers will pick you up Monday morning at seven."

I don't respond. I walk quietly up the stairs only to slam my door so hard it shakes our house. Mom's voice filters up through my vent. "She'll be fine, Dan. I promise."

I scream into my pillow. She is clueless.

CHAPTER FIVE

I drag myself out of bed at twenty to seven. My legs ache from jerking me awake all night long. Stupid dream ladders.

Grabbing my best sports bra and an outfit that I welcome to be destroyed, Marissa's advice echoes in my mind, "What if you meet a guy? Or what if you're painting the home of a modeling agent?"

I doubt either of those things will happen but I throw some mascara and eyeliner on anyway. At least I can look decent when strapped to a gurney.

I hate walking into the unknown. It sucks. All I know is that this job will be dangerous and hot. I grab a granola bar from under my bed, hoping it will help calm me down. A motor sputters into the driveway. I run down the stairs to head off my new coworker from meeting Mom. That would be horrifying.

But Mom's already waiting for me at the door. I pray she won't come outside with me. She hands me a water and lunch with a smug expression on her face. I take the water bottle but refuse the lunch. She's not winning everything. Our exchange is silent. About time.

A battered white pickup truck idles like a snoring troll in our driveway. Metal ladders stick out of the truck bed and a small sign hangs loosely from chains over the side of the bed, "Purposeful Painting Inc." The sign swings in the breeze, banging loudly against the truck. I'm pretty sure that is illegal. The business doesn't seem legit at all.

A young guy sits in the front of the truck, sipping from a coffee cup, wearing a painter's hat and a pair of sunglasses. He has a strong jaw and stubble. I look at his arm, bent up toward his face on the window ledge. He is tan and muscular. A goofy smile spreads across my face. Maybe the summer won't be a complete waste after all. I climb into the passenger seat, thankful I put on mascara.

"Good morning, Lucinda," the driver says in a mocking tone.

I stop breathing.

No way. He takes off his sunglasses. Two piercing green eyes stare back at me. I don't even try to hide my groan.

Justin.

He laughs. "What?"

I roll my eyes before hitting my head against the seat. To any other girl in school, this would be Heaven. To me, it's a humiliating nightmare.

"Awesome party the other night, huh?" he prods.

I shrug. There's no way I'm giving him info to use

against me. I pull out my granola bar, taking a bite so it's impossible to speak.

Justin stares cockeyed at the granola bar and my water bottle. "Is that all you have?"

I swallow. "Yup." Justin raises an eyebrow. "It's all I need. Seriously, I'll be fine."

Justin shakes his head and turns off the engine.

"Um, are you listening? Let's go. I'm fine." It's only been three minutes and already I want to strangle him. He never listens.

Justin jumps out of the truck, bee-lining it for my front door.

"What are you doing?" I jump out, following.

"Getting you lunch." He looks me up and down, shaking his head. "You won't survive the day without it." He pushes open my front door and walks right in. The nerve. I run in behind, reaching the entryway only a few seconds later. Justin isn't waiting for me. I throw the kitchen door open and want to die.

Justin's shaking Mom's hand. "Yes. Mrs. Zwindler. It's great to finally meet you. My mom reads GardenLush.com every spring to prepare for the flowering season. She loves your blog." Justin smiles at Mom and she flushes. Even my mom falls for his fake charm.

It always surprises me when people say they are a fan of that blog. To me, the blog is just an extension of her gardening therapy, helping her recovery. It is a constant reminder of what my birth caused. Babies are supposed to bring their mothers joy. I just brought mine postpartum depression that turned into years of darkness.

But Justin's compliment makes Mom glow. "Oh, she's a fan? Would you like to take her some samples of a promotional product?" She reaches into a sack, not giving Justin a chance to say no. She pulls out three palm-sized, moist bags. "These are tulip bulbs wrapped in a rich new fertilizer. They use cow and goat manure as well as catfish eggs." She hands the three lumps to Justin. He looks down at his hands, now holding tulip bulbs and poop. He raises his eyebrows at me. Mom doesn't notice; she's oblivious as to how weird her gardening fascination is.

"Tell your mom to plant them this fall. They will be the most beautiful tulips next year," Mom explains. Justin flashes Mom a thankful smile. Fearing what he'll say, I jump in.

"Justin," I almost growl at him. "Let's go."

"Lucinda, be polite." She takes a slow, therapy breath. "I apologize for her rudeness. She's not normally so frank." Justin nods, occasionally glancing down at the bags in his hand. He's actually speechless. I grin and make a mental note: To make Justin shut up, add poop bags.

Mom continues, "You see, this job is not exactly her choice … but her father and I believe it will do her well." I cringe as Mom tells way too much information.

"I understand, Mrs. Zwindler." Justin recovers, now holding the bags of poop like hacky sacks. He casually starts to juggle them. "I promise I won't judge her character off this first week alone." He flashes his crooked smile.

"Thank you." Mom pats my back as if she's done me a favor. I go stone cold, hating her touch on my shoulder. It takes all my strength to not shove it off. She turns back to Justin, her hand still resting on my shoulder. "So, what can I do for you?"

"Lucinda needs a lunch."

Did Justin want me to hate him for eternity? Only my parents have the right to call me Lucinda. And even then, I hate it.

"Heavens." Mom opens the fridge, pulling out my lunch bag. "I tried to get her to take it, but she refused." She hands the bag to Justin. "Thank you for thinking of this. Her father will know she is in good hands when I tell him."

"Mothers always know best," Justin responds with another flashy smile. Mom smiles back, not understanding that he's mocking us from our fight the other night. Justin looks at me. "Okay, *Lucinda*. Let's roll."

"Sure." I quickly grab Justin's arm and try dragging him through the door. He finagles his way out of my grasp, returning to thank her for the tulip poop bags. I can't listen anymore. I storm out of the house, seeking refuge in his crappy white truck.

Why did he have to meet Mom? Why did she have to give him poop?

This was the cherry topping of my humiliation. I knew I'd get a call from Marissa asking how I let Mom give Justin poop. How does anyone explain that?

Justin opens the door, chuckling.

"Well," Justin begins as he turns the ignition. "That was fun. When my uncle called and told me who I was picking up, I was thrilled. After your little show Saturday night, I knew I needed to meet your Mom. She's famous, ya' know?" He tosses me a poop bag. "And that! What a great welcome gift." He laughs as the truck clanks down the driveway.

I refuse to look at him. I act more interested in the crack in the windshield.

Justin turns on the radio and, to my surprise, he stops bothering me. We listen to JSTP's morning show. A woman calls in and complains about having a fat bridesmaid. I hate listening to any talking on the radio. Isn't the radio for music? But I endure it. At least it makes him stop bothering me.

Justin pulls into the driveway of a small rambler house. I breathe a sigh of relief. One story—I won't be dying today. Part of the house is a dirty, pale yellow while the other part is a rich grey. I hope the new color is the grey. The yellow looks like pee. Five guys sit on buckets in the driveway, all my age and relatively attractive.

Justin stops the car and touches my arm. My instincts yank it away. "Sorry." He seems offended. "I just wanted to let you know that I'll help you out today."

"Why?" My voice is a bit too harsh.

He replies, meeting my tone. "Well, I assume you know nothing about painting and you'll need my help."

"I don't want your help."

"Fine." He climbs out, leaving me alone in the truck. Not wanting to look lame, I force myself to follow. I trail him toward the group of guys. They all stand as I approach.

"This is Lucy," Justin begins. I wait for him to provide further introductions. He doesn't. Instead he ditches me, grabbing paint and a bag of brushes before walking away and setting up at the front door. I stand alone in front of a group of cute guys. Marissa's dream. My nightmare. They eye me and I know I'm being judged. But I don't have to be. I have Zach. I stand up straight, meet each gaze without a smile, and their eyes dart away. Message sent— I'm taken.

"Hi," I say as they examine the asphalt. The tallest guy is the first to recover from being caught in total *ass*essment mode.

"Hey." He walks forward, extending his hand. "I'm Troy, project manager." Got it. My boss. He points to each of the other guys. "That's Luke, Emmanuel, Jake, and Alex." Jake shoves Alex off balance. After the brief introduction, Troy tells them to get started. They all gather supplies from the truck and go separate ways. Troy walks right past me.

Am I supposed to grab stuff to start or wait for instruction?

"Um, Troy?" I ask, forcing myself to follow him like a helpless puppy.

"Right, sorry. You're working with Alex." He scans the yard. "I think he's in the back. You'll be his protégé." A sigh of relief slips from my lips. *A protégé*. I can handle that. I'll be like Alex's assistant or something. Troy grabs a ladder from the truck bed and easily tosses it over his shoulder. "I'll bring your ladder down for you." I eye him as he tosses the clunky metal over his shoulder. Is he going to help me move it all summer?

When we reach the backyard, Troy drops my ladder, waving Alex down. Alex hops off his ladder from much too high, keeping his ear buds in as Troy gives an instruction in whispered tones. He nods, still bouncing to the music, until Troy leaves.

With Troy gone, he bounds over to me, taking out his ear buds. "I'm Alex. I've never gotten a protégé before." He's upbeat, holding up his hand for a high five. I give him a hesitant slap back. "I can't believe they trust me with this."

45

My confidence soars.

"Not that you should be worried … I'm awesome." He smiles at me, and it is genuine. He can't be over fifteen.

"Thanks. Where can I start? Near the ground?"

"Ha. No way, girl. If I start you there, you'll never get up that ladder." He nods to the humongous metal structure leaning against the house.

"I'll be fine," I lie. "It'll be nice to just get the feel of the paintbrush before climbing up that thing, you know?"

"Nope. I watched Troy make that mistake with Luke. Look at him, always clinging to the ground." Luke stands, grounded, painting the edge of a lower windowsill. "He only paints up high when he's forced. He's a slacker." He puffs out his chest. "My protégé won't be a slacker." Tapping the ladder, he lifts his eyebrows. "You know you want to."

I take a deep breath. I can already feel my feet flying through the air.

"Come on." He motions with his hand.

I take a step back. Nope. I'm not getting up on that thing. It's over fifteen feet tall.

Alex watches me, his fingers tapping his lips. "Okay. What if I can promise that the ladder won't move and there'd be someone here to catch you if you fall?"

"Alex, there's rarely anyone to catch you when you fall," I say matter-of-factly.

He looks at me blankly, not quite understanding if I'm talking about falling or life. His face scrunches up. He's thinking too hard. I can't have that.

"That's why they call it a fall. If people caught you, wouldn't they call it a catch?" I try to lead him astray. He smiles. It works.

46

"Okay. Then, at worst, you'll have a catch today." He beams and holds out his hand. He has a little dimple in his right cheek. "Come on … please? The boss'll be pissed if I don't get you on that ladder." Alex is so sweet and too young. I can't make him suffer. I take a breath and walk up to the ladder. I can at least try.

I reach up, grabbing the middle of a rung. Alex moves my hands to the side rails. "It's easier this way. Don't worry. I'll stand at the bottom all day if I have to." His voice drops to a whisper. "Don't tell anyone, but I hated the ladders in the beginning too."

I like Alex. He is good people.

"Okay." I clear my mind with the same deep breath I used to take before every free throw. "Here we go." I start climbing. I don't need to be told not to look down. Thankfully Alex knows better than that. But I can totally imagine him staring at my butt. Good kid, but still a guy.

"Great," Alex says. "Now stop. You're halfway. How does it feel?"

"Ugh, okay."

"That's as high as you have to go today." My stomach relaxes. I can deal with this. "Tomorrow we'll work higher up." I let myself look down. At most, it'd be like an eight-foot fall. Not fatal, just a broken arm.

"Now come back down and I'll set your supplies up nice."

I take extra caution stepping back down the ladder. I can hear Alex behind me, taking supplies out of a huge bucket and moving around the base of my ladder. When I get down, the ground has transformed. Large drop cloths cover the grass. A variety of brushes and rollers are arranged on the ground. He grabs one and hands it to me.

He shakes his head and grabs another. I hold it and he nods. Alex assesses the remaining supplies. He knows his stuff.

"How old are you?" I have to know.

"Fourteen. Almost fifteen."

Younger than I thought.

"You look older than that," I offer. He straightens his shoulders, making them broader. He's kind of adorable. "You know a lot about this painting stuff, huh?" I give him a little ego boost. I need an ally.

"Of course I do." He hands me a small bucket of paint while he climbs up my ladder. He holds out his hand, and I hand up the bucket. "I've been with the company since it started."

"When was that?"

"Two summers ago." I must look confused because he continues to explain, "Family connection. At first I just hung around watching. Then I got so annoying they had to give me a brush … and then a paycheck." He laughs as he hooks the paint holder to the underside of the ladder. "Not many thirteen-year-olds can purchase their own HD flat-screen TV." He tightens the paint holder. "Now I'm saving for a car. I'm technically only allowed to work five hours a day so I help out the other three."

"You want to work full time?" I blurt. My cheeks burn. This is my first job and I already dread every hour.

"Absolutely. An outdoor gig, hanging out with friends, listening to music, building muscle without thinking about it, and getting paid? Sweet deal." He climbs back down the ladder, switching places with me. I climb back up. He hands me the brush. "Dip the bristles in only a third of the way." I do. "Yup. Now gently wipe the excess off on the inside lip of the bucket. Now brush with the grain of the siding. Not up and down, but side-to-side." I do. The grey paint goes on smoothly. I smush the paint into a crack in the board, covering up all traces of the ugly yellow. Perfect.

This isn't as bad as I thought. It's kind of hypnotizing. Alex shuffles his feet at the base of my ladder. I bet holding my ladder all day is probably as miserable for him as me being on one.

"Alex, you can let go."

"Really? Are you sure?"

"Yup." I nod to the ladder set up a few yards away from mine. "You won't be far. I'll holler when I need help with a refill."

"Awesome. You're already doing great. A natural. But don't tell anyone that. Tell them I taught you everything there is to know, okay?"

I laugh, gripping the ladder. "As long as you keep me alive, consider it a deal."

"Can do." He winks playfully and bounds away. The kid has energy. He scales his ladder to the top, with supplies in hand. He steadies himself, plays with his iPhone, and puts in his ear buds. Mental note: bring music tomorrow. He bobs his head in rhythm. A smile seems permanently glued to his face. He really does love this job.

Assessing the siding in front of me, I carefully re-dip my brush while clutching the ladder. I reposition my grip and begin to cover the wood. Back and forth. I let my mind slip into blankness. It feels nice.

Back and forth.

Progressing down toward the ground isn't so scary. I manage to unhook the paint bucket and move it with me.

This isn't too horrible.

The sun gets hotter and the air stickier. Alex takes more frequent water breaks and eventually takes off his shirt. My tank top glues itself to me. I want to just wear my sports bra but there's no way I'd put myself on display here. And, worse, they'd probably think I thought I was super hot or something. I'd just be embarrassing myself.

The heat gets more suffocating with each stroke of my brush. We're on the sunny side of the house. My only solace comes from knowing that eventually the sun will pass over and our sunny side will turn to shade.

Like Alex, I start taking sips of water between each board I paint. I don't know what causes me to sweat more, the sun or climbing up and down because of my thirst. Staying hydrated is a work out in itself. My progress slows.

I sigh as I take my last sip of water. Dehydration, not a fall, would kill me.

Just as I debate asking Alex for a sip, Troy comes around the corner. "Break time, take twenty," he shouts. There is a gas station a few streets away. I can run there, buy more water, and be back in time. I nearly jump off my ladder, surprising both myself and Alex.

"Whoa. Careful!" Alex calls as he climbs down his ladder. "Overconfidence can destroy you." I think of Justin. Yes, that sounds about right.

I don't waste any time. "Right; I'll remember that." I pick up my water bottle and jog past Alex. "I didn't bring enough water. I've got to run to the gas station."

"But you won't have time to eat something." He has run to reach my side. He motions to the other guys, all sitting on the lawn eating out of their lunchboxes. I look down at my watch.

"It's ten. When do we eat lunch?"

"One."

"I can make it. I'll be fine." My stomach growls in protest.

"Lucy, you should eat. You'll get hungry."

"I can last three more hours. Water is way more important."

Alex motions toward the house's hose. "Use that, water's in our contract." I scrunch my nose. "Come on, like when you were a kid, remember?"

The thought of the metallic taste grosses me out. Plus, a trip to the gas station helps me avoid Justin. "No thanks. I'll just make a quick run. I'll be back." Alex doesn't say anything. He stops running, shaking his head. Troy approaches him. Alex explains, "She wants to go to the gas station. I can't stop her."

"Well, she better come back."

"She will." Alex says confidently.

Wow. The idea hadn't occurred to me to just leave. Why not? I hold the answer to that question in my hand: my phone. GPS. I'll be back because I have to be. I bet Mom is watching where I am right now and wondering where I'm going, about to jump out of her computer chair and get in the car and chase me down. I start to jog. Mom now has total control, everything she wanted.

I arrive back as Troy shouts, "Back at it, men!" He looks at me as I pass him. "And Lucy."

How nice to be included.

I drink half of one of the water bottles on the way into the backyard. I'll definitely be using that hose in the next couple of hours. I climb up my ladder where Alex has already prepped my supplies. My stomach growls again.

Ugh, this will be a long three hours.

I brush back and forth, grey over yellow. My stomach growls just enough to distract me from hitting a rhythm. I climb up and down the ladder to grab sips of water. Alex has somehow clipped his water to his ladder, saving him from going up and down. I'll have to ask him about that during lunch. The sun is right over us now. In only an hour or so it will move to the other side of the house. Shade. The front and back of my tank top are soaking wet. It is unusual for me to sweat so much. I'll bring two tops tomorrow.

The water finally settles my stomach. I fall back into my painting rhythm and my mind drifts to Zach. Should I call and apologize for my mom at the party and explain her crazy need for control? He'd agree and comfort me. Maybe he'd even stop over to sit with me outside and talk? I can already smell his cologne.

The back of my throat burns; I'm thirsty again. I climb down the ladder. My head feels a bit fuzzy. I take a long sip, feeling sleepy and unusually relaxed. I take another sip, closing my eyes for a bit. My stomach seems to turn over. I drank too much. My hands start shaking.

I bend over, my hands on my knees. *Collect yourself, Lucy.* Too late. The water comes back up. My eyes go fuzzy.

"Lucy?"

The ringing in my ears drowns Alex's voice.

CHAPTER SIX

Water. Water everywhere. Wet. My eyes jolt open.

Justin stands over me, spraying me with a hose. "She's awake." Justin leans down. He puts one arm around my shoulder and the other under my knees and swiftly picks me up.

"Put me down." I push away from him but he holds on. The world turns. "Now," I insist.

Justin refuses. He throws me in the front seat of the truck, reaching over and buckling me in. The truck lurches as something lands in back. Alex. My whole body trembles. A Pixy Stick is dangled in front of my face. "Eat this."

"No." I move Justin's arm away. "I'm not hungry." My stomach stings. Who can eat when they feel like this?

He pushes the Pixy Stick back in my face. I snatch it

and throw it out the window. There. My head pounds, I bury it in my knees. My stomach heaves and yellow liquid follows.

Justin groans.

The stinging in my stomach ends. I lean back to rest my eyes. Better. I don't want to deal with Justin anymore. I'd rather sleep.

***

"Mild hypoglycemia and moderate dehydration." I wake to a deep voice. A line of tubing disappears into my hand. Wires lead from my chest to squiggles on a computer monitor. I've watched enough of Discovery Health Channel to know it is my heartbeat. An older man stands with his back to me at the foot of the bed, my bed, I guess. A stethoscope hangs around his neck. My parents sit on chairs in the corner. "She'll wake up shortly and probably feel woozy and exhausted the rest of the day."

The room spins. He's got that right.

"Will she be okay?" Mom asks.

"Oh sure," he chortles. "We will observe her the rest of the day. If she's stable, she can be discharged this evening."

"I'm sorry. I wasn't expecting this."

"It's okay, Sarah," Dad says. "It's not your fault. The boy said she refused to eat."

Justin. Of course he'd tell my parents this was my fault.

"Dehydration and a little low blood sugar can come on very fast in this heat, especially when you aren't used to working in it," the doctor offers the information to Mom as comfort. I'm sure it just makes her feel worse. "Now if it wasn't for that boy, she would have been in much worse shape." The doctor chuckles again. "Did you know he poured a Pixy Stick into her mouth while she was passed out?"

What? I don't remember that.

"He's a smart guy. He may have saved her from a seizure."

Mom gasps. Great job, doc. You successfully gave her a new reason to manage me. Dad places his hand on Mom's shoulder. "We'll thank Justin. Maybe have him over for dinner?"

"No." The word flies out of my mouth. All three turn toward me. Mom rushes to my side, grabbing my hand. I jerk my hand away from her. I don't need her fakeness right now.

"Honey. You're awake."

"Obviously," I say.

The doctor continues, "Another side effect you may notice is some additional attitude and aggression. She apparently hit that boy rather hard across his face when he carried her into the emergency room." He winks at me. "If you could have heard what she yelled at that boy …"

"I can imagine." Mom stands up from my side and glares at me as she crosses the room. She's given up fake appearances. Good.

"Of course, this all may just be a side effect of being a teenage girl, too." He looks at me and winks. I don't like him. I hate when people attribute actions to "being a teenager." Anyone who views someone as a life stage instead of an individual with thoughts pisses me off.

"Excuse me?" a female voice says.

"Come on in, Esther." The doctor pulls the curtain

open and an older, plump nurse walks in with a small box.

"Hi, Sweetie." She puts the box on my bed. "I just need to poke your finger to test your blood sugar, okay?"

I wince. I hate needles.

"It'll be quick. Promise." She puts a small little box against my middle finger. *Click.* A sharp dagger digs into my flesh. She squeezes out a drop of blood onto a small pink paper. "Done." She places the paper into the machine. It beeps. "Seventy," she says to the doctor. Then she turns back to me. "How about some juice?"

My mouth does feel dry. "Ok." She leaves the room. Her steps are soft on the hard white floor.

"Well, Lucinda," the doctor looks down at me. His white bushy eyebrows bounce as he speaks. "We'll watch you closely, probably let you go home later tonight. How would you like that?" He pats my hand. I suppress the urge to ask him to stop. He turns to my parents. "She's going to be just fine."

"Oh thank you, Dr. Forts. Thank you so much." Mom shakes his hand. She gives him too much credit.

I look down at the line in my hand, vaguely remembering a strong hand holding my arm down while a needle jabbed my skin.

"She needs a bolus, now." Esther's voice filters through my memory. She's the one who took charge.

Now, my parents stand at the foot of my bed, looking down at me. "I'm fine." I roll my eyes.

"Why didn't you eat?" Mom asks, her sweet tone she had around the doctor now gone.

"I wasn't hungry."

"We can't even trust you to take care of yourself. Why don't you think?"

"Sarah, maybe not now." At least I have one compassionate parent.

"Yeah, Mom. How about we wait until I get out of the hospital?"

Dad pats my foot. "You too, Lucinda. Not here."

"May I come in?" Esther peeks around the curtain. Dad eagerly pulls it open for her. Esther walks in with three containers of juice in hand. "Cranberry or apple?"

"Cranberry please." She hands it to me. "Thanks."

"Well, Sarah and Dan, I need to do some vital signs and a physical assessment on Lucy." Esther looks down at me and smiles. "I bet Lucy wouldn't mind some privacy."

Mom interrupts, "Oh, it's okay."

No, it isn't. I look to Dad, raising my eyebrows. He gets the hint. "Honestly Sarah, I'm hungry. How about we go grab a snack while Esther watches Lucy?"

Esther smiles. "Yes, don't make more work for me, Dad. I don't want another hypoglycemic patient today."

"Good point. Come on, let's find a candy bar." He wraps his hand around Mom's and leads her out the door.

"Do you know how much high-fructose corn syrup is in a candy bar?" Mom's voice echoes down the hall. I roll my eyes and Esther chuckles.

Esther places a blood pressure cuff around my arm, squeezing it like a boa constrictor. "Thought I'd give you a break, honey." She nods toward the door. "It's hard being sixteen and in the hospital with your parents around."

"It's hard being sixteen in general." I sigh, laying my head back on my pillow.

She pats my arm. "97/68."

"Is that good?" I ask.

"Just fine for a woman your size." I smile. A woman.

She places her fingers on my wrist, resting them where my blood bounces. "I'm actually surprised it's so normal. I thought it might be a little high now that you're remembering some things." She whistles. "You made quite a scene in the ER."

"Yeah, I'm sorry." I hope I haven't said something mean to her. She's nice.

"No apologizing. It was the best part of my day—listening to you call that guy names as you went in and out of consciousness. And that punch! Whoop! He didn't see it coming!"

"Did I really hit him?" I try to hide my smile. At least I have that …

"Right across the face." She nods while counting my pulse. "The best part though was when you woke with him sitting next to your bed. You looked him right in the eye and told him his head was so big it would explode."

"It will someday," I mutter. "Was he mad?"

She shakes her head. "Nope. He just laughed." Of course he did, laughing at a girl in a hospital bed. He's probably already texted everyone about it. I hate technology.

Esther pulls up a chair. "So, I know you can hold your own with the boys, but how's everything else going?"

"Um, okay." I lie. She raises her eyebrow, catching me. I am too exhausted to exaggerate on the lie. Honesty seems easier. "Okay, it's crappy."

She leans back in her chair, hands folded on her lap and ready to listen. "Tell me about it." So I do. I tell her about everything: Marissa, sneaking out, the party, Mom's yellow hat, Zach, and the new job. I even talk about basketball.

Esther nods along with my words. "That's a lot to deal

with. Hang in there. Sixteen can suck, but it can be oh so good too. More independence. Dating. Love. Knowledge." She pauses. "Sixteen is really just the beginning of your journey."

She gets it. Now why can't Mom and Dad get it too?

CHAPTER SEVEN

A half-eaten bowl of Kung Pao chicken and an untouched orange juice rest on my bedroom floor. A nasty combination. I need to text Zach. We haven't spoken in four days. I can't really blame him after Mom's show the other night.

Me: Hi Zach. Sorry about my mom the other night. She's crazy. I did have fun at the party with you though. Want to hang out soon?

"Lucy?" Eric's light voice calls through my door.

"Come on in." My little brother is the only person I ever welcome into my room. But he has to ask first.

The door creaks open. Eric wears matching frog pajamas. With red jelly on the corner of his lips and blond hair in a curled mess, he looks like a five-year-old prince.

"What's up, bud?" I swing him onto my bed. My right

shoulder protests in pain. My wrist hurts even more. Crap. Wasn't fainting, fighting, and the hospital enough? Of course the painting job gets the final say. I stretch out my shoulder as Eric looks at me with a scrunched nose; his thinking face.

"-othing up." He stands up on the bed to poke at the Band-Aid on the back of my hand. "You got a shot?"

"A little one." His lips turn into a frown. "But it didn't hurt at all. It just helped me get better."

"So you're -ot sick?"

I give him my best reassuring smile and answer back overenthusiastically. "No, bud. I feel great!" I stand up and do our crazy dance, a complex set of movements that involves spinning and arm flailing. My shoulder muscles beg to be ripped off. He giggles and dances too.

"Good Lucy. -ot sick."

"Good. Lucy *is* **n**ot sick." I correct him. He has been working with speech therapy on annunciation and full sentences all year. I bend over and tickle him into a fit of giggles.

"Lucy is not sick!" He says between gasps. The doorbell rings and he pushes me away. His new chore is opening the front door and he takes it very seriously. I pretend to hold him captive but let go when I notice his smile turning into frustration. He clobbers down the stairs. "No, Daddy. -y job!" I close my bedroom door, only hearing muffles from below.

Dried sweat cakes my skin. Nasty. I step into the shower, using my loofah like iron wool on the visible layers of dirt on my skin. There, clean. I grab some jeans and a tank top off my floor and throw my hair back in a bun. It's time to get out of this house. It is only ten in the morning. Marissa is definitely still asleep. Maybe Eric will want to walk to the park with me?

BZZZ. My phone. Zach.

Zach: Crazy is right. Grabbing burgers with guys tonight. You and Marissa in?

My heart relaxes. I had no idea it was so tightly wound. He still wants to see me.

Me: Sounds yummy. I'll check with Marissa. But I'll be there.

Zach: Oh, you'll have more fun if Marissa comes too. It'll get boring.

My heart twists again. Rejection.

But maybe Zach is right? I imagine myself sitting at the end of a table filled with his lacrosse friends. I'd have no idea what to say and look like an idiot. I send Marissa a quick text. She'll say yes; she rarely turns down an opportunity to hang out with a group of guys.

What to wear? I find my favorite tank top wrinkled with a peanut-butter smear down the front. I gather the rest of the dirty clothes that carpet my floor and bring them all downstairs to do laundry. Eric's voice chimes from the kitchen. Talking to himself again. Cute. I swing open the door, but it doesn't open more than an inch. I hear a low grunt and then the pressure releases, allowing the door to swing open.

My stomach drops. Justin is blocking my view of our white-and-black checkered floor.

Perfect. Am I even wearing makeup? Not that it matters around him. Barfing in front of him trumps not wearing mascara any day. Humiliation.

Justin holds a truck in hand. Eric sits next to him, pointing to his trucks and explaining, "That truck is Bert."

Justin looks up at me and flashes his favorite smile. "Have you met Bert, Lucy?"

I roll my eyes, "Really, here?" His light laugh rolls as he smashes Bert into a gold matchbox car. The screen door opens and Mom and Dad walk in.

"Lucy, I was just about to call you," Dad says. Justin stands up and Dad pats his back. Excellent. They are buddies. "Justin stopped in to check on you." Dad smiles at me indicatively.

No, Dad. Way off.

Justin picks up on my Dad's smile and interjects, "Well, actually, my uncle sent me. As the owner he feels it's important to check on any employee who falls sick or gets injured on the job. He has a business meeting," he explains.

Mom speaks in her fake sweet voice, "Well, isn't that nice? You're lucky, Lucy, working for such a great company."

Working? As if I still am? Whoa. I must've missed something. What about the hospitalization? It never even occurred to me that I'd be returning.

"So," Justin looks at me. "How are you feeling?"

Eric answers for me. "Good. Lucy is not sick. She's all better!" He looks up at me, so proud of his sentences.

I pat him on the head, "That's right, buddy. I'm all better now." Eric seems satisfied and zooms a car into Mom's foot. She scoops him off the ground and cuddles him in a hug; he sticks his jellied face into her neck.

My eyes dart away. I don't get to have any memories of doing that with Mom. Her depression stole all opportunity from me. My preschool friends' moms used to do the same rocking hug after our holiday concerts. But Mom couldn't even make it to hear me sing. She just sat empty on the couch, waiting for nothing. The only fun memories I have is when I was Eric's age and we watered plants together every day. Her therapy had started. She'd get off the couch, teaching me about each plant and we'd talk to them while watering, encouraging them to grow. But when she finally got better, I was too old for those sorts of hugs.

"Anymore fainting?" Justin asks.

"Nope. I'm one hundred percent."

"When do you feel able to return to work? Any restrictions?" Justin acts so professional in front of my parents.

"Umm …" I look at Dad. He shakes his head and looks toward Mom. I can't believe it. They're still expecting me to do this.

"How about I'll pick you up tomorrow and we can see how you handle it?" Justin offers.

I'm defeated. "Fine," I mutter. At least I won't have to be stuck at home with Mom all day. There's no way she's going to let me hang out at the pool with Marissa if I'm not well enough to work. I open the kitchen door, hinting at Justin to leave.

Justin takes my lead. "Well, Mrs. Zwindler. It was nice to see you again. Mr. Zwindler, always a pleasure." My parents respond with enthusiastic goodbyes. Why does he have to act so perfect around them? He's so fake. Justin looks back at me. "Lucy, I have your lunch bag in my car."

"Right," I sigh. Why didn't he just bring it in with him? I walk out, leaving him behind. He can follow when he's ready. I sit down on the front porch; his appreciation for the fertilized tulip bulbs floats out the window. His mom is apparently very excited. Yeah, right. I picture the tulip bulbs abandoned in a trash can or, more likely, flung onto the side of the road.

Finally, the front door swings open and he steps out alone. "So, Lucind-"

"Don't call me Lucinda." I stand up, crossing the lawn to his truck.

"Why not? It's your name."

I groan. "Just don't."

"No problem. Lucinda is too proper for you anyway. You threw up in my front seat. A Lucinda wouldn't have done that."

I cringe. Justin opens the passenger door. I walk over, bracing myself for the smell of vomit. Instead, a lemon-fresh scent greets me. Scrubbed swirls decorate the floored upholstery.

"I'll pay you back. How much did it cost?"

He lifts his eyebrow. "What cost?"

"The interior cleaning."

"Oh, nothing." He shrugs. "I did it myself."

"You cleaned up my puke?"

"Someone had to do it." He shrugs again while reaching under the seat to grab my lunch bag. "So," Justin chuckles and looks back at me with a smug look on his face. "I learned a lot about you yesterday."

"Really?"

"Oh yes."

"Like what?" I want to ignore him but I can't. I need to know.

"Well, you have more to say than you let people know. Also, you are not my number-one fan. And you throw a good punch." He points to his eye. I step close to him, he smells like mountains. I breathe through my mouth. A light crescent bruise rests under his red, broken-vesseled eye. I hadn't noticed it before because it is easier to find comebacks when I don't make prolonged eye contact.

"Sorry." I apologize before I can think. "You probably deserved it though." I don't want him to add the knight-in-shining-armor complex to his ego.

"Yeah, I'm sure." I can't tell if he is being sarcastic or not. Does he actually feel like he deserved it? Because he did.

He lets his bright green eyes linger on mine. I look away. I'm not falling for that charm. We stand in silence for a moment. He pulls out his phone, returns a text, and checks the time. "Well, I've got to get back to the house. Alex hasn't shut up about you. He thinks this is his fault. He's dying to find out if you are okay."

"He told me to eat and drink from the hose. Not his fault."

"Right, that's what I told him. You're the one who decided to run a mile and refuse to eat. Smart choices, Zwindler."

"Just leave, okay? I already have to deal with you tomorrow."

He jumps in the driver's seat and rolls down the window. "We'll see if you can handle it." He winks the eye I punched. I wish I had punched harder. "Lucy," Justin throws my lunch bag out the window toward me. It lands just short of my feet. "Bring food. Don't be a liability." The truck sputters away.

CHAPTER EIGHT

Zach smiles when he sees me get out of the car. With his arms wrapped around me, we sway in the parking lot while he talks with Matt, the junior lacrosse captain, about upcoming practices. I love it. Things are simple with Zach. He doesn't need to say hello or ask how I am. He knows I need him the moment he looks at me. It's nice to know I'm dating a guy who automatically opens his arms when I need it.

"Come on, lovebirds." Marissa tugs on Zach's arm. "Let's eat." Zach un-wraps his arms and takes my hand.

"Sounds good," Matt adds quietly. He walks out in front of us, confident in walking alone. Marissa positions herself next to Matt to chat, leaning in toward him and casually bumping him with her arm. She laughs and tosses her hair over her shoulder. Matt smiles back, becoming more and more interested in whatever she is talking about.

I sigh. I like Matt. He's in my math class and never asks stupid questions and takes perfectly formatted notes. His kind smile becomes a loose, goofy grin around Marissa. I wish she would have chosen another guy to flirt with. Matt isn't the type of guy that deserves to be treated like a toy.

It takes my eyes a moment to adjust to the dim lighting in Old Minnie after we walk through the door. Deep mahogany booths are the only seating option and in the corner stands a large, carved bar. Off of the dining area are pool tables and old arcade games. Top-40 music covers the constant hum of conversation. It's the perfect neighborhood bar and grill. Marissa's choice, of course.

We all slide into our booth. I grab Zach's attention, before his teammates can.

"Zach," I touch his arm. He puts his hand over mine. "How was practice today?"

"Awesome, the guys killed the drills. We're gonna be unstoppable this year. Right?" Zach high-fives Chaz across the table. I re-touch his arm, bringing him back to me.

"How was your day?" he asks.

"Honestly? Kind of crappy. You wouldn't believe what I've been through."

"I bet. Your mom's a crazy mess. I'm sure you've had a hell of a time."

I groan. "I know, right?" Zach is good at sympathizing. "They actually made me get a job."

"Really?"

"Yup. I've been painting for Purposeful Painting Inc. It's basically boot camp."

"Oh, that's like Justin's crew, huh?"

"Yup."

"Well, that must suck. What an egomaniac."

"I know. He seriously drives me crazy. The way he's always pulling his hands through his hair. What's with that?"

Zach pauses, his temple throbbing. "He thinks he's a god. The moral absolute," he says as he squeezes his hand around the salt shaker. I love that I'm dating a guy who sees through Justin's crap. Zach's hand turns red, his knuckles white. Will the shaker break? I haven't ever handled Zach when he was angry and I don't want to tonight. I want tonight to be relaxing.

"He's totally not worth it." I scan the room for a distraction. I notice an advertisement on the table top for their new two-pound burger. I point to the ad. "Zach, do you think you can handle it?" He's the competitive type; easily distracted by a challenge. I watch his grip loosen on the salt.

"With my appetite?" Zach often brags about his stomach being a bottomless pit. "Babe, I'd need two." He throws a rolled-up piece of his napkin at Miguel, getting his attention. "Are you guys in? How many can we eat?" Zach stands up and flags the waitress down.

Matt and Marissa join the booth, pulling up two chairs to the end of the table. Zach orders everyone the burger. He orders himself two. Marissa protests, it'll totally ruin her figure. Inevitably, all the guys check her out.

She leans her chair in toward Zach. "You can't make me eat it," she says slowly. Wait, is she fake flirting with Zach for a reaction? I watch her quickly pull away from him. No. That was just her way of trying to be in control.

Marissa is acutely aware of her sex appeal. She switches spots with Miguel because she can't be comfortable in her skirt on a chair. Miguel doesn't protest as he eyes Marissa's legs. She sits kitty-corner on the booth from me now, smartly positioning herself between Matt and Chaz, who have huge biceps. Marissa bats her eyelashes. I seriously thought they only did that in old Hollywood films.

She's having a blast.

The burgers arrive and loud, competitive chaos follows. Zach easily wins the chowing competition. Marissa doesn't touch hers. I eat a quarter of my burger and that's only because Zach cheered me on. The meat sits heavy and slows everything down. All I want to do is go back to Zach's arms around me and talking. Will Zach and I ever get time alone? A chance to connect?

The odds are not in my favor. Zach and Matt are running new offensive strategies by Chaz and Miguel. I barely understand what they're saying. Lacrosse is a mystery sport to me. I prefer games played on a court, like basketball or tennis, rather than a field. Marissa keeps trying to interject her thoughts about new ideas for shots for the school yearbook. They ignore her.

"Enough, men. Why don't we play a little pool?" Marissa stands up and stretches next to the table. "Will someone teach me? I need a teammate." Marissa turns, bending down to grab her purse to make the perfect butt view. I blush for her. Chaz and Miguel stand, shoving one another out of the way. Matt looks at me. I cuddle close to Zach. I want to stay. Matt nods, pushes his chair away from the table and follows.

We are finally alone. Zach looks down at me and smiles.

"So," I don't know where to begin.

"So?" He lightly cups his hand on my chin, tilting it up

toward him. "So," he says again. He looks me in the eyes before bringing his lips to my mouth. He moves his hand around my back, holding me and pressing himself to me. His mouth moves too fast and my head starts to spin. I grab a breath during one of his pauses, trying to reorient to the situation.

We are in a family restaurant. Making out in a booth.

In front of everyone.

I lightly press my hand to his chest. "Zach." He moves in closer, kissing me farther into the corner. I pretend to laugh. "Zach, not here." I push my hand against his chest a bit harder. I don't want to be *that couple*. He tries kissing me again but I duck away.

"Fine," he says, pulling away from me. "So?"

"Can we just talk a bit?"

He shrugs. "If that's what you want." His hand moves back to the salt shaker. He starts pouring salt out in a little mountain on the table.

"It's not that I don't like kissing you. You're really good at it." I nudge him. He gives me his crooked smile. "I just want to tell you about the hospital."

"The hospital? What happened?" The salt mountain grows larger. I scoot closer and interlace my fingers in his salt-shaker free hand. I tell him about the fainting and the emergency room. The salt shaker is almost empty so I skip everything about my parents. When I get to the nurse's part, his eyes drift toward the billiards room. I have to admit, he isn't the best listener. I change topics mid-sentence, trying to reel him back in.

"So then I guess I punched Justin. He's got a big black eye," I exaggerate.

Zach's attention returns. "That's my girl. I knew I liked

you for a reason."

I knew I liked you for a reason. Was he trying to remember this whole time why he liked me?

"Listen, how about we go play pool? I'm amazing. You can be on my team." He stands up and holds out his hand.

I hold in a sigh. That's the last thing I want to do. I know guys aren't like characters in the movies that sweep you off your feet, but it'd be nice if he had a bit more patience for my story. But there's no use forcing someone to listen. I reach out, allowing him to lead me to the other room.

Marissa yanks me aside when we arrive. "What's wrong with you? I just saw you completely smothered by Zach at the table—"

"I know. I made him stop so people wouldn't get uncomfortable."

"No. That's not what I mean. Why do you look so depressed? You just kissed a super hot guy. Smile or you'll lose him." I take a deep breath. Sometimes Marissa can be too pushy. But there's no way I can confront her here. Not now. She's always apologetic when I point it out to her in private. She doesn't do well with confrontation in public. So, I give her my best smile.

"Good," she whispers.

Drama avoided.

"Who's up for a new game? Teams?" Zach announces. "So Lucy and I versus Matt and Miguel?" I scan the room, looking for a way out. I suck at pool. I spot a familiar bushy head of hair. Alex smiles and waves at me.

"Actually, Zach, I need to go take care of something." I nod toward Alex waving at the other end of the room.

"Oh, is that one of your new painting geeks?"

"Something like that." I want to say that he is actually nice but the look on Zach's face makes me stop. He glares at Alex, obviously not a fan.

"Suit yourself. I'm not really into hanging out with kids."

"Want to win a game with me?" Marissa asks Zach.

I bite the inside of my cheek. This is so wrong. I don't need to watch Marissa fake flirt anymore, especially if it involves Zach. I'd rather hang out *with kids.*

Alex's smile grows as I walk over. At least someone likes me.

"Lucy, you're alive!" He gives me a quick hug.

"Yup." I hug him back.

Alex turns and taps a cute freckled girl on the shoulder. "Sally, this is Lucy. Lucy, this is my girlfriend Sally." I smile back. Her rich red hair is fixed in a cute, chopped bob, which her flowing tank dress and Converse shoes only accentuate. She has that 1950's glamorous build to her in cute, punk clothing.

"Your boyfriend tried to save my butt the other day," I explain. "He's a smart guy." Alex beams and Sally looks up at him with green doe eyes. I wonder if that's how Zach and I look together.

"Smart? Are you sure you've got the right guy?" She nudges Alex in the side and he laughs. She's playful, perfect for him.

"Sally's a genius and loves to let me know it." Alex turns to her. "Lucy's the girl I've been telling you about. The one who got sick. You know, the girl who punched Justin in the hospital."

"How'd you know I punched him?"

"I was in the truck bed. When Justin came out of the

ER, he had a bag of ice on his eye. He told me to shove it. Solid punch, Lucy." He puts his arm around Sally, being a good boyfriend. She is his priority.

"When are you coming back?"

"Tomorrow. Don't worry, I'm going to be the best painter ever," I lie.

"You ready for that ladder again?" he asks as he rubs Sally's shoulder.

"Absolutely, all the way up." Alex's friends shuffle behind him, pool sticks and chalk in hand. "Well, I'll let you go. See you in the morning?"

"Bright and early."

I return to Zach's side and watch him win their doubles game. He puts his arm around me and I blush. He loves wrapping his arm around me. Marissa winks at me on the way to the restroom.

"Darts?" Zach nods toward the board across the room where a group of guys have gathered. Throwing a dart in front of all of those guys doesn't promise a shining moment for me. Or for Zach.

"Uh, not really. But, listen, that doesn't mean you can't go play." I'm a super-relaxed girlfriend. "Wouldn't bother me a bit."

"Really? Awesome." He dashes across the room and grabs the darts out of Matt's hand.

And there I am again, standing alone.

So, I go to the bathroom. Something to do.

I sit alone in the stall reading graffiti. *Jenny <3's Danny. Payton is a whore. Today, I will make a change!* The walls are a mosaic of proclamations of love, life advice, and insults. My right thumb nail is rather sharp. I think about carving in my own life statement. What should I say? *Don't fall off* *ladders.* Not amazing but whatever, it's something to do while Zach plays darts. I start carving the *D*.

A clicking pair of high heels pass in front of my stall and the sink turns on. I see a pair of Converse sneakers pass in front as well. Why did I choose the middle stall? It always feels weird knowing people are standing right in front of me while I'm peeing. Thankfully, I'm just carving the wall.

"Excuse you." It's Marissa's voice.

"Oh, I'm sorry. I didn't realize the sink would spray you." The voice is gentle and sweet. Converse shoes. Sally.

"Yeah, you wouldn't realize that, would you? You are just a stupid, ignorant … like … what? Twelve year old?" Marissa is looking hard for a fight. Sally looks more like an eighteen-year-old than her true fourteen-year-old self. If Marissa accused twelve, that means she's jealous.

My abs tighten. A jealous Marissa meant for a nasty confrontation. I pick my feet up off the ground, not wanting to be there.

"Oh." Sally isn't prepared with a comeback. She shows weakness and Marissa pounces.

"What are you doing in here anyway?"

"Uh, going to the bathroom?"

"Well, this is the girls' bathroom."

"I know." Oh sweet Sally. She is going to have to do better than that.

"Do you? Because with your hair, I'm pretty sure you're an altar boy from the 1800s."

"I—"

"Actually, no. If you were, you'd be skinny. I'm sorry," Marissa's heels click closer. "I was mistaken. You look more like a state-fair swine. All those pink, red, and disorderly freckles."

Marissa is really stretching for insults. This only strengthens Sally's case for being gorgeous. But, at fourteen, how can she know?

"Let me guess," Marissa continues. "You had an entire burger for dinner?" Marissa waits for an answer which, thankfully, Sally doesn't provide. "You did, didn't you? Honey, if you want to look great like me, you can only eat a few bites." Marissa's heels click toward the door and then the door squeaks closed. Finally.

The sniffing starts. I watch the Converse shoes cross in front of my stall. The stall next to mine creaks open and shut. Her sniffing grows more urgent. The toilet-paper holder clangs against my stall's wall. She sobs and blows her nose.

I want to give her privacy but I can't. As far as she knows, she and Marissa were alone. The thought of being fourteen and having a senior rip you apart while her junior friend listened is enough to destroy any girl. She doesn't need to know I was here.

I wait with my arms hugging my legs up on the toilet seat, barely breathing. Sally sniffles and her occasional sobs sound like they could be my own.

The toilet-paper roll clangs against my stall's wall. One last sniff before Converse shoes walk out to the sink. Water splashes, the best way to calm a tear-stained face. The door squeaks open and shut. I'm alone.

I release my grip on my knees and my insides collapse. I should have opened the stall door and told Marissa to stop the moment she said "Excuse me." I should have given Sally a hug and comforted her or at least explained how Marissa works. But no, I picked up my feet, hugging them to my chest on a toilet seat. How have I come to this?

I wash my hands out of habit and return to the pool room. My gut churns. Sally sits on a stool, Alex standing behind her giving her a slow, rocking hug. A smile is plastered on her face, trying to hold it all together. Alex whispers in her ear and she temporarily drops her smile, nodding. He takes her hand and leads her from the room. I'm impressed. He's an in-tune boyfriend.

I jump when a hand suddenly rests on my shoulder. It's ridiculous how easy I jump. But after that year of the seniors torturing me in the locker room, I just can't help it.

"Marissa and I are going to run out to her car." Zach rubs his chin.

"Yeah, you know my front tire? How it screeches when I turn left? Zach says he'd take a look at it."

"Oh, okay." Her front tire did squeak. "I'll come watch." I'd love to see Zach looking over a car. Guys like that.

"No need." Marissa points me back to the pool table. "Stay, play, have fun."

"Yeah, you can stay here, Lucy. It'll be totally boring." Zach pulls me to him, his hands around my waist, and gives me a kiss. "I want you to have a good time tonight." He smiles down at me and my knees go weak. "Go play pool. I'll be right back and then I can show you how to throw darts." I nod. "Just you and me." He kisses my cheek and then he and Marissa are gone.

I end up at the pool table, fighting a daze. I don't want to play pool. I want to hang out with Zach and Marissa, watching Zach work on the car. His kiss threw me off. No. I want to be with him. I should be with him. As I turn to leave, I bump into Matt.

"Sorry."

"It's okay." He has two pool sticks in hand. "I was just coming over to see if you wanted to shoot with me?" Matt holds out a pool cue.

I relent. Zach will be back soon anyway. "Okay, I suck though."

"Doesn't matter. We're just going to shoot. Any ball, any time, any pocket."

I smile back at him. That, I can do.

I like shooting pool with Matt. He is quiet and simple. He says exactly what he is thinking but never too much. We talk about math class and the final exam. He got a B+ in the class. I tell him I got a C.

"What?" He straightens up in disbelief. "You always aced every pop quiz and test."

"How'd you know?"

"My last name is Yates. Y before Z. I always correct your exams." No wonder I always corrected Shaun Anderson's paper. "So, how did you get a C?"

I cringe. It is one thing to have your parents call you out on your grades, but a classmate?

"Homework." He looks at me with one eyebrow raised. "I hate busy work." It's a lame excuse.

"Yeah, busy work sucks. I get that. But, I figure, if you can't bring yourself to do it now, you'll just have to do it later. Life happens that way."

Is he talking about homework or is he being more philosophical? Maybe he's saying I won't get into college, so I'll have crappy jobs the rest of my life. Or does he mean that life is always filled with busy work, so get used to it?

I shoot the number four ball into the left, back pocket. Or, maybe, just maybe, I'm thinking too much.

"I bet your parents were pissed, huh?" he asks.

"Yup. Grounded."

"Is that why your mom crashed Watson's party? You snuck out?"

I blush. I didn't know Matt had been there.

"Exactly."

Matt takes a shot, sinking two balls. "Then what happened?"

"Oh." Other than the nurse, no one has asked me that before.

"You don't have to talk about it if you don't want to."

"No, it's just. No one's really wanted to know." I hate that this is true.

Matt looks at the door that leads to our cars, where Zach and Marissa are. "Really?"

"Yeah."

"Well then," he rests his chin on top of his pool stick. "What happened?"

"They made me get a job." And so I start my story. Matt nods and "uhuh's" with me through my whole story. When I get through the hospital part, he simply says "that sucks," and he means it.

It feels so good to tell someone who listens. Before I know it, I'm telling him about Justin and how he is driving me crazy mad.

"Oh, don't sweat it. Justin's awesome."

I scrunch up my face. I was worried he'd say that. My respect for Matt falls a few notches. Why can't regular people see how Justin is only crazy in love with himself?

Matt opens his mouth to explain but I never hear it.

Marissa and Zach walk in together. Marissa announces, "Ten o'clock, Lucy. Curfew. Gotta get you home or your mom will kill me."

I want to crawl under the pool table and die.

Matt scrunches up his nose, studying Marissa and me. He walks with me to the door, pulling me aside as Zach and Marissa leave. "Why her?"

"It's a long story. She's not that bad. I mean, she is, but she isn't. She saved me."

"Saved you?"

"Again, long story." Marissa honks her horn. "I'll see you later?"

"Yes. At my birthday party, okay? Don't miss it. I'll text you."

Honk.

"Absolutely."

Zach waits for me outside Marissa's car. He opens his arms and I wrap myself in them.

"Thanks for the dinner," I say, trying to sound intriguing.

"Yup. No sweat." He pulls out of the hug and looks down at me with a relaxed grin. "I had a fun night."

"Me too." I lie.

"I'll call you tomorrow night, okay?" He opens the passenger door for me and I slide in.

"Oh, okay." The goodbye is too quick. Marissa starts pulling away and I haven't even had a chance to kiss him. *Oh, okay* is the best thing I can come up with. Mental note: plan boyfriend goodbyes in advance.

"I so need a boyfriend." Marissa hits the steering wheel.

"You will snag the right guy, soon." She looks at me

like I'm crazy. "The Justin plan." I smile, thinking about how annoyed Justin will become with her reckless pursuit. He deserves it.

"Of course. But that's not now. With my calculations, it'll be a month before I can seal that deal. That's like half the summer."

"But it's worth it, right? I mean, Marissa, we're talking about Justin here." I suppress my gag. Marissa looks mad and lonely. If I can eliminate at least one of her emotions, the drive will be much more tolerable.

"You know what? You're actually right. Justin is worth the wait. I need to focus, set my eyes on the prize, you know?"

"Exactly. Pursue him with all you've got."

"Hell, yes." Marissa giggles and puts her foot on the accelerator. Crisis averted.

How does Marissa live with her emotions constantly oscillating? Flirtatiousness. Jealousy. Loneliness. Excitement. Keeping ahead of her exhausts me. I can't let her dwell; it'd be too easy to slip onto her bad side. I don't want to be the lame friend with a ten o'clock curfew. Will I ever achieve a status she is happy with?

But then I think of Sally and wonder if I even want to.

CHAPTER NINE

Justin's white truck sputters up my driveway. His door flies open and I wave him back. No way am I letting him come in. I can't let him infiltrate my life further. Who picks up people at the front door anyway? Normal people wait in the driveway. Somehow Justin stays on top of the social pyramid when he clearly doesn't play by the rules. It pisses me off.

"Good morning," Justin says as I open the passenger door and shove my stuffed bag under the seat. Justin snickers. "I see someone decided to come prepared."

"Better than not."

"Like the other day?"

"You could have given me more of a warning of what to expect."

Justin puts the car in reverse. "Hey, I offered you help.

You didn't want it."

"But you knew that would happen, didn't you?"

"I hoped not. I was banking on you listening to Alex." He looks at me out of the corner of his eye. "But you're more stubborn than I thought."

I purse my lips. "I wasn't stubborn. I was thirsty. You can survive for a month without food but only a few days without water." He laughs at me. My fingers clench. "I'm serious."

He waves my comment away. "Well, despite your survival facts, Alex should have stopped you."

"To his credit, Alex tried. He did."

Justin shrugs and pulls onto the exit for the Cross-Town Highway.

"We aren't going back to the yellow house?"

"Nope. We finished it yesterday. Starting a big project today, an association of homes. We'll be based out there for a month or so."

"Where is out there?"

"Minnetonka. About a fifty-minute drive."

Forty-six minutes to go.

"Get comfortable." Justin turns on the radio to some news station. The news is growing on me and it keeps Justin silent. He's much more tolerable that way.

I zone out, watching the people in the cars next to us, all rushing. A man passes us on the right talking on his Bluetooth, already working for the day. A woman applies lipstick and sings while driving a red minivan that looks like an opossum, hood slanted like a nose to the ground. Toys litter her backseat. She seems happy to be having the drive alone.

Mom got rid of our minivan when I started on the high

school basketball team. She called the van her "Tween Bus." Filled with middle school girls, lip gloss, magazines, iPods, basketball bags, lotions, and ribbons, it earned its name. The van was old, with bench seats and no CD player, which is exactly why Mom bought it. She couldn't handle our chatter and music. I guess I can't blame her for that.

My heart aches. I really miss those girls. I drifted away during freshman year. I didn't want to have to answer their questions—they were too good at asking them. I stopped answering phone calls and stood them up for our basketball dates. Eventually, the calls stopped coming. Instead of talking on the phone, I sat alone in my room and cried. What did I expect, them to rescue me? No one could rescue me from that situation ... except for Marissa, and she did.

No. I don't need to feel lost today. What I need is confidence, dignity, and the ability to not fall flat on my face. I scroll through my iPod, skipping Marissa-made playlists and select Mozart. I crank the volume down, the perfect background track. He seems to fit the weather and general vibe of the day.

I peek at Justin, who sits back relaxed, attentively listening to the newscast. I wouldn't have pinned him as an NPR listener. He hasn't shaved this morning so his extra-thick stubble highlights his square jaw. My stomach flips in a girly way, and I make myself focus on the windshield. Okay. So what? He's gorgeous but still a jerk. I shift my eyes toward the clock, thirty more minutes, and then close them to rest.

NPR features two doctors and two nutritionists debating the Gluten Disease. I peek at Justin who's strumming his fingers on the steering wheel, like this is a really great song. The NPR mediator takes a brief break and switches to a commercial. A frail voice cracks through the speakers. "I want to be a football player. Not have leukemia." Another voice adds, "I was a ballerina ... until leukemia." Soft music begins to play, making my heart ache. Crap. I'm such a softie for these advertisements. I wait it out, listening to the celebrity call for action to help Children's Leukemia Research. I thumb my phone, feeling guilty. But it's not like I even have a credit card to give anything with. Heck, if I gave money every time I felt moved, my parents would be broke.

Justin, on the other hand, grabs his phone off the center console and scrolls through his contacts, pushing send.

Ha. He hadn't even noticed the commercial. He's probably calling Jennifer, arranging a hot date for the night. How insensitive! Not that I was planning to call in, but still.

"Kate, hey!" Justin's voice is smooth. "Great to hear your voice again too." He pauses, scratching that fabulous stubble. "Naw. I don't want to go on air in Phoenix. Just put me down for the usual."

On air?

The NPR mediator returns, announcing the next segment, a live research conference on Children's Leukemia Research from Phoenix.

Holy crap.

He's donating!

"We should definitely catch up. When are you in town again?" He motions for me to open the glove box. He points and smiles at a small black notebook and pen. I hand it back. Seriously? Is he always this prepared?

"A month? Great. I'd love to help. What's your cell?" He jots her name and number across his pad. "Fantastic. Thanks for the opportunity. You've got my number?"

Stupid question. Of course she does. He's freakin' Justin Marshall.

"Sounds good. Have a good one," he says before hanging up.

That short conversation adds a whole new dimension to Justin. He's a regular donator. But why? How?

He hands the notebook back to me. "Thanks."

As I place it back in the glove box, a political advertisement for his dad catches on my finger. Ahh, right.

"So? Are you commissioned to donate to research facilities on behalf of your dad's campaign or something?" The question flies from my mouth before I can stop it. Horrible, rude. But then again, it is Justin. It's not like he hasn't ever been blunt with me.

Justin's green eyes snag my breath with their intensity. "No," he says. "I donate my own money and time to leukemia research."

"Are you prepping for your own run for senate soon?" This all makes sense. A future politician. He's smart, keeping his record clean. Already building a foundation.

"Ah, I see you have me all figured out."

"Pretty much. It's not a bad thing to be so transparent though. I'm sure you'll make a great senator someday."

"Do I have your vote?"

Ha. "Probably not."

"I didn't think so," he says with a slight smile. "I'll have to change that, huh?"

"Good luck trying."

Justin nods as he switches into the right-hand lane, before slowly pulling off to the shoulder of the road and throwing on his hazard lights.

"You better not be giving me a campaign speech or something. I'm locked in here. Totally not fair."

His green eyes find mine again. "Lucy, what do you know about my family?"

"Why are we on the side of the road?"

"Just answer the question."

I sigh, debating how much it's appropriate for me to reveal. From Marissa's obsession, I already know far too much. "Well, your dad's running for governor. Your mom runs charities." He nods along. "Doesn't your sister have a home design business or something?"

"Sort of. Fashion, actually."

"Right. You kind of have the perfect family." It's true. Everyone knows it.

"We all love each other and aren't afraid to show it." His words fall gently.

"You're lucky." Bitterness bites on my tongue as my stomach clenches. My family dynamics are so far from that.

"Yeah, well, tragedy brings a family together."

I swallow. "What happened?" My stomach tightens. I can't believe I asked that.

He nods to the radio. "My older brother, Jackson, died from leukemia when I was four. He was seven. I was his bone-marrow donor. I gave it twice. … It never took."

My hand flies over my mouth. I'm such an ass. Here he's been being real, and I've been a total jerk. I reach out and touch his arm. "I'm sorry for your loss and that that happened to your family."

Justin blinks the redness away. "Yeah, well, our family doesn't really advertise it. We give quietly. It's not that we aren't proud or wanting to keep the memory of Jackson alive. It's just our thing that the media doesn't need to know about." He smiles at me, but not his fake smile. It's real, relaxed.

"You must think I'm horrible, assuming you donated for political gain."

"It's an interesting insight." He glances down at my hand still resting on his arm. Oh, right. I pull it back as he says, "You never know what the future may hold. But, preferably, I'll go into the business of medical research." He shifts the truck into drive and pulls back onto the highway.

Silence hangs between us. It sucks. This is the first time I've ever wanted Justin to speak to me and I've given him every reason to close up. I take a deep breath. He's got to at least know I care.

"I really am sorry about your brother."

He nods. "Thanks. That means a lot. It's alright though. I'll see him again someday." His confidence surprises me. I don't know any guy who talks about faith so frankly. "In the meantime, I've got my sister and my parents. We're lucky." He pulls back onto the highway. "Tell me about your family."

I freeze, not knowing what to say. My relationship with my parents isn't like his. He wouldn't understand it. I mean, how am I supposed to complain about Mom controlling my life when he has such a different perspective?

Justin watches me. "That's okay. We've got the whole summer."

I shrug.

"So, what's it like dating Zach?" He asks instead. "I bet you've never felt so appreciated." His sarcasm can't be missed.

"Seriously, you follow up your story with that?"

"Aw, come on. It's got to be awesome to listen to him talk about his lacrosse stick constantly." He snickers at his implication.

"It's not like that."

"It's Zach. I don't care what you think, kid. But it's like that."

I actually huff. Kid? My blood pressure rises. I want to throw my iPod at his face. "Thanks," I say with as much confidence as I can fake.

"For what?"

"For reminding me why I despise you."

He chuckles while I reach over to turn on the radio, flipping it to my favorite music station. I turn the volume up and settle back into my seat. I can feel his eyes on me. He chuckles again.

I hate that chuckle.

Justin relents, leaving me to my thoughts and my top-40 music.

Lacrosse stick.

No. Zach isn't like that. He likes to make out but he never hinted at more than that. My legs grow antsy. Is he hoping for it, though? He's a year older than me. Maybe that's his goal? A hole carves out in my stomach.

Marissa lost her virginity on a beach during spring break in Panama City. She kept saying how fun it was to fool around and that it's essential to do before seventeen. "A girl needs experience before she finds *the one* so she can do it right." I totally agreed at the time. But now that hole has doubled into a huge pit. She'd made it sound so casual and free.

Can I do that with Zach? Immediately I taste bile in the back of my throat. I swallow it.

No. That's something I can never give him. I'm not ready for it. I couldn't be that girl even if I tried. I sigh and Justin glances my way. I sink down in my seat.

My face heats. Not even in theory am I ready for sex.

***

The universe is kind to me. My first few days back on the job are uneventful. I manage to stay on my feet and the ladder. Alex welcomes me like an eager younger brother, claiming me as his partner for the entire project at the association.

The association is larger than I'd expected. Seventeen single-family homes with extensive landscaping strategically positioned around a community pool, park, and tennis court. Alex explains that these homes are considered a pioneer in home associations in the Twin Cities. Each home is at least three thousand square feet and, unlike the association where I live, each home's exterior and floor plan are completely unique.

BMWs, Porsches, and Escalades decorate many of the driveways. Luxury living. I picture myself spilling a bucket of paint in one of the beautifully landscaped gardens below. My lack of gracefulness does not accompany "luxury" well.

Thankfully, we don't start with paint. Alex scores one of the power washers and some scrapers to restart my education. He meticulously shows me how to power wash and follow up with the scraper, scraping away any loose paint that the wash did not remove. Once I am proclaimed proficient, Alex leads us in a rotation between power washing and scraping so our arms won't get too tired and we won't get too bored.

I enjoy power washing. Blasting away old paint is as satisfying as picking off nail polish. I love the loud, constant hum from the air-compressor supply. It leaves me alone with my thoughts and sometimes, when I'm lucky, the sound will take them away as well. Whenever I get tired, I play the *William Tell* Overture. It may as well be a power-washing anthem. I forgot how much I enjoy classical music. The songs used to be part of my morning pre-game ritual. They relax me like nothing else.

Alex and I prep ten houses in three days. At the end of each day, I climb back into Justin's truck and pull my hat down over my eyes. Justin, as exhausted as I am, seems to get my message and leaves me to myself on the drive home. He listens to ethereal rock music that's strangely beautiful and always lulls me to sleep. It seems that as long as I work hard, Justin is willing to leave me alone. After two pleasant drives, I start to hope that maybe Justin is finally done bothering me and we can maintain this casual, professional relationship.

It isn't until the third night when I finally collapse into bed that I have a nagging feeling of disappointment. I toss and turn, trying to find a comfortable position. I'm exhausted. Why can't I fall asleep?

The disappointment answers me. Isn't the real question why isn't Justin being annoying anymore?

Justin hadn't done anything on the drive that morning

to bother me, other than occasionally glancing my way. I turn to the window, looking out at the tree I climbed down just two weeks before. Am I not interesting to him anymore? My heart sinks deep into my chest, hiding away.

Why did he stop? I ache with a sense of loss.

I take a deep breath, accepting what my instincts know to be true. Somewhere, deep inside me, I enjoy having this annoying relationship with Justin. Whenever he pisses me off, at least I know I'm noticed. And now Justin is bored with me and I'm left with a hole in place of his attention. Attention I never wanted in the first place.

I close my eyes and visualize this new void inside of me. I don't need to fill it with something else. I just need it to go away. I watch the void get smaller, a trick Mom explained to me enthusiastically after one of her therapy sessions. I never asked for clarification but I knew that whatever void she was trying to shrink was something I had made.

I curl up into a ball. I take slow breaths in through my nose and out through my mouth, allowing each breath to leave my body with a piece of this void. My heart beat slows as I watch the void disappear.

As I drift in and out of sleep, I think about Justin's charming smile and rolling laugh. I visualize his strong forearms and washboard abs. He's gorgeous. I forgive myself for my stupidity. I'm only human after all. Any girl would feel this way if she was stuck spending the summer with Justin. Isn't that what I want? Just to be like every other girl?

A tear rolls down my cheek.

I catch one last fleeting message from my heart as I drift to sleep.

When exactly did my life goal become being ordinary?

***

BZZZZZ. I wake up covered in sweat. My head hurts. Talk about fitful sleep.

As my head's fog drifts away, I remember the ache I felt the night before. I search for the void and am thankful I can't feel it anymore. My muscles relax. I'm so thankful that morning brought reason. I don't need Justin to make me feel complete. I take a moment, standing up straight and adjusting my swept bangs.

I don't need him.

Why would I need him?

Why would I want him?

I pull out my phone and find Zach's number. I have a great boyfriend.

I thumb the call button as it highlights his name but then catch the time. Six twenty-eight. Somehow, no matter how much I know Zach likes me, I can't picture him wanting to get a call from me this early.

My phone vibrates.

Justin: Get your butt out here. Or would you rather I come in?

What the hell? Twenty-eight minutes early. I text back as I press the puffy part under my eyes with a cold rag.

Me: Learn how to read a clock.

Justin: Either come out or your Mom can drive you.

Never. I can't face Mom's smug look when I explain why I missed my ride. Or worse, be stuck in traffic with her. I throw clothes on and brush my teeth in the kitchen as I shove some random protein bars and crackers in my bag. It'll have to do.

I yank open the passenger door with as much annoyance as I can portray. I throw my light bag under the seat and heave myself up into the truck. "If I end up in the hospital today, it's on you."

He smirks. "I think you'll survive." He looks at me out of the corner of his eyes and then rolls them in a dramatic fashion. He laughs to himself. My chest heats.

"Why are you so early?"

"Better than late."

I fake a yawn. "Pretty sure I'd prefer late."

"Then Zach's perfect for you, huh?"

I open my mouth to retort but no words come out. My snappy comeback is tangled up in emotions. He is so annoying. But he is bothering me. Why did my heart grow warm when he laughed? And, more importantly, was he going to do it again?

I must have a stumped look on my face because he actually does laugh again. My heart skips a beat.

"What? Nothing to dish out this morning?"

My tongue finally finds words. "No. I'm just wondering if it is worth it."

Justin turns toward me. "Oh trust me, what you have to say is always worth it."

I bite the inside of my lip as my heart flips. No. I push the flips aside. I'm not going to allow myself to misinterpret what Justin means.

"I'm sure," I throw in some sarcasm before putting my head phones on and looking out the window. As each car drives past, I search for reason.

Justin is dating Jennifer, the perfect girl. He has no

interest in me. Plus, I have Zach. I think of how Zach would lean in toward me while he spoke. It feels like sunshine when Zach turns his attention on me. I think of him pressing me into the corner booth and kissing me while his strong hands hold the small of my back. My stomach flips and I smile. My heart just needed to be realigned.

I pull out my phone to type Zach an email. Too early to text. "Hey," I write. "Just thinking of you. We should hang out tonight. Maybe go to a movie? I would have texted but I didn't want to wake you. Hope you're sleeping well!"

I fumble with the keys as I consider how to sign the email. Texting is awesome because no signature is required. Email makes it trickier. A dash would seem too impersonal. But love, love you, or even luv u, can be misinterpreted. I settle for the cheesy "<3 Lucy." Up until this moment I'd always rolled my eyes at the use of <3. But as I type it, I feel a growing appreciation for the cliché symbol.

I push send and lean back in my seat. Moments later, my cell buzzes.

Zach: Out running. Let's grab dinner. I owe you— remember?

Me: Absolutely. That'd be great.

Zach: Awesome. Romano's. Pick you up at 7.

I smile, thinking of that romantic corner in Romano's.

"What's with the silly grin?" Justin's voice cuts into my thoughts. He is so nosy. I can approach this two ways: either refuse to acknowledge his question or brag about my date. I choose the shallower approach.

"Just planning a date with Zach," I say.

Justin scrunches up his nose. "Oh, still seeing *that guy?*"

"Um, yes. Not much has changed in the last week." I mock his cackle.

Justin won't take his eyes off me, making me shift in place. "Didn't I tell you not to see that guy? He's not worth it."

Like hot water on dry ice, I steam. Why would I listen to him?

I readjust myself in my seat so I can face him square on. If we crash, we crash.

"You can't tell me who to date. I make my own choices. Zach's a great guy. I choose him." I glare at Justin with venom. He needs to back off, now.

His serious expression slowly becomes more relaxed. Hint taken.

"So you go against the advice of a wiser, older man?" He laughs.

My heart flips. That damn noise.

Justin turns back to the road, leaning back in his seat with a huge smile on his face. His smug smile pushes me over the edge.

"You are so full of yourself. Yup," I taunt. "I said it. full of yourself. You aren't God!" The adrenaline flies through my system. "What on earth would give me any incentive to listen to you? You are an egotistical, pompous ass!" The words are sweet relief flying off my tongue.

"I am, am I?" He sucks in his cheeks, nodding slowly. "I assume this is not a random conclusion?"

"Hell, no. It's well studied, I assure you."

"So you've been studying me?" He chuckles and it vexes me despite the beauty of its roll. Maybe being around Justin is good? It's a great reminder that we are not compatible.

"I won't dignify that with an answer, as I'm sure your head will explode."

"So you have?"

"For real? You are seriously clueless. Listen to me. Get over yourself. You're not royalty."

Justin studies the glare in my eye and his smile fades.

Good. Comprehension.

He shrugs. "At least I'm not as clueless as you, Lucy."

CHAPTER TEN

Justin doesn't talk to me the rest of the day which is great, because I can't stand him. But I do find a white plastic bag filled with three water bottles and a breakfast sandwich at the bottom of my ladder before our morning break. His version of apologizing? That or he doesn't want me to faint again. He also took care of lunch, buying the entire crew pizza. We downed eight pizzas in ten minutes.

As Alex and I power wash, I occasionally sneak glimpses of Justin priming the house behind me. He usually spends the day listening to music, joking around with the crew. Today he paints iPod-free and only once squirted Emmanuel with a hose. He never glances in my direction. He doesn't even say goodbye when I climb out of his truck at the end of the day.

He's acting like a child. I want to shake him. He

deserves every word I said. And now he's punishing me? I hate how his silence is worse than his taunting.

Mom picks up on my agitation the moment I walk through the door. She stands at the counter, soaking bulbs in some new concoction while mud drips from her gardening boots onto the hardwood floor. Her look of concentration reminds me of a kid enthralled in their first science experiment. It would have been cute, except she is supposed to be a mom.

Sadly, her concentration is not deep enough to miss me as I pass by.

"How was your day, Lucinda?"

I take a deep breath before turning around. A few nights ago, I begged Mom to stop treating me like a child. Her response was "Of course, Lucinda. I will never call you Lucy again." She knows I hate my full name. By using Lucinda, she picks at the fresh scab. I take another deep breath. I am so not in the mood for this.

I turn around to face her. "Fine." I force myself to smile at her with all the pleasantries of a stranger. I can't handle this if it doesn't go smoothly. "How was yours?"

"Great." She motions to the table for me to sit with her. I opt to remain standing, leaning against the wall with my arms crossed. "What's wrong?" she prods.

"Nothing's wrong. Why do you always assume something's wrong, Mom?" I uncross my arms, attempting to appear casual. In control.

She brings her hands together in front of her center as she breathes in slowly through her nose. Therapeutic breathing. I get lots of this.

"Well," she begins, "as your mother, I'm in tune. I know what that look in your eye means. What happened?"

My blood seethes. She's in tune? No way. "Maybe you're just imagining this *look* so you have an excuse to talk to me?" I roll my eyes before I grab an apple to toss around. "Nothing's wrong, okay? And even if there was, I wouldn't dream of telling you." My stomach ties in a knot. That was a total bitchy thing to say, but it's the truth. She has no right to know everything going on in my life.

"Lucinda, now that isn't fair. I'm your mother. If something is wrong, I need to know."

"Nothing is wrong. And you don't need to know my problems," I snap back, harsher than I intended. I look at the door out of the corner of my eye. My exit isn't far.

Mom glares back at me before standing up and crossing the room where a vase with pink carnations and white lilies sits on the counter. "Fine." She forces a smile back at me. "These came for you today." She pulls the card out and hands it to me. I quickly examine the envelope's seal. It hasn't been broken.

"Thanks," I say slowly, for both handing me the card and, for once, not violating my privacy.

The card is embossed with roses bordering some scratchy, boy handwriting. "Lucy, I can't wait for our date tonight. I'll see you at 7. ~ Zach"

See, Zach is a great boyfriend. I wish Justin was here so I can shove the flowers in his face.

"Will you at least share who the flowers are from?" Mom asks as she wipes the mud off her boots and the floor.

I opt for honesty, knowing that a refused answer would only land me in a situation where we would fight over whether I would be going on the date.

"Zach." I hand her the card. "My boyfriend," I add for emphasis.

"Oh," she scans the card. "And where are you going?"

"Romano's."

Mom wanders over to her bowl of bulbs and garden potions. "Well, since you have been working at painting and are being accountable for your whereabouts, that should be fine."

I clench my jaw. I haven't asked her permission, yet she feels obligated to give it. I don't need her permission. Thankfully, reason comes to my rescue. She's giving me permission. I take a deep breath, holding in my real response. If I fight this, I definitely won't be sitting in a secluded corner with Zach and a plate of Chicken Marsala.

This isn't a battle worth winning. So I simply nod and make my exit.

***

"Hey, Pretty." Zach smiles at me and my stomach flips over.

"Hey, you." You? Is that really the best I can do? "Thanks for the flowers."

"No problem. I think I was due to send you some." He winks at me. I catch Dad and Eric watching us pull away through the living-room window. Eric waves. I don't wave back.

"So, what did you do today? Pool time with Marissa?" Zach begins.

"I wish. But my painting job totally ruined those summer plans."

"Right, right. How's that going?"

"It's fine. Hard work but I'm learning."

"I bet. I feel bad for you. Spending the whole summer with Justin. Staying away from him?"

"We barely speak," I say truthfully.

"That's my girl." Zach pulls out his phone. "Sorry. I owe someone a text."

I watch as he texts while driving. I hate that this makes me so nervous. His eyes never leave his phone yet we are driving sixty-seven miles per hour. Marissa always texts while driving and I'm still not comfortable with it. I clutch the door handle and pray we won't hit anything or anyone. He explains he was arranging another captain's practice for this weekend.

I hide my sigh of relief in a steady breath when Zach pulls us safely into Romano's parking lot. He meets me in front of the Jeep and wraps his warm hand around mine, leading me into the restaurant. We are immediately seated at a small table up front near the window. I mask a bit of disappointment when we aren't given that table in the back corner. Goosebumps prickle my arms as I scan my menu. Something hums above me; of course I'm sitting right under the air-conditioning vent.

I eye the women around me. Only a few wear cardigans while most endure the temperature to show off their outfits. Fashion obviously outweighs comfort in the dating world. I smile at Zach, determined not to let the temperature ruin my date or my outfit.

Zach reaches his hand across the table and intertwines his fingers in mine. I willingly allow him to dominate the dinner conversation. He talks about lacrosse and shares his hopes of getting an athletic scholarship. I reassure him and he squeezes my hand in response. Zach seems gentler without his team around. He keeps eyeing me and from time to time, tells me how beautiful I look.

Zach's attention and the dim lighting lull me into a romantic haze. Every time he repositions his hand in mine, a chill wanders up my spine.

After dinner, he suggests a walk in the park. The sun is almost set and brilliant colors fill the sky. Soon the lamp posts will light as the sky darkens. He puts his arm around me as we walk the paths toward the river. He slides his hand into my back pocket.

My face warms. It feels awkward having his hand there and I know we are now one of those silly couples with their hands on one another's butt. But, somehow, it makes me feel good knowing that I am Hand on the Butt worthy.

I can't wait to tell Marissa.

Zach walks me over to a bench behind a hedge, completely private.

"We can watch the sunset best from here," he whispers in my ear as we sit down. His skin is so warm next to mine.

It's like I'm living out a scene in a movie.

Zach pulls me close to him and we cuddle silently as the sun slips away. The extraneous noises of the park die down as well. Our secluded bench might as well be a deserted island.

My heart pumps in my head. The feeling of Zach's hand rubbing up and down my arm is electrifying. I shudder in anticipation.

Zach pulls me close to him and presses his lips softly to mine. It's unlike any of his kisses before. Maybe this is the real Zach? I can't get enough of the tenderness of his kiss.

I respond with the same pressure, letting him know this is the type of kissing I like. I pull my fingers through his hair as he pulls my waist closer.

He continues to kiss me, the passion increasing. His hands wander up and down my back. I am lost in him. Somehow, he moves me from the bench onto the grass below. He presses his body into mine and his hand wanders up and down my thigh.

His kiss intensifies, pushing his tongue into my mouth with a bit too much force. It becomes too much and I need a moment to breathe. His weight is crushing. I push away from him as his hand wanders up my top. He keeps kissing me, a bit softer now, supporting more of his weight as he leaves his hand resting on my waist.

I return his kisses but my mind is racing a million miles per second. How far does Zach want to go? How far am I willing to go? I think of Justin's *lacrosse stick* comment in the car. Zach's body presses back into mine and the crushing weight returns. I try to take a breath but can barely fill my lungs. I'm not imagining things. It really is hard to breathe.

Suddenly, his hand is up my shirt, resting on my bra. The moment his fingertips reach inside the cup, my instincts take over. Adrenaline surges before me and suddenly I'm pushing him off of me. Too much and too soon.

Zach looks confused for a moment. He leans in to kiss me again, this time grabbing my neck and pulling my head to his while he shoves his tongue down my throat.

I pull away, gasping. "Stop." This time he relents. He sits beside me, pulling his hands through his hair.

I move a foot away, trying to grasp what just happened.

"It was just too quick," I whisper. I want to be ready for this, but I'm not.

Zach purses his lips together.

I wait, not knowing what to say.

"Okay." Zach takes a deep breath. "That's fine." He stands up and walks away.

I force myself to follow.

"I'm really sorry, Zach. I'm just not ready for that." I rest my hand on his arm. "Not yet, but someday." I try to reassure him even though I know it isn't true.

He nods and pulls out his phone, answering a text before looking my way.

"I should probably get you home."

"Yeah," I mutter. I check my phone. Nine forty-six. Every step away from the bench makes me feel more like a lame, little girl. I wish I could have just shut my eyes and done a little bit more. At least I wouldn't feel like such a prude.

I study him out of the corner of my eye while he responds to another text, gnawing on his lip. He doesn't seem angry, more disappointed. I can manage disappointment. I just need time.

I break the silence on our ride home. "I had a really nice time tonight."

"Yeah? That's great." He speaks in more of his boisterous tone, although I can tell it is a bit forced.

I fill the awkwardness with comments about how well he manages his team. The texting never seems to end. He smiles and launches into some team politics. I agree with whatever he says and compliment him whenever possible.

But really, I just want to cry. I hate myself.

When we reach my driveway, he doesn't move from his

seat. I eye my house, not blaming him for not wanting to walk me to the door. I lean in toward him and give him a quick kiss because I know my parents are watching.

"Thanks," I whisper.

"No problem."

"I'll call you tomorrow?"

"Yup, cool."

I climb out of the car and pop inside to let Mom and Dad know I'm home. The last thing I need is my parents freaking out and punishing me for missing curfew when I was just hanging out outside.

I go straight to the basketball court off the side of our garage. I curl up with my back against the garage, right under the hoop. I look up through the circle of netting and study the moon.

And then I surrender to my tears.

I hate that I have to cry about Zach. Why can't I be more like Marissa? I don't have to go all the way but I could have at least done *something* more. What's wrong with me? I'm sixteen. I should be able to handle this.

My old purple street ball snuggles behind our front shrub. I crawl over and grab it, the rubber tread like massage therapy to my palm. The only thing that feels right, but I can't do it anymore. I hug it like an old teddy bear. Pathetic.

Maybe I can take just one shot. With wet cheeks, I stand up. Deep breaths. I just need to dribble out to the spray-painted three-point line, square up and shoot. But my chest squeezes the air out of me. My legs want to dart inside to my room. Sweat condenses on my palms and the ball slips through, bouncing away and back behind the shrub.

My heart stutters. Almost did it. But not even close. A sob erupts from my chest. I clamp my hand over my mouth. The windows are open. I can't let them know I'm out here, crying.

I thought I left this long ago.

BZZZZ. My back pocket vibrates. My phone, unknown number. Zach must be calling from home.

I steady my breath, grasping composure.

"Hello?"

"Hi, Lucy." The voice on the other end is higher than Zach's and not as forceful. "It's Alex."

"Oh, hi Alex." I sit up, a lame invisible attempt to sound collected. I rub my eyes. "What's up?"

"Just calling to let you know Luke, Emmanuel, and I will be picking you up in the morning. Justin won't be able to make it."

"Oh, that's fine. Same time?"

"Yeah, pretty much." Alex pauses and I take a deep breath. "Hey, are you okay, Lucy?"

"Of course I am," I say to Alex in the peppiest voice I can manage.

"Oh, okay. You just didn't sound like you, ya know?"

"It's the phone … it always does that to my voice. Don't worry about it."

"Okay," he draws out his pause. He doesn't believe me. "Well, alright. I guess I'll see you in the morning."

"Sounds good. Seven a.m.!" I say in my best cheerleader imitation.

I push end call on my way back to the front porch.

Justin won't be driving me tomorrow. He can't ask me how the date went. I grasp this small relief and then my brain runs wild as I walk inside. Would Justin have even asked after our argument this morning? He gave me the silent treatment all day and now he isn't even going to pick me up.

Is he that upset with me?

What have I done? It seems like no matter what I do in life I always do it wrong. I thumb my phone, hoping it will vibrate with at least a text from Zach. After a few minutes, I put it back in my purse. I don't know what I would say to him anyway.

I pace in my bedroom. My skin itches like I've done something wrong. I think of Zach's body pushing me against the ground. My skin crawls. I fill the bath and climb in, hoping to soak away whatever is making me feel so wrong.

Even my body knows I'm failing at everything.

CHAPTER ELEVEN

Alex pats me on the back when I climb in Emmanuel's minivan the next morning. Like a brother, he knows exactly what to do. He doesn't ask me much as we make the long drive. In fact, most of the way he argues with Luke over the best boy bands of all time. I have to hand it to Alex. He's one confident kid. He even has me smiling by the time we pull into the association.

The crew operates differently without Justin around. Troy walks around a bit more confidently, which is weird considering he is always our project manager. He seems very pleased with himself as he barks out orders. Oddly, the more orders Troy gives the less the guys seem to listen. They act like elementary school kids with a substitute teacher. Whenever Troy turns his back, Alex and Luke throw water on one another and Emmanuel mocks Troy with surprising accuracy. I welcome every distraction as I find myself searching the grounds for Justin, even though I know he's not around.

Troy sits beside me during our breakfast break. He lounges backward, with his left arm supporting him behind me. "It's like managing two-year-olds, I swear." He wipes his brow. "You can never take your eyes off of them." He motions toward Luke, who is trying to balance the handle of a paint roller on his palm.

I laugh politely as I notice Troy inch closer. I shift my weight to my knees, purposely leaning a bit away and giving myself space.

"Yup. This is my second summer as project manager," Troy continues. He looks around the complex and whistles. "A year ago, I managed only single-family homes. But, seriously, look at me now."

I bite my lip. Wait. Is Troy hitting on me? I cock my eyebrow. Like this? He leans in closer, mistaking my look of disbelief as a look of interest. He keeps looking at me intently, waiting for me to respond to his business accomplishment. "Yup—impressive," is about all I can manage.

I look away from his uncomfortable stare and catch Alex's eye with a pleading glance. He takes one look at Troy and rolls his eyes. Alex crosses the lawn and plops down in front of us, extending his legs out and in between us. Troy glares at him but Alex plays oblivious.

I owe him, big time.

"So, what's up Troy? When do you think we'll start tackling block three?" Alex asks.

"Next week."

"Why?"

"Because three comes after two ... "

"Right. That makes sense." Alex nods my way, "Isn't she doing great? I'm a great teacher, huh?"

Troy sits up straight and turns to me. Instantly his flirtatious demeanor disappears and his eyebrows furrow. I cross my arms in front of me before he gives his assessment. "Yes. She's competent in the basics and has potential. But her edging technique should actually be nurtured along a bit more."

Alex rolls his eyes from behind Troy. "Yeah, okay. I'll work with her along the edges." I mentally review my edging technique. My edge lines are actually cleaner than Alex's and Emmanuel's. Alex mouths, "You're fine," to me.

"No. Again, all business here, but your edge lines are not the best example." This time I roll my eyes in Alex's direction and smile. Troy turns back toward me as I smile, again misinterpreting my message. Troy returns my smile and winks. "In fact, I think I'll take over her coaching from here Alex."

"What? No way. She's my protégé."

I back away from Troy. "No really, Alex is doing great. I like learning from him."

"See, I'm doing great. Plus, you won't be able to manage if your attention is on Lucy."

"I'll manage."

"Troy, no really," I interject.

Troy holds out his hands for me to stop talking. "No, it's okay, Lucy. You can hang out with me and really master this painting thing." He looks in Alex's direction and directs in an overly authoritative tone, "You've done a great job. I'll send you all the new protégés to master the basics. Thank you for your help."

Alex bites his lower lip. "Fine." He stands up and brushes off his jeans. "Sorry, Lucy," he says before he walks away.

Troy looks at me. "Sorry for what?"

"It's an inside joke." I don't turn back to look at Troy. I watch Alex kick an empty bucket. I feel Troy lean in toward me, the smaller space making me uncomfortable. I stand up, turning my back away from Troy as I brush the fresh-cut grass off my butt. Somehow I'll find a way back into Alex's responsibility.

Troy puts his hand on my shoulder, "Great attitude, Lucy. Let's get going. Guys, break's over!" he bellows through my ear canal. His voice rattles down my spine.

As the morning wears on, I'm forced to conclude that Troy is a good guy, just not my type. He keeps making lame jokes, laughing too much at himself and over-praising me. Nothing he tries makes me remotely interested in him. The poor guy is spinning his wheels.

Luckily, I have a boyfriend. I fill most of our conversation with "Zach this, Zach that." I really want him to know that I'm taken. But Troy is clueless. He misinterprets every polite smile I give him, leaning in closer and closer throughout the day. Eventually, I revert to purposely messing up the basics in hopes that he will send me back to Alex.

I keep looking at my watch. It is already one o'clock and Troy still hasn't called lunch break. I notice the other guys slowing down, every so often looking in Troy's direction. I hope Troy will notice my stomach growling but he seems too focused on my trimming technique. I start to feel a bit woozy so I take matters into my own hands. I'm not going back to the hospital.

I climb down the ladder and lean in toward him. I take a deep breath and bat my eyelashes. I know I look ridiculous. I suck at flirting. Alex lets out a distinctive laugh from the scaffolding above.

"Troy," I say softly, "Do you think we can take a break?" I bat my eyelashes a bit more.

He looks at me with a dazed expression on his face. I can't believe it worked. He obviously does not interact with girls that often.

"Oh, right." He looks down at his watch and swears. "Guys—lunch!"

I jump off the ladder and leave it for Troy to take down, give him something to do other than ogle me.

Alex runs over and slaps me on the back. "Thanks! I swear—Luke's head was turning into a roast-beef sandwich. I'm starving!"

I laugh. "It's the least I can do considering I got you demoted."

"Yeah, well, that's for now. I'll figure something out. The boss will eventually notice that the productivity has crashed. Troy will be forced to give up training and go back to managing." He pats me on the back. "I will, however, miss the entertainment. Watching you react to Troy is hilarious."

"Ha ha. Funny." I playfully shove him away as I catch Troy eyeing me from across the lawn. I smile at Troy only to make Alex laugh. This will be a game that will no doubt carry us through the summer. I settle myself with my PB and J, gigantic water jug, and granola bar under a shady tree. I inhale my food and lean back to close my eyes. It feels so good to not be moving.

Moments of last night filter back into my mind. I lean in toward Zach at the restaurant and we walk hand-in-jeans-pocket through the park. The tender kiss that turns into lung-crushing force. I watch myself push him away and my lower lip quivers as I follow him back through the park. How did a night that started so well end in disaster?

My eyes itch and my throat tightens.

No. This will not happen here. I close my eyes tighter, allowing one tear to fall. Only a few more hours before I'll be home and I can call Zach and explain myself. I'm certain he'll understand. But how will I explain?

The loud clank of a familiar motor interrupts my thoughts. I don't even have to open my eyes.

Justin arrives.

I listen to Troy greet Justin. Their voices drop and they have a quick, hushed exchange. I open my eyelids only slightly to try to catch Justin's mood. Justin palms a basketball as he finishes his discussion with Troy. Troy shifts in place as they speak. Justin smiles and pats him on the back before throwing the basketball at Luke, only to steal the ball back immediately. Justin doesn't seem upset at all. Maybe I was just imagining yesterday? I watch everyone else rise from the shade to go greet Justin. The street soon becomes a basketball court, without hoops.

I sit awkwardly underneath the tree. I'd be avoiding Justin if I didn't stand up and join them. But, if I do, I risk Justin blowing me off. I survey our equipment, trying to find something legitimate to tend to so I don't appear rude, just busy.

My eye quickly rests on the stack of empty water bottles. Perfect.

I walk over to Justin's truck and grab a wagon out of

114

the bed. Justin catches my eye as I pile the empty bottles into the wagon. He takes a moment to smile at me, which results in Troy stealing the ball from him. I smile back and give a quick wave before motioning to the empty jugs of water.

Obviously I have very important work to do.

I haven't filled the water before. I remember Troy briefing us about a water fountain in the pool area that the association welcomed us to use. I pull the wagon down the street and up the pathway to the pool. I can't help but feel like a little girl as I haul the little red wagon around. If only I had some lemonade.

The pool complex is empty. It is a beautiful pool, shaped in a large L and surrounded with trendy loungers and umbrellas. These people live in style.

I find the water fountain on the opposite side of the pool house. I lean against the cool brick wall, filling each container with precision. I eye the pool, imagining how refreshing it would feel to dive in. I toy with the idea when the sound of the pool gate opening removes my chance.

A familiar giggle echoes off the cement around the pool. A splash soon follows. "No, you didn't. Come here, you!" The voice is instantly recognizable—Marissa. I have no idea why she's here but there's no doubt that Marissa has a flirtatious agenda.

Another splash and another squeal.

I finish filling the water bottles, wanting to reveal myself to Marissa before I interrupt anything too intimate. Marissa works quickly with guys.

I'm right. Marissa has pressed her new guy into the corner, where she wraps her arms around his neck and starts kissing him. I open my mouth to clear my throat but then I notice the sandy blond hair that Marissa's fingers are pulling through. Her hands resting on familiar biceps.

Zach!

Marissa is making out with Zach.

I don't know what to do. I stand there witnessing their slow kiss turn into a passionate make-out moment. I want to scream at them. I want to run away and hide. But all I manage is a gasp.

It is loud enough to make them take their tongues out of one another's mouths.

Marissa whips around, giving me, their interrupter, an annoyed expression. I watch as recognition dawns on her. She swims away from Zach and readjusts her bikini.

My eyes rest on Zach who doesn't seem to need any time to process the situation. He nods up at me. "Hey, Lucy." He reaches over and pulls Marissa back in front of him.

"Listen," Marissa begins. "I was going to tell you."

My shocked silence is replaced with livid anger.

"Bullshit." The words spew from my mouth. Zach moves toward the stairs, slowly climbing them and walking toward me. "How long has this been going on? How long?" I shriek.

Marissa shrugs, adopting her catty face that I have seen her use on way too many victims. "About as long as you've been dating." Her voice has that horrid edge, the one that allows her to step all over you … the one she used on Sally in the bathroom. She follows Zach out of the pool and ties a towel around her waist. She wraps her arms through Zach's. "It started getting more *intense* the night at Old Minnie." She giggles and looks up at Zach. "Remember, out by my car?" Zach nods.

"Oh. My. God." I feel like I have been slapped across the face. "You really are a jealous witch, aren't you?"

Zach takes a quick step toward me. "Dude, Lucy. It's no big deal."

I glare at him. "No big deal? Are you crazy? You cheated on me."

Zach shakes his head. "Come on, Lucy. We barely even dated."

"What?"

"Ok. Let's be honest here. We were never really together." He shuffles uncomfortably. "I mean … come on. You know what I mean?"

"No. I don't."

"Damn it. Come on. I sent you flowers last night. I took you to a nice dinner. I even tried to be romantic in the park."

I nod. "Yup. I remember that. Sounds like dating to me."

Zach shakes his head before replying in a condescending tone, "How do I make this clear?" He rolls his eyes. "Fine. Make me say it." He takes a deep breath and I brace myself for what I know is coming. "I sent you flowers and you gave me *nothing* in return!" He pulls Marissa close to him.

Marissa pretends to gasp. "Oh Lucy, you didn't?" She leans into Zach's body.

Zach shrugs at me. "You won't put out."

My stomach revolts. Bile rushes up my throat. I swallow it as I try to find something to say. My heart races and I can't see straight. The creaking sound of the gate saves me.

"Zach." Justin's voice bounces off the concrete. He

suddenly is in front of me. "What are you doing here?"

"My uncle lives here. He lets me hang whenever I want." Zach shrugs and motions toward me, "And, after last night's disappointment, I needed some time with a real woman." Zach grabs his bag and towel off a lounger.

Justin takes a step toward Zach as if he is going to hit him. Without thinking, I grab Justin's hand and pull him back.

Marissa seizes the opportunity to exit. She whisks past me, pulling Zach along with her. "Sorry it didn't work out between you. I really tried to teach you, Lucy." She shakes her head. "You never even went down on him. My God, I didn't know you were that clueless."

"Well at least she's not a slut," Justin interjects.

Marissa looks back at Justin. "Oh, come on, Justin. You know you'll be thinking of me in bed tonight."

After this? Yeah right. There's no way Justin will want to be with her.

"You always knew this was coming, Lucy. Just accept it and move on," Marissa says with a wave as she opens the gate and steps out with Zach. "See you around."

Zach wraps his hand around her waist, tucking his fingers into the side loop of her bathing suit bottoms.

They walk away in slow motion.

Adrenaline pumps through my body. My hands shake violently yet my legs become noodles. Justin catches me as I crumble. He eases me to a lounger.

How can Marissa and Zach do this to me? The bile returns and this time I can't push it back down. I turn away from Justin, throwing up all over the cement.

My boyfriend cheated on me with my best friend.

I want to laugh. Best friend?

Marissa is such a manipulative bitch. How did I not see this coming?

And Zach! I wouldn't *put out*. I can feel his body forcing me against the ground in the park. I start to tremble, wrapping my arms around my knees. Holding myself tight.

Justin brushes my bangs out of my eyes. That caring movement sends me into an ugly cry.

I can't process anything.

Mad. Betrayed. Used. Insignificant.

Lost.

I close my eyes and tuck my head down in between my legs. I sob.

How can this happen to me? What did I do to deserve this? I dry heave.

Just minutes after Zach made out in the booth with me he was feeling up Marissa in the parking lot. My empty stomach turns and fills with betrayal. No wonder Marissa wanted to get me home. They were hooking up.

CHAPTER TWELVE

Warm pressure around my hands brings me back to reality. "You need to stop shaking," Justin urges. My hands rest in his palms. I keep my eyes averted from him. I'm so humiliated. His fingertip rests on my chin, slowly tilting my head up so I'm forced to look at him.

"Lucy, I'm sorry this happened to you."

My heart skips and immediately my mind whirls. I cannot stay in the pool complex like this forever. I need to collect myself. I sit up straight. "Yeah, well. I'm sorry too."

He lifts his eyebrow while he sweeps my bangs out of my eyes. "Why would you be sorry?" His thumb rubs my wrist. My hands have stopped shaking in his. My heart pounds against my rib cage. I need to increase the distance between us before I lose my senses.

"Well, the barf, again." I lean away from him as I

motion to the ground behind me. "I'm sorry for that."

Justin smiles and releases my hands. He also leans away from me. "Well, yeah. You owe me big time." I nod. I know I should laugh but I can't force it.

"Well, that answers that." Justin stands up and extends a hand, pulling me off the lounger. Once I am on my feet, he drops my hand from his.

"What answers what?" I rub the palms of my hands against my legs, attempting to erase the memory of his hands. My heart is so confused.

"For a second I thought you weren't going to be okay." Justin hands me a water bottle. The water cools the burn in the back of my throat. "But if you can talk about barf, somehow I know you'll make it."

"Right," I manage. I take another drink. My mouth tastes horrible. "Do you have any gum?"

Justin grabs the wagon full of water bottles and opens the pool gate. "In the truck."

I eye the gate, not wanting to walk through. I know the moment I step through I am leaving the crime scene, which means I have to face my new reality. I have to start processing being betrayed and used. Face being alone.

Justin catches my hesitancy. "Listen, Lucy," he motions toward the gate. "I'm not saying it'll be easy. But, I can promise you that your life will be much better without them." He waits for me to move. I bite my lip and step through the gate. He pulls the wagon behind us.

"So, I'll just run this out to the guys if you want to wait in the truck. I'll take you home."

Home. I think of climbing in my bed and hiding under my covers. I could cry as long as I need. Just the thought of the freedom to cry brings tears to my cheeks. And then

I think about my parents. What would they do if they heard me crying in my room all afternoon? Mom'd just barge in, demanding to know what was wrong.

I can never share this with her. She wouldn't understand. My pain would become her prize, her *I told you so* moment.

"No." I shake my head. "Not home."

"Why not home?"

"I just can't go there."

"Then where?"

I look up the street where Alex is dancing alone to his head phones while painting window trim. "I'll stay here."

"You want to work?"

"Yeah, I already missed one day for illness. I don't want to get fired."

"I promise you won't get fired. I'm taking you home." Justin turns and starts walking ahead of me.

"No, really. I want to stay." I briefly touch his arm so he will look at me. "I need to stay," I whisper. "I need the distraction." Tears well in my eyes.

Justin lets out a light breath. "Fine. We'll see how it goes."

"Thanks," I say.

Troy approaches us as we drop off the water wagon near the supplies. "Justin. What took you so long?" Troy walks up to me and puts his hand on my shoulder. "Did you get lost, Lucy? I started to think you were ditching more of my training this afternoon." He smiles at me playfully.

I glare at his hand on my shoulder and rudely shrug it off. My left hand begins to shake. Being hit on is the last thing I need. Troy, not taking a hint, steps closer. I eye the truck. Maybe I do want to go home.

Justin reaches out and touches my shaking hand. I take a deep breath. He casually steps between Troy and me. "What's this about you training Lucy? I thought she was Alex's protégé?"

Troy shuffles his feet. "Well, she was. But I thought she needed more specialized attention than he can give." Troy shrugs, "I've got the best technique so I thought I'd show her the ropes. She's learned a lot. You should check—"

Justin holds out a hand to interrupt him. "I thought I made it clear that Lucy was to train with Alex."

"Oh, come on. You know she's learned all she can from the kid. Let me take her to the next level." Troy's undertone is clear.

"No. You stick to managing." Justin clenches his jaw.

"Fine. I'll go get Alex."

Justin shakes his head. "No. That won't be necessary. Lucy will hang with me the rest of the day." He nods toward Alex, "Alex is killing the top trim. No reason to interrupt him."

Troy glares back at Justin. "Fine, man. You're the *boss*." Justin swears under his breath and gathers our supplies.

"Wait. What just happened?"

Justin shakes his head as he hands me a bucket full of rags and brushes.

"You told me Troy was project manager."

"He is." He grabs a ladder off the driveway and effortlessly throws it over his shoulder.

"But he called you boss."

"Hmm, caught that part, huh?" Justin scrunches up his face.

"Yeah. That's pretty hard to miss."

Justin turns toward me, a look of defeat on his face. "Well, that's because I am. Troy's my project manager." He shrugs. "I'm the owner."

"Wait? What? Why didn't you tell me?"

"Because I didn't want you to know." Justin sets up the ladder against the house and motions for me to climb it.

I start climbing the ladder, meeting him at eye level. "Why not?"

Justin meets my gaze. "Honestly, I thought you'd tell Marissa and then the whole school would know." Marissa's name is salt in my open wound. I grimace.

But he has a point. Marissa can't keep a secret.

Justin continues, "The company is my own thing, no expectations from anyone but myself. Everything else I do," he shakes his head, "people just know too much, you know?" I do. Justin was always the hot topic at school. I never imagined it bothered him though.

"I guess I can see that." I climb higher and look down. "Then who's the guy that knows my dad that got me the job?"

"Uncle Alex. He had a conference call with your dad the morning after the party and he mentioned it to me. He's kind of the adult face of the company to give it some credentials." He nods toward the center of the association. "I'd never have landed this gig if it wasn't for him."

"Uncle Alex? As in …?"

"Alex's dad."

"Cousins?"

"Yup." I look at Alex, effortlessly perched on top of an

eighteen-foot ladder. He has lighter hair than Justin but his frame is similar, just in a fourteen-year-old form. I think of his laugh; they have the same tone. I shake my head. "I don't know how I missed that."

"Eh. You see what you want to see." He's right. If I'd have known Alex was Justin's cousin, I never would have been his friend. I look at Alex. He really is my only friend. He's always been so welcoming where Justin seems determined to drive me nuts.

That's what is odd. Justin is being so nice to me. Maybe he really does care?

Justin hands me a paintbrush before setting himself up near the base of the ladder. I climb the rest of the way up before turning around and looking down at Justin. "You know I wouldn't have told, right?"

"Told?"

"About you owning the company."

Justin shrugs. "Well, now I do. But, I'm still glad I didn't tell you."

"Why?"

"I didn't need to give you further reason to find think I'm *full of myself*."

I groan and he smiles in his taunting way.

"Justin. Please, lay off. Not today, okay? I don't know how much more I can handle."

"I know. That's why I'm staying right here." He nods toward the bottom of the ladder. "There's no way I'm letting you go all vomiting, jelly fish again. Your relational woes will not ruin me. I'm not going to be sued by your parents for unsafe working conditions."

"So, that's it then?"

"That's what?"

"Nothing," I mutter before returning to trimming.

My heart sinks. I thought he was being attentive because he cared. Knowing his attention stemmed from legal purposes makes me feel even emptier than before.

I look over at Alex, who is dancing with his brush on top of his ladder. They may be cousins, but Alex would never have said that.

I am a potential liability to Justin. Not a friend.

I bite my lip as I paint, focusing on every detail of my brush stroke. I start feeling numb. At the pool complex I didn't feel alone with Justin at my side. Now, with Justin below me, I feel completely isolated. I was a task to manage.

And then there's Marissa and Zach. That's how they always look at me too, an annoying task to attend to, at best, a means of entertainment. I'm Marissa's pet project. She felt threatened the moment I started drawing attention from Zach. No wonder she always insisted on calling him for me—she was setting a nice trap for him. She couldn't handle me being the center of attention, for once.

And Zach makes my skin crawl. I think I always knew that he was just one of those guys, after any girl who would put out. The moment he realized I wasn't going to give him what he wanted, he welcomed Marissa onto his lap. The thought of them together literally makes me gag. I look down at Justin who is listening to his iPod, thankful he didn't hear it.

Marissa and Zach are repulsive.

I cling to this feeling of disgust as the day wears on. It's the key to holding on to reason. Occasionally, worthlessness and humiliation attempt to redirect my thoughts. But I won't let them. I can't let them. Not now. I will deal with them later. Not here.

I'm not going to cry here.

Justin doesn't let me out of his sight the entire afternoon. Occasionally, I catch Troy glaring at him from across the courtyard. At least I don't have to deal with him anymore. I concentrate on the angle of my brush. Each new stroke covers the dulled paint with a bolder red. I completely lose myself in painting because Troy yells, "call it" much sooner than I anticipate.

I climb down the ladder. Justin stands waiting at the bottom, his hands on his hips. "So, now can I take you home?"

"No. This is all business, right? I didn't fall. I'm not a liability. I'll catch a ride from Alex and the other guys." I can't help but return the sting of his legal approach.

"Fine. I've got to go deal with Troy anyway."

"Wait," I call out to him. "Why were you so insistent that Alex train me instead of Troy?"

Justin lifts his eyebrow. "Isn't that kind of obvious? You're the only girl on the crew. Alex's in a relationship, which made him the safest choice. I didn't want to deal with everyone hitting on you. I don't need a sexual-harassment lawsuit too."

His words cut deep. That's seriously all he cares about, huh? This stupid painting business. Why can't I be somebody to him? To anybody?

I'm not going to cry. I'm not going to cry. I'm not going to cry.

My eyes counter my thoughts, welling with tears, tears that Justin definitely notices. He pauses briefly before I blink them away. He opens his mouth to say something but Alex bounds between us.

"Way to save Lucy, man. I don't know how much more

we can take of Troy's macking style." Alex playfully nudges me in the side. I turn to him and force a smile.

"So, are you going to ditch me now that your old ride is back?"

Justin opens his mouth to speak but I beat him to the punch.

"Nope. I'm heading home with you. Justin's got stuff to do."

"Your dad is helping me with another business proposal," Justin explains.

"Oh, so she knows now?"

"Yup."

"Finally. We were all getting sick of your secret. It seriously sucks to pretend to listen to Troy, man."

Justin shoves Alex's shoulder. "He's still your project manager."

Alex picks up my supplies. "Sure. Whatever you say, boss."

"Well, maybe if you'd have listened to him you'd have finished more than one house. Come on. You're killing my productivity!"

"Oh, trust me man. Past nine o'clock, Troy's attention was focused *elsewhere.*" Alex nudges me again. Under other conditions, I may have felt flattered. But instead the insinuation crawls down my throat and into my lungs.

My body is freaking out.

Suddenly, I am watching Marissa and Zach making out in the pool again. A ringing tone deafens my ears as I remembered seeing Zach pull Marissa into a hug. I gnaw on the inside of my cheek. The iron taste in my mouth is revolting. My fingertips vibrate.

A hand on my back. Alex. "Whoa Lucy, are you sick?"

My heart bangs inside my head as my legs buckle. Footsteps vibrate the ground near me. Another hand is placed on my shoulder.

"Why didn't you force her to drink more water?" Alex accuses. "You made her work too hard."

Justin doesn't reply. He just leans down toward me. "Are you okay?" he whispers in my ear.

My spine becomes jelly. His whisper throws my heartbeat out of my head and into my chest. I briefly open my eyes and the ground starts to spin. Ever so slightly, I shake my head no. I glue my eyes shut as I feel my stomach begin to turn. Not again.

"I'll go grab some water and food." Alex's hand leaves my back but the pressure is instantly replaced with Justin's other hand.

"Take a deep breath," Justin guides.

I listen, concentrating on making each breath wash the nausea away.

A cool rag falls in my hand. I press my face into it.

You're okay. You're okay. You're okay.

My stomach relaxes. I sit up straight, taking a sip from a water bottle held under my lips.

"Justin. I don't know about this," Alex begins. "Look. She won't stop shaking."

"Just give her time." Justin squeezes my shoulders.

I open my eyes, looking down at my hands and arms which are shaking in involuntary spasms. "Are you having a seizure?" Alex asks with wide eyes. He reminds me of Eric and it provides just enough of a distraction for me to refocus.

"No," I force myself to smile at him. "I don't know what happened. Probably not enough water." I take the water bottle that he holds out in front of me and draw in a long sip.

"See," he accuses again, looking over my shoulder back at Justin. Alex surveys me with his fingers lightly covering his mouth like how Eric would analyze his chances before asking me to play. A horn beeps. "Are you going to help me get her to the van?" he asks Justin.

"No, I can walk. It's fine." I start to stand up but Justin's hands push me back down.

"Don't worry about it, Alex. I'll bring her home."

"No way. You said she was going with me." They acted more like brothers than cousins.

"Do you seriously think you can handle her if she ends up like this again in that van? Emmanuel will freak out if she starts puking."

"No. I won't puke, I'm fine."

"See?"

"Alex. No."

"But …"

The van honks again.

"Go."

"Fine." Alex kicks the dirt. "I'm sorry, Lucy. I hope you stop shaking soon." He leans down close to me to whisper, "And, no offense, I kind of hope you throw up again in Justin's truck."

I nod, closing my eyes at the mere mention of throw up. "If I do, I'll make sure it's a good one."

"Thanks," he pats me on the back as he goes.

With Alex gone, I become acutely more aware that Justin's hands are still on my shoulders. A different type of adrenaline takes over. My shaking intensifies.

"Lucy," Justin voice is husky. "What am I going to do

130

with you?" His hands rub my arms. "Relax," he urges.

"Right," I turn toward him. He grabs my hands in his, deciding to make the shaking stop on his own. Justin's hands are so warm. My heart pounds against my chest. I close my eyes, urging my shoulders, arms and hands to relax.

"There you go," Justin says. I open my eyes to find his green ones wide with worry. "I shouldn't have let you work. Bad call. I'm sorry."

"No, it's fine. It just hit me, that's all." I pull my hands back out of his. He nods and stands up with me, putting his fingers over his lips as Alex had.

"So, am I going to have to carry you?" he teases.

***

I curl up in bed and, for the second night in a row, silently let my tears overwhelm me. I pull my blanket over my head, welcoming its darkness. My thoughts become a fuzzy void that seems to dull my pain. Time slips by, only marked with the occasional creak of my door and light pressure of a hand on my thigh. I shift away from Mom's touch, desperately hating being brought back to reality.

I must have fallen asleep because at ten o'clock the ringing of my cell phone wakes me. It's Justin. I answer without thinking.

"Hello?" I say, not able to mask my groggy tone.

"Sorry, were you asleep?"

"In a way, yes, but not really."

"Right, of course." Justin pauses awkwardly on the phone. "So, tomorrow's a work day."

"I want to go to work."

"I'm not going to hold it against you."

"No, really." I look around my blank-walled room. Did anyone with a personality live here? "I can't stay here."

"Well," Justin wavers.

"I promise I'll be just fine."

Justin sighs. "How about I'll pick you up but we'll play it by ear, okay?"

"Sure, whatever gets my mind out of this place, you know?"

Justin's musical laugh turns my heart. "Right. I'll see you in the morning."

"Thank you." I'm unable to mask my sincerity.

Justin's voice echoes my tone. "Lucy, you know you are going to be okay, right?"

"Yeah," I squeeze my eyes shut. "I just need to work through it."

Justin doesn't respond right away, providing an awkward moment of silence that I don't have the energy to fill. "Sleep, Lucy. I'll see you in the morning."

"Sounds good." I push end call before Justin can change his mind.

I drag myself out of bed to brush the rotting taste from my mouth. I catch my reflection in the mirror. My face is uncharacteristically pale and greasy while wisps of hair fly away from my ponytail. Dark circles have found a home under my eyes.

I look like a troll.

I groan, realizing that most of the day Justin has looked at some version of this girl in the mirror. It's not like it really matters though. I turn the shower on extra hot. I need to start over again. My mind keeps replaying Zach's arms around Marissa's waist and her cackling giggle. I can't take it anymore. I seek relief, allowing my thoughts to drift to Justin.

I picture Justin's smile, accentuated with his stubble and jaw line, and my heart flutters. My hands tingle as I remember Justin's palms in mine. I sigh, knowing that part of me is falling fast for him. I can't deny that his tenderness today has sent my heart haywire. I blast the top of my head with cold water. I have to be sane about these feelings. Justin is taken, in love with Jennifer. I have no chance.

But somehow, knowing that a future with Justin is impossible makes it easier to like him. It's risk-free.

I climb out of the shower with my mind feeling warped. How Justin drives me crazy yet simultaneously melts my heart confuses me. I sigh as I pull a brush through my hair. Maybe it's because I have to be real around Justin? I can't hide my sarcasm, sass, and annoyance from him when I try. Something about him unarms me. I'm not used to thinking and acting so freely. No wonder I'm confused. I don't know how to be me.

I crawl back into bed, holding my own hands as I let that small part of me remember again the warm pressure of his palms. The memory eases me into an odd but peaceful sleep. Only once do I wake, to the sound of my door closing. Dad's snoring crackles from down the hall. The spot next to me on the mattress is warm. Someone has been sitting there.

Mom.

CHAPTER THIRTEEN

I wait on my front step the next morning, holding my knees up against my chest. Random butterflies try to take flight inside me but I catch each one, blushing as I shoo them away. These will be the only blushes of the day. I can't allow more.

The clank and sputtering of Justin's truck announces his arrival before he pulls around the corner. I hop off the front step, not wanting him to feel the need to greet me. He rolls down his window and smiles. A butterfly takes flight. Damn.

"Good morning Lady Barfs-a-Lot," he taunts from his window.

A quick frenzy of rage squashes the butterfly with its thumb.

"Wow, have I ever told you how hilarious you are?"

Sarcasm seeps out of my mouth like lava.

Justin leans over and opens my door from the inside. "Nope but I'd love to hear it. You know me. Just can't get enough."

I roll my eyes. "Yeah. I'm pretty sure I caught that about you."

Justin stretches, his hand reaching over and blocking my face. I push it out of my way. "Well, I've got to nurture my ego if I'm going to maintain it." He chuckles as he throws the truck into reverse.

"So," he continues, "Yesterday kind of sucked, huh?

I attempt a laugh. "Pretty much the lowest I can go."

"Naw, I wouldn't say that. I think yesterday was a step up for you."

"In comparison to?"

Justin shrugs, "The day before."

"So you liked me barfing and totally freaking out over—?"

"Being Marissa's oblivious drone," Justin states harshly. He looks at me, gauging my reaction. I work hard not to flinch so he will continue. "Trust me. That look was not becoming on you."

"Well, I'm happy to have climbed your ladder of approval, barf and all."

"I'm glad you finally did too. I was worried I'd have to bring you to your senses."

"Oh? With what plan?"

Justin grins. "I had a few ideas. But, their way was much clearer than anything I could have come up with."

I don't grin back. "And when did you decide I needed your help?" This isn't funny.

"At the pool that first day."

"When I was waiting for Zach?"

"No, earlier when you were reading a magazine next to Marissa. I've known her since elementary school. Everyone knows her general philosophy on relationships. You seemed like a victim of one of her master plans."

"That's one way to put it." I bite the inside of my lip. How can he talk about this so casually? Her betrayal is still an oozing wound.

"And then I saw you pathetically waiting for Zach. You needed help. I had to save you."

Pathetically. Great.

My heart tugs. What he says doesn't feel right. I turn away from him and look out the window. My mind starts piecing things together. "Wait, so I was a project for you to save?" The situation mirrors Marissa's original attempt at saving me.

He looks confused at my question. "No. That's not what I'm saying."

"I *needed* you to save me? You planned to bring me to my senses?" I shake my head. "Sounds like a project to me."

"No. I mean, well kind of. But it wasn't like that."

"How wasn't it?"

"I was going to help you."

"That's exactly what Marissa said."

Justin throws his hands up in the air. "Oh, come on. You know I'm not like her."

"No, you aren't. But doesn't that make it worse?"

"How?"

"She's vain. But I thought you had a sense of humanity."

Justin looks back at me blankly. "Well yeah. That's why

I wanted to save you." He says a little too slowly.

"Okay then, let me ask you this. What were you planning to do with me after you saved me?" As the question comes out, I realize how desperately I need to know the answer. Where does he see this unique relationship going? Are we going to be friends? Or, now that the *project* is done, would I just go back to blending into the background?

Justin doesn't answer. I watch his jaw clench. I desperately want it to open with a response. Instead, Justin focuses intently on the traffic.

"Whatever," I say under my breath.

The truth of the moment hangs between us. I reach over and turn on the radio, hoping the noise will chase the awkward truth away.

As we continue to drive, my conscience picks away at me. Did I really believe that Justin thought of me in the same manner as Marissa? I glance back at him, catching him as he glances away from me. He takes a deep breath and relaxes his jaw, pulling his hand through his black hair.

The answer rises from my gut. No. Justin doesn't think of me that way. I am someone to him. I just don't know what someone means. That butterfly I'd squashed earlier resurrects. I push it aside. No. That isn't possible. Justin is dating Jennifer. But, friendship? Yes. That I want. In fact, I absolutely need it.

Justin is right—I was Marissa's drone. I shamefully followed her everywhere. Even when I had an idea, I never initiated it. I didn't need to when Marissa controlled everything. I press my hand to my forehead. How did I become so passive? That needs to change. I look at Justin and swallow a lump in my throat. The change needs to start now.

"Justin," I begin. He glances at me. "Listen, I'm sorry." Please let him understand. "I know you aren't like her. I just," I take a deep breath. "I guess I'm on edge, not having a lot of recent experience with trust."

"Yeah, I get that. You're kind of …"

"Broken," I volunteer, and he nods. "I shouldn't have asked you what you planned to do with me." Justin lightly furrows his brow in confusion. "It doesn't matter to me because," my heart pounds in my chest, "I already know what role I want to take."

Justin becomes rigid. "Listen, Lucy …" He takes a deep breath and I realize he thinks I'm about to throw myself at him. He's going to give me his let down speech.

I laugh, interrupting him. "Oh, no. No." I laugh again, trying to cover up that little butterfly shouting *yes*! from inside. "Not that." I shrug, "Just friends, that's all."

His face relaxes. "Good." He sounds a bit too relieved. "I mean, not that … well … you know. I just want to be friends with you too. Anything more would kind of ruin it, right?"

Splat. That butterfly commits suicide.

"Yup, totally." I say with convincing confidence.

"So, friends, Lady?" he offers.

"Absolutely."

"Well, just so you know," he leans in toward me, "I take friendships very seriously." Now I look at him confused. "So, if something of my friend's is broken, I'm the type of friend who helps them fix it. Understand?"

I smile, "Do I have any choice in the matter?"

Justin shakes his head.

"I didn't think so."

***

The weather couldn't have been crueler. Ninety-seven degrees with seventy-eight percent humidity. The air is so thick I swear I can chew it. Alex, to a point of annoyance, makes me take too many water breaks. My progress slows. I start waving Alex off every time he motions for me to climb down and grab a drink of water. I am determined to pull my weight with this job. The white trim needs my help. Every brush stroke covers up the cracked paint beneath. I willingly let it symbolize myself, tenderly brushing away the cracks. Proving that somehow I will find a way to heal.

"Lucy, water break," Alex calls again. I shake my head, leaning in closer, making another clean stroke over dull blue paint. "Fine, suit yourself."

"Lucy." Justin's voice. I instinctively turn around, following it to its source. The moment I see him I wish I hadn't. He holds a huge bucket of water. "You wouldn't," I gasp.

He smiles wickedly. "Of course I would." He tilts the bucket back and throws the water in the air toward me. The cold water hits me like a ton of bricks.

I take a deep breath before jumping off the ladder, completely soaked from the neck down. "What the—?"

Justin shrugs and walks over, patting me on the back. "Alex here told me you were refusing water break and so I thought I would take matters into my own hands."

Alex shrugs next to him, he moves just like Justin. "Sorry, Lucy. You needed it."

"Betrayal," I mutter.

Justin slaps me on the back, "Oh come on, *friend*. You'll get over it. I'm sure." He smiles in a way that makes his dimples pop. A goofy grin creeps across my face. My hand flies over my mouth to hide it.

Troy yells, "Break."

"Finally," Justin says. "It's time to buy him a new watch. I'm starved."

Alex brings me my lunch box, he owed me. I ring the water out of my tank top. Now that the shock has worn away, I actually don't mind it. It's refreshing. I lie back on the grass in the sunlight, a feeble attempt at drying myself in the high humidity. I close my eyes, listening to the rhythmic bounce of the basketball on the street. The sound is as comforting as rain. My mind drifts back to yesterday. It seems so long ago.

I brace myself, waiting for the memory to overwhelm me. I take a deep breath as the harsh words and images filter through my mind. I wait for the nausea but it never surfaces. I check my hands. Steady as a rock.

I look at Justin helping Luke with dribbling. I smile.

He's right. I'm going to be alright.

***

I abandon all of my worries in my work. I don't notice the air turning an orange color until Alex throws a rag at me and points to the sky. Wind whooshes past us, making my bangs whip and sting my cheek. I pull out a bobby pin from my waist band and sweep them out of the way.

The sky is beautiful. Orange, pink, and yellow hues dance in the clouds. Everything is quiet. Our usual chatter echoes the sky's mood, dying away into silence. I look at

Alex, who keeps looking up at the sky and back at Justin. The rest of the crew does the same. Justin and Troy stand near the truck, listening to the radio.

The wind picks up, large tree branches creaking in protest. Alex looks at me and shouts over the wind, "I'm going to go talk some sense into them. This meeting deadline stuff is bull if we're gonna get blown away." Luke and Jake follow him to the truck. Emmanuel shrugs at me from the scaffolding across the courtyard before turning back to his portion of the siding.

I dip my brush back into the white paint. My ladder sways a bit to the right and I grab the eve of the roofing, holding on to steady myself, the ladder, and my paint can. I glance at Justin and Troy, hoping they'll make the decision to call it a day. Justin leans in through his car window, trying to hear the radio over everyone's opinions. Troy looks at the sky, his arms crossed and shaking his head.

The large oak tree behind me startles me with a creak. As I glance back, one of the thick branches bends from stress. I instinctively tighten my grip, this time with both hands, onto the roof's edge. Immediately, a gust of wind hits my ladder. My fingers dig into the roofing as my feet meet the air. The ladder clangs on the sidewalk below. *Crack*, the tree branch crashes to the ground.

I scream, struggling to find a ledge of the siding to dig my feet into.

Alex drops his water bottle and runs toward me. I dig my fingernails into the shingles and tighten my muscles. I look down, a two-story fall to the ground.

"Hold on."

"Catch her."

"Shit."

I struggle to maintain my grip; my wrists feel like they are going to snap. A new ladder bumps up beside me. An arm wraps around my waist, pulling me over to the ladder. "It's okay. You can let go." Emmanuel's voice reassures me. "Seriously, I've got you."

"Let go." Justin's voice shakes from below.

Another gust of wind hits the side of the house, jostling Emmanuel's ladder. I cling to the roof even tighter than before.

"Emmanuel. Get her down before you both fall. Now."

"Come on, Lucy, let go." The ladder starts to sway below us. "We've got to do this, now."

I let go. Wind whooshes around the corner toward us. Branches crack from the trees. I cling to Emmanuel as our ladder falls to the right.

"Don't let go." Emmanuel instructs. He wraps both arms around my waist.

The fall takes forever. I close my eyes, allowing Emmanuel to lead. He hesitates a moment before he jumps, pushing me out in front of him. I brace myself for impact. But it never comes as another set of arms wrap around my waist, pulling me away from Emmanuel. *Thud.* Emmanuel slams against the ground.

Luke pulls me into his body and eases me to the ground. Justin rushes to Emmanuel's side. My heart pounds—*move, Emmanuel.* Justin turns him over but he doesn't respond. Justin shakes him and leans in close to check for a heartbeat. My throat tightens.

Justin presses his head against his chest. Alex steadies Emmanuel's neck.

I stop breathing.

Suddenly, Emmanuel's arm whips up and grabs Justin's shirt, dragging him down. Emmanuel punches Justin in the nuts. Alex bursts out laughing as Justin rolls to the side, gasping for air.

Luke lets out a breath before letting me go. He pats me on the back.

Emmanuel stands up. "Serves you right, Justin. Deadlines my ass. You almost killed us!" Emmanuel calls to me, "Are you okay?"

"Yes, I'm fine. Thanks."

He shrugs, looking back at Justin who still lies on the ground cupping his groin. "Someone has to be thinking, right?" He rolls his eyes before holding out his hand to Justin, pulling him off the ground.

I turn around to Luke. "Thanks to you too. How exactly did that work?"

"Emmanuel's from California. He loves to surf. He just rode the ladder down like a wave and handed you off before he hit the ground." He points at Justin who's still crunched over and groaning. "I'm pretty sure his fall was more to prove a point than anything else."

Alex tugs on my arm. "Man, woman. Do you ever have a normal day?" He pulls me into a hug before giving me his signature pat on the back.

I wonder the same thing.

The wind picks up again. I jump at the sound of abandoned ladders crashing to the ground. The oak tree gives another protesting creak as its branches bend above us.

"Alright. Call it," Justin yells. "Get your stuff and get home. Safely," he adds.

Everyone breaks away from the huddle, grabbing

everything in their path. I walk over to my ladder, grabbing its edge. My fingertips and palms protest in pain as I swing it up and over my shoulder. I search for my paint can, finding it in the daisies which are now splattered with white paint. The roof's edge hangs above me where only moments before I'd been dangling. I can't help but shudder at the what-ifs.

The oak tree makes a popping sound, jolting me out of my state of shock and awe. I readjust the ladder over my back. The ladder seems so much heavier than earlier that day. I watch the guys in the distance effortlessly throw their ladders and supplies into Justin's truck bed. For the first time, I really do wish I was that large He-She-like creature that the senior girls called me. I could use the strength today.

I focus on Justin, climbing into the truck bed and surveying the supplies. The rest of the guys have taken refuge in their vehicles. Thankfully, the changing weather distracted everyone from my struggle. I don't want any more attention.

I dig my feet into the ground, determined to get my ladder to the truck on my own. I refuse to be lame and leave it behind. But the oak tree urges me to with every creak. It doesn't understand. I don't always want to be the damsel in distress. I need to do this on my own.

Sheets of rain pour from the sky. The sound is near deafening. I readjust my grip on the metal. My palm stings as if glass has cut me. The ladder slips through my palms, crashing on the sidewalk below.

I bend over, determined to do something right. Surprisingly, the ladder lifts with ease. I look up as Justin takes it from me, swinging it over his shoulder. He pushes me in front of him toward the truck.

Damn. I'm sick of being so hopeless and weak.

Boom. A cannon of thunder.

Justin throws the ladder in the truck bed and pulls me around to the front. I reach up, grabbing the door's handle only to be rewarded with pain shooting through my palms. Red blood drips down the side of Justin's white truck.

Justin gasps as he reaches past me and grabs the handle, opening the door and lifting me onto the seat. White pellets fall on Justin's shoulders and it's like I'm stuck in a popcorn maker. Justin stands outside, oblivious to the hail and rain. He turns over my palms, searching for the cause of the blood. I look at my hands with the same curiosity.

My fingertips are scraped and raw, already swollen and bleeding. Large calluses have been ripped from my palms. Small holes weep blood in their place. Two deep cuts are positioned on my right palm where blood seeps freely.

Justin removes his hands from mine. He takes off his shirt, pressing the wet cloth into my palms. I close my hands around it and focus on the white fabric changing red. The shirt stings but I hold it tightly. It's a good distraction from Justin's abs. The door shuts and a moment later the other opens. Justin slides in next to me.

He grabs my wrists, pulling my hands back in his. "Lucy, crap." Water drips down my face. I am pretty sure it isn't from tears. At least, I hope not.

The sirens blare and the wind gusts pick up. Justin swears, dropping my hands, turning the ignition and throwing the truck into reverse. The radio broadcast continues, "Severe Thunderstorm Warning in effect."

"Thunderstorm warning? Look outside." Justin shouts

at the radio. I glance through my window. Clouds swirl above us as Justin speeds away from the neighborhood. He pulls onto the highway. We're flying with a few other cars at over eighty miles per hour.

"That's a Severe Thunderstorm Warning for Hennepin County." The radio voice reiterates. A siren blares from the radio. "Update: Tornado Watch in effect for West Hennepin County." I roll down the window for a clear view at the sky. The clouds drop lower, spinning in opposite directions above us. "Justin, the clouds …" Cars stop and drivers run down into the ditch.

The truck screeches to a halt with them. I turn, fumbling with the door's latch. "Forget it," Justin shouts over the wind. A bush blows past my window as he pulls me over his lap with one arm. He throws the door open, pushing me out of the truck and into the ditch.

Justin shoves me against the ground. I duck, covering the back of my head like they taught me in elementary school. I feel more pressure over my head as Justin's body presses over me. Two women scream as the sound of a train approaches. Cars scrape against the pavement and smash into one another. Justin lies next to me, one hand over my head. The train drowns all noises.

I hold my breath.

CHAPTER FOURTEEN

The train roars. Sour iron particles coat my tongue. Dirt. My throat swells. There's no way this is happening. Justin's hand presses down harder on the back of my neck. "HOLD ON," he yells in my ear.

To what? I grasp a fistful of grass.

Metal screeches cut through the wave of noise. The tornado has arrived. A vacuum attaches to my ears. My brain is being sucked out. My feet and legs lift, suction dragging me across the grass. Shit. I'm gone. I scream, grasping for more grass but ending with fistfuls of mud. Suddenly, a huge pressure falls on my body.

Hot breath blows against my neck. Justin.

The wind sucks harder, but I don't budge. It dampens as leaves and branches surround us. Justin grunts. His breath is wet and rapid on my neck. I pray.

The roaring of the train disappears as quickly as it arrived. Justin's breathing slows. He waits a moment before rolling off of me. I open my eyes, looking straight into the branches of a tree. I didn't even hear it fall on us. The trunk hangs suspended above our ditch, between the road and its base. We army-crawl out from underneath. I sit up, surveying the damage. Justin's truck stands untouched but a few cars are flipped over and one has been thrown against the concrete barrier. Trees are flung through the noise-barrier fences, exposing backyards and houses with partial roofs.

"Is everyone okay?" a man nearby yells.

Justin's eyes are glazed and his mouth hangs slightly open. Totally frozen. "Alright here," I yell out, responding for us. I stand up, still clasping Justin's shirt in my hand. Justin stays on his knees, pressing his face into his palms. I turn toward the screaming next to us.

I run to the group of women huddled on the ground. "Are you okay?" They cling together. I pull them apart, quickly assessing for injuries. All are breathing and uninjured. Just rightfully terrified.

I check for passengers in the two flipped over vehicles.

"The red one's mine," a man shouts from the ditch.

"And the white one's ours," a woman says as she places her hand on my shoulder. "We're all accounted for."

"So everyone's alright?"

"It seems like it. Everyone's fine." She looks up to the sky. "Thank you," she whispers. Her eyes fall on the bloody t-shirt in my hands. "You, on the other hand, what happened?"

"It's nothing." She lifts her brow. I further explain, "I'm a painter and the ladder blew out from under me. I had to hold onto the roof."

"My, brave girl." She motions to the people still in the ditch. "You were the first up checking for injuries and here you are the injured one." She turns to her car and kicks in the passenger side window. "Luckily for you, I'm always prepared." She crawls down on the pavement and reaches into the glove box, pulling out a first aid kit. "Now, how about we get you out of the middle of the highway and fixed up?"

We return to the ditch where Justin still sits frozen, hands behind his head with his eyes closed. Maybe he actually is injured? My heart races as I rush to his side. I put my hand on his shoulder, "Are you okay?"

He reaches up and grabs my hand. Not letting go, he rises. He touches his forehead to the top of my head before pulling me into his bare chest. My heart leaps into my throat.

"Lucy," he breathes. "I'm so sorry."

Justin's chest is warm and I feel safe in his arms. I want to stand with him like that forever. But I can't. Justin is not mine to have. Only this morning he made that perfectly clear. I feel his heart thud. Millions of butterflies take flight. And that's when I know I have to push away. I have to protect myself from this certain heartbreak.

I put my hand against his chest. I push back lightly as I step away, putting an appropriate distance between us. He steps back too but takes my injured hands in his.

The woman from the white car flashes her first aid kit to Justin. Justin nods, directing us toward his truck, holding both my hands along the way. The woman climbs in behind me, sitting in my spot while Justin goes around to the driver's side while I perch on the center console.

She unravels Justin's t-shirt from my hands. "So," she looks past me to Justin, "how'd this happen?"

"I told you," I interject, "the roof."

She smiles at me and pats the back of my hand. "I know dear. I just want to hear his side of the story. I'm interested in knowing how you ended up hanging off a roof's edge."

Justin takes a deep breath. "I've been asking myself the same thing since the moment I saw her dangling."

"I see." She unwraps my hands. "So, her ladder fell, you stopped painting and got stuck in a tornado?"

"That's the basics of it," I answer for Justin.

Justin shakes his head. "No. You're forgetting why you were up there in the first place. I wanted to finish the house before taking cover. I put you at risk."

"No," I shook my head at the woman. "He didn't. He was listening to the radio and the storm came on suddenly. He had no way of knowing the wind would knock down my ladder."

Justin throws his hands back, pulling at his hair and shaking his head. "And then you know what happened? I was so worried about getting her down that I forgot to hold the base of the ladder that was used to get her from the roof." He hits the steering wheel. "Of course it would blow to the ground!" The woman's eyes grow wide and she starts looking at my whole body for injuries. "No, she's fine. Someone caught her." Justin explains.

The woman lifts up my hands, "You call this fine?"

"Of course not." He places his hand on my shoulder as he leans over me, almost whispering to the woman. "And then," Justin starts laughing in a crazy way, "I totally forgot her. I was so worried about getting everyone and all of our supplies to safety that I forgot her." My stomach sinks with the words *forgot her*. Why am I so easy to forget?

Justin continues, "I told people to pack up and head home. Then another ladder hit the ground. I look back and realize she thought she had to drag her eighteen-foot ladder back to the truck on her own."

"Hmm," the woman begins. "That would explain these." She points to the deep cuts on my right palm.

"The ladder slipped when it started to rain. It cut me." I turn toward Justin. "It's not your fault that I grabbed my own ladder. I wanted to. I'm always such a burden, a liability," I add. "After falling in front of everyone, well, I—"

The woman lays her hand on my arm. "You wanted to prove yourself."

"Something like that. Yes."

She pulls me into a hug. Her compassion surprises me. I usually avoid stranger hugs but, in that moment, a hug from someone attached to no emotional confusion is exactly what I needed. She releases me before laughing. "I was right. You are a brave girl."

I laugh back. "Or severely crazy."

"And apparently easy to underestimate," she aims her comment at Justin. She opens her first aid kit. "I need to disinfect your wounds and abrasions." She points to the dirt from the ditch that has managed to finagle its way in. "I'm not going to lie. This is going to burn." I nod, watching her take out a small bottle of hydrogen peroxide. "Do you want me to count?"

"No, just do it." I look away, waiting to feel the cool liquid burn my skin.

"See," she says to Justin, "brave girl."

I flinch as the cool moisture hits my skin. I cringe and close my eyes as the burning penetrates the cuts. The burning intensifies as the air bites at my palms. I suck in my lower lip. Justin's hand squeezes my shoulder. I want to shake it away. This needs to stop. My heart aches.

A dry cloth pats my skin and the burning subsides. "There," the woman says. She places a piece of gauze over each palm and bandages my fingers before wrapping each hand with an ace bandage. "This is a little bulky but it will do for now." She smiles down at me, "You'll need to stop in at the doctor to get some ointment and better bandaging. You may need stitches on the long cuts." Sirens blare next to the truck as a police car pulls up. "I need to go report my wreck," she says as she opens the door.

"Thank you," I offer.

"No problem. I gladly serve the brave my dear." She smiles at me. "And you," she looks at Justin, "be more aware. She deserves it."

"Of course," Justin jumps out of the driver's side and back into the rain, where he helps the woman out of the truck. I wave goodbye as I slide down onto the passenger seat. I examine my bandages. They look like very ugly oven mitts.

I greet Justin with a clumsy wave as he climbs back in.

"Lucy," he begins.

I put my hand up for him to stop. I can't let him tell me how he feels. I don't need more of a reason to like him or dislike him, depending on the direction he takes. I rush through his apology for him. "I know. You're sorry. Don't beat yourself up about it." I wave my clumsy hands again in his direction and smile. "I've got a new set of boxing gloves. I can do it for you." He doesn't crack a smile. "For real though. You're forgiven. Don't worry about it."

"Thanks."

"Remember, today was way better than yesterday." I roll my eyes dramatically. Justin's chuckle rewards me.

"Lucy, that's not saying much. Nothing was worse for you than yesterday."

"Nope. Not true."

"Oh?"

"I was worse off the day before, remember? I just didn't know it yet." I smile at him, teasing him about our earlier conversation. He doesn't respond so I try another approach. "So, can I ask you a question?"

"You don't need to ask permission."

"Good. Just checking." I hold up my bandaged hands. "Can I have the day off tomorrow? Doubt I can paint like this." Wiggling my fingers, I ignore the resulting pain.

Justin turns to me and laughs, "Sure, you can have two days off."

"For real?"

"Why not?" Justin looks over at me and flashes his mischievous smile. "Joke's on you though."

"Why?"

"Tomorrow's Saturday."

CHAPTER FIFTEEN

My parents freak out when I arrive home in bandages. I explain my story, eyeing Justin to leave out all of his guilty details. If I want to keep painting, I have to convince my parents that this was entirely my fault. They buy my story without question. Mom thanks Justin a million times before Dad insists we leave for the doctor. She invites Justin to come with. He declines, explaining he has already made dinner commitments.

But she won't take no for an answer. "Please stay. You rescued our daughter again. She's been too much trouble for you, Justin. Come with us to the doctor and we'll take you out to dinner."

Justin shakes his head. "I'm sorry, Mrs. Zwindler, but I can't. It sounds lovely but I have a dinner date with my girlfriend tonight."

Jennifer. A perfect gut punch.

I hold my smile steady as my heart deflates.

"Fine." Mom laughs. "I see you can't be persuaded." She looks over at me and back at Justin. "You need to find Lucy a guy like you. After what that Zach boy did to her, she needs someone great."

"Mom," I interject. She holds out her hand to silence me.

"No, Lucy. Let me speak." She turns back to Justin. "Good guys usually have good friends. Match her up, will you? After what she's been through, she could use a good date." Mom giggles as she leads Justin to the door. "Think about it. We welcome anyone you bring through this door."

"Mom. You aren't arranging a marriage. Let him leave." I stand up, forcing a smile in Justin's direction. "Have a nice date with Jennifer tonight," I add, proving to him that I am satisfied with our friendship.

He waves goodbye before closing the door behind him. A large part of me protests at his absence. But that part can wait. My blood churns and I swing around, glaring at Mom. "Was that really necessary?" I snap.

"What, honey?"

"You know what. Here I am your bleeding, injured daughter, sitting in your living room. And, what do you do? Try to get me a date!" I stand up abruptly, crossing the room toward the stairway.

"Be careful," Dad urges from the couch.

"No! Shouldn't she have the decency to know what is appropriate?" I turn back to Mom. "Are you determined to humiliate me every chance you get?"

Mom steps in front of me, blocking my exit. "Lucy, be

reasonable. I was only opening a door—"

"To what, Mom? Another humiliating saga of my life? Give me a break! I was cheated on yesterday. Trust me, that wound is fresh enough without you pouring alcohol in it." I push past her and walk up the stairs. "If you don't care about me enough to notice those wounds, then I can't expect you to really care about these." I wave my clunky bandaged hands.

We glare at one another. My labored breathing is the only sound in the room. I refuse to move my eyes from hers. I'm not backing down. Dad moves toward Mom and grabs her hand. She shakes it away before storming out of the room, slamming the kitchen door behind her.

"Lucy, you need to see a doctor," Dad insists.

"Not with her."

Dad shakes his head, always refusing to choose sides. He pulls his keys and wallet from his pocket, holding them out to me. "Then go on your own. But at least go."

"Fine." I snatch the keys out of his hands. I glare back at the kitchen door. "Why, Dad? Why did she have to do that?"

"She cares about you," he offers.

"Well, she has a wicked way of showing it." I walk past him. He snatches my arm pulling me around to face him.

"Listen. I know you don't get along with your mother right now but you don't have to go out of your way to intentionally hurt her. We didn't raise you that way."

"Sure, Dad. Whatever. I'll stop intentionally hurting her when she stops doing the same to me."

"You know she isn't being intentional." He takes a deep breath, "Your mother's off the mark sometimes, you know?"

"Right. That's the nice way to put it, Dad. She's a lunatic. I've never known her another way." A gasp comes from behind the kitchen door. I don't care.

I try to wiggle my arm loose from Dad's grip. He tightens it. "Get out of here, Lucy. And don't come back until your head is on straight. Try having a real conversation with your mother and I sometime. Without the snark." He shakes his head, disappointed. "I'm serious. Don't walk back in this house without compassion for your family. You aren't welcome here if you can't learn forgiveness and understanding."

"But Dad, you know she's being completely unreasonable. I mean ... who does that?"

"That may be true. But let's discuss it. Not yell at one another. We're always open to a real conversation about our relationship with you." He nods toward my hands, "Good luck at the doctor. I hope you'll join us later."

He flips off the light and swings open the kitchen door to find Mom. I stand alone in the dark with his car keys and wallet resting on my bandaged hands. I fumble with the door handle, holding back more tears. It seems like I'm always crying lately. At least it's an improvement over barfing.

I turn the ignition in Dad's car and peal out of the driveway. Why does Mom have to be so cruel? Does she really think a good boyfriend will solve everything? Just magically fix the betrayal I felt the day before? And pleading to Justin to get me a date. It's as if she was created to ruin me.

I can't handle her anymore.

A few cars sit scattered in the urgent care parking lot. I blot the wetness from under my eyes. I guess it doesn't really matter what I look like anymore. When I enter the building, a nurse glances up from her desk, drops her pen and rushes to my side.

I knew I looked horrendous.

She directs me into a back room where I wait for the doctor. She probably misinterprets my crazed appearance as shock from my injury. The fluorescent lights hum above me and hurt my eyes. I swing my legs back and forth with my eyes closed.

This day needs to end.

The doctor examines my hand, remarking how beautifully the wounds have already been cleaned. He suggests stitches on the two deep cuts, leaving the decision up to me. He tells me I am going to scar either way, so I might want the scars to align.

After my day, the thought of someone sewing my flesh together doesn't seem so bad. I shrug, handing him my palm as I grimace into my shoulder. He quickly sews me up before sending a nurse in to finish bandaging my palms. I leave urgent care with flexible and less glove-like bandages. I drive aimlessly, not yet ready to go home per Dad's standards or my own.

Why does Mom always have to be so awkward? Why can't she understand that she is socially inappropriate? I have tried approaching her calmly, with concern. I have tried ignoring her. I have tried yelling at her. She never gets it.

I pull the car into an empty parking lot. How can Dad expect me to find compassion for her? She doesn't seem to have any for me. I lean my head against the steering wheel, remembering her hand on my leg the night before, my packed lunch in the fridge, and her look of worry as I walked through the door this evening.

I relent. I don't have enough energy to rationalize against the truth any longer. Mom does care. I just chose to ignore it.

My new troll appearance stares back at me from the rearview mirror. Why can't I just be nice to her? Why do her unintentional moments of humiliation outweigh her kind gestures? Why can't she just sit down and talk to me? Or, even better, listen?

But why didn't I know how to sit down and do the same?

I groan, hating my conscience. This isn't my fault.

And, that's when it dawns upon me. Just as our issues aren't exclusively my fault, they aren't hers either. We are both responsible for what we've become. I will try harder. I'll start small, showing her compassion in the ways she showed me. I rub my cheeks as my eyes grow heavier. I can do that. I turn the key in the ignition. That will have to be enough for Dad. I'm not ready for a group share, but I can start being better.

***

I maintain a low profile at home that weekend. I sleep a lot between loads of laundry and trying to do small things for Mom. I organize the gardening magazines on her desk, walk Eric down the street to his friend's house, and vacuum the stairs. I doubt Mom really understands what I am trying to do but it does seem to keep her out of my hair.

While I am folding laundry, our home phone rings. I usually ignore it but recognize Justin's number on the caller ID. The white receiver is thick and foreign in my hand and the curled cord is so restraining. I won't be able to pace as we speak. I take a deep breath before answering.

"Hello?" My voice weakens at the end. Crap. I sound nervous. I sit down on the blue wingback chair, hoping it will help give my voice stability.

"Lucy, why didn't you call me back?" Justin's voice, even in frustration, makes my heart pound.

I speak slowly, containing the rush of energy through my system. "Sorry. I didn't know you called."

"Was your cell broken?"

I'd purposely left my phone in my purse all weekend. That small—well, now large—part of me wanted Justin to call. I couldn't have my phone taunting me. I didn't want to be that girl hovering over her phone, waiting for a boy to call. I'm pathetic enough already.

"Nope, I just haven't checked it. What's up?" My legs itch. How do people talk without pacing? "Can you drive yourself to work tomorrow? I've got some errands I want you to run." His words sting. I thought he was calling to check on me.

"Sure," I say lightly.

"Great. I'll text you all the info you'll need for the morning."

"Okay, sounds good." I force the rhythm of my voice to sound upbeat.

"Alright. See you tomorrow afternoon."

The phone clicks before I can say goodbye. I keep the receiver up to my ear, softly hitting it against my temple to the dial tone. I'm completely helpless to this stupid heartache. There is nothing I can do. I can't flirt or dress my way into his attention. I wouldn't even try. Justin has a wonderful relationship. I'm not like Marissa. I would never try to screw that up. I just need a distraction so I can move on.

I wander up to my room to check my phone. I have missed two calls from Justin and two texts. One's from Matt.

Matt: Sorry about Zach. You're better off. Please still come to my party, next Friday. Don't forget, you promised me during pool at the restaurant!

I read the message but don't respond. Crap. I did say I'd go. I'll have to cancel. There's no way I can handle being anywhere with Marissa and Zach making out.

I scroll to the next text.

Justin: At Rivervalley Library, please pick up books that I have on reserve. They are expecting you. Then stop at Target and pick up home design magazines and a notebook. I'll pay you back. See you 9ish.

I fumble through my desk for a pen and post-it to make a clearer list. The bottom drawer is jammed. With a pen, I slide out the offender. My essay on *Pride and Prejudice* falls to the floor. The red C- seems larger than before.

C-. That sucks. I curl up on my window seat and scan the essay. The format is perfect but the content is absolutely laughable. It's obvious I haven't read the book. A C- was generous. I can't believe I wasted Mr. Taden's time with this. On the last page, I discover a short note scribbled in red pen. "Lucy, you try to sell yourself short but your potential shows through. Please re-do before the last day of school."

My gut sinks. I'd never taken the time to look past the grade.

I pull *Pride and Prejudice* off the above bookshelf. Boring

Victorian figures sit ghostly together on the cover. The binding has never been creased. I ruffle the pages, smelling them. I used to be able to pick a good book by its smell. This book smells old and flowery. It's worth the read.

I believe I've found my distraction.

CHAPTER SIXTEEN

The morning drive to work is an eternity without Justin bothering me. I double park him as punishment. The guys are on their breakfast break when I arrive, but I won't allow my eyes to linger to pick Justin out from the group. But his dark hair and neck muscles are pretty hard not to notice. I give a quick wave in everyone's general direction before fumbling with my keys. Crap. No pockets. I pull down the visor, pinning them to the garage door remote.

"You do know Luke likes to steal cars, right?" Alex teases, reaching in through the window and grabbing the keys off the visor. He slips them into his pocket before he opens my door. "I heard about your hands. That sucks, huh?" I step out of the car.

"Totally."

"Can I see?"

I laugh. "Seriously?"

"Please?" he pretends to pout.

I shrug, carefully uncovering my palms. Alex holds the gauze for me so he can get the full picture. He whistles. "No fair. Those are gonna be wicked scars!"

"The doctor said something like that."

"Sweet. And such an awesome story to go with them. Falling off the roof followed up with being run over by a tornado." He whistles again.

"Now, don't pity her too much, Alex." Justin smiles, taking the gauze out of Alex's hands. "You should probably keep these wrapped up if they're going to heal, right?" He takes my left palm, holding it in his large hands, and starts pulling the gauze around it. My heart pounds violently against my chest.

This needs to stop.

"Don't worry. I've got this. I've been doing it all weekend." I pull my hand from his and finish the wrapping myself. He takes a step back, eyeing the backseat. "The stuff's in the trunk," I say. He nods, reaching in my car and flicking the trunk release switch. Three thick volumes about Victorian homes, the Target bag, and a few books on business economics sit in the trunk.

I pull my water bottle out of the car. "So, can I go work with Alex today?"

"No, not today."

I secretly rejoice, knowing that after the accident he would want to be my partner.

"Oh, okay." I act casual.

"Actually, I'm going to have you do some research." He taps the volumes of books.

"Wait, I'm not painting?"

Justin raises his eyebrow. "Do you really think I'd let you paint like that?" he nods toward my hands.

"But I'm fine. I can move them without issues!" That's a lie. They sting like crazy when I bend them. But I don't care. I need to paint; it's weirdly relaxing.

"Sorry. No way. It's not happening." He hands me the notebook from the plastic bag and the first volume about Victorian homes. "I need you to read this and take notes on anything pertaining to the exterior of Victorian homes, what materials they used, and what compounds were in the paint."

I open the cover. A cloud of dust poofs in my face. "Seriously?"

He nods. "And when you're done, I need you to read the other two."

"And then I can paint?"

"Well, after you complete your art project."

"You're kidding, right?"

Justin shrugs. "It's a job that needs to be done."

"What's the art project?"

"Well," he holds up the second volume and flips through it, "While you are reading, take time looking at the homes' exterior colors and inside details. Flip through the magazines you bought and rip out any similar looks and colors. Save them for me."

"Like a collage?" I say sarcastically.

I am unprepared for his chuckle so naturally my heart melts. Justin smiles at me. "Actually, that's a good idea. That way they'd be all together." He looks at the notebook. "Just put them in the back of the notebook for now. I'll bring glue tomorrow."

"Tomorrow?"

"Of course. You don't think you can finish this in a day, do you?"

I shrug, "I could if I wanted to."

Justin rolls his eyes. "Well, don't. I'm hoping this will last you the week." He nods toward the house. "Then you can paint."

I look down at the volume in my hand. "You know this sucks, right?"

"Yup. That's why you're doing it and not me." He pats me on the back as he walks away, calling out to Troy in the distance.

Settling myself under a large shady tree on Dad's emergency blizzard blanket, I open up the first volume and balk at the faded print. My nose itches from the dust. Justin wasn't kidding. This really may take all week.

The book is surprisingly interesting. Each chapter was dedicated to a Minneapolis or St. Paul historical home. I become engrossed in each home's history, learning about the families that lived there, fires, new additions, and even a few murders. Occasionally I come across a line about siding or paint color and I force myself to stop and jot down some notes. At the end of each chapter, I rip out a few colors that match the photos, stuffing them into the back of the notebook for the collage.

I used to meticulously create collage book covers with Marissa at school. It was torture, but I never let on. It was something to do during study hall.

I rip out a photo of a dark red lamp, crumpling the edge a bit as I put it in the back of the notebook. It's amazing how satisfying it is.

I really do hate crafts.

During my breaks, I spend a lot of time at the base of

Alex's ladder complaining. It takes all my strength to avoid Justin. A simple glimpse at his tan arms is enough to send me reeling. Everything feels so raw right now. I can't be near him. My feelings would be too obvious.

Troy ends the day as I finish the first volume. I slam it closed, avoiding the dust. My butt aches from the grooves of the tree roots. Justin is crazy if he thinks I'll do this a full week. Tomorrow, I'll be more efficient, finishing both books so I can start painting again on Wednesday. And screw the collage. There's no way I'm doing that. He can just sort through the photos himself.

Justin walks over to me as I pile the books in the trunk. He leans against my car, shifting uncomfortably. "So, listen," he begins. "It probably doesn't make sense for you to come out here super early tomorrow since you're just reading and stuff."

I hold up my notebook and flip through ten pages of perfectly outlined details, "You call this *just reading*?" Talk about under appreciation. All of the butterflies that have taken up permanent residence in my heart cringe in unison.

"You know what I mean, Lady." Justin follows me to the front seat. I pull open the door, fumbling with the visor for the keys.

"Crap. Alex." I turn around just in time to see Alex and Emmanuel's van pull away.

A jingling noise tickles my ear. "You may need these," Justin holds them out to me.

"Thanks."

"So, what I'm saying is that you can drive yourself tomorrow, alright?" He pats the top of my car as I turn the ignition.

I want to say that it's not okay. I like driving with him, not only because he makes me go haywire but because it makes me part of the crew. Now I'm just going to be the girl who shows up to read, curled up under a tree.

But I smile instead. "No problem."

"Great. See you tomorrow." Justin hits the roof of my car one last time before stepping away.

I drive home feeling discarded. It's so easy for him to decide I should drive myself. I miss our morning banter. He probably doesn't even notice it's gone.

I look forward to curling up on the living room couch and pulling out *Pride and Prejudice* from my bag. I shake my head in disbelief. In less than a week, my whole social life has shrunk, now fitting neatly between the pages of a classic novel.

It's also time for a new look. There is no reason to be dressed for manual labor if I am going to be stuck under a tree reading all day. I trade in my shorts for my favorite floor-length maxi skirt and my pony tail for loose waves. The mirror reveals a comfortable yet feminine me. Marissa would have hated this outfit. She doesn't believe in casual skirts; she says it's just an excuse to be homely.

I twirl, watching the last tier of the skirt fly out. Freedom. Marissa is wrong. This look rocks. And, whoa, seriously … what twirling a skirt can do for my mood. Mental note: wear more skirts and twirl more often.

Marissa can shove it.

I pull into the work utility lot feeling oddly confident. Yes, I would be isolated all day but at least I felt good about myself. Justin's lack of attention can't change that. I settle under the tree, this time bringing a few pillows for my butt and back. Troy calls for break as I open the second volume. I don't join them. This project is ending today.

I start reading about the James J. Hill House, one of the largest and most prominent mansions in Minnesota. I barely start my outline before a tap on my shoulder interrupts me. "Hey, Lucy." I look up, shielding the glare of the sun. Troy smiles down at me.

"Hey. What's up?"

He shrugs and sits down. I smile politely, turning toward him while simultaneously shifting to a friendly distance. He looks at the pillows and nods to my skirt, "You've kind of got an Arabian princess thing going on here, huh?"

I laugh. "Yeah. I guess so."

"It's a good look for you," he adds as he leans back, doing his characteristic move of placing his arm behind me. "So, I was thinking," he smiles at me before continuing. "Do you want to grab dinner later?"

I blink in confusion, not expecting such a direct approach. "Well, I mean," my brain searches frantically for an excuse.

"Obviously, I heard about Zach and Marissa." He reaches his hand over to touch mine. "I'm sorry about that. Let me make it up to you."

Score. Troy has no idea he's just given me the perfect excuse. I pull back my hand politely. "Thanks but—"

"Don't say no."

"No, it's not that. I just, well …" Stumbling. Crap. Get the words out. "It happened only last week." I smile at him politely. "I need more time, you know?"

I watch Troy process my request, hoping he'll take it the way I mean and not literally. "Okay, I get that. Time I can give you." He stands up, wiping the grass off his butt and not trying to hide his disappointment. I smile at him politely in an effort to cover up my inner cringe. I'll need to be clearer with him in the future.

I look down at a photo of the James J. Hill mansion so I don't have to watch him walk away. The grand stone walls blur. Troy is a nice guy. There's no reason I shouldn't have said yes. I have no lingering feelings toward Zach, other than disgust. I study Troy out of the corner of my eye. He's attractive. Outgoing and a good leader.

Then my eye catches Justin spinning a basketball while laughing at Luke. My stomach flips.

But Troy doesn't make me feel that way. I refocus on Troy, willing some butterflies to take flight. Nothing happens. I picture myself cuddled up on the couch against Troy's chest. I feel no hint of desire.

I look back at Justin. I wonder if that is how he feels about me. Thankfully, I haven't put myself out there with Justin like Troy just did with me. I wouldn't put Justin in such an awkward situation—or myself for that matter. I turn my attention back to the book, pouring myself into the James J. Hill mansion's history, welcoming its distraction.

***

"You know you can take a break, right, Lady?" Justin's voice interrupts my work flow. "It's three o'clock."

"Already?" I set the third volume aside.

Justin sits down and I try not to look excited. "Yup. You didn't even flinch during lunch break. It was like you were—"

"In my own world," I offer.

He nods while drinking from his water bottle. "Yeah, that's how my parents always describe me when I'm reading."

I shrug. "Honestly, it's nice to escape."

Justin picks up the notebook, flipping through the pages. "Crap. You're almost done?"

"I told you it wouldn't take long."

"That's over four hundred pages of reading."

"There were pictures."

"In less than two days." He winks.

My heart. Stops. Whoa.

"What am I going to do with you tomorrow?"

Must. Recover.

"Lucy?"

"Let me paint?" I offer.

He sighs, handing me my lunch box. "Maybe."

"Really?"

"We'll see."

"Come on. I can't sit here all week."

He nods down toward my hands. "How do they feel?"

"Great!" I wiggle my fingers at him. My palms sting but I don't care.

"Impressive."

"So, I can paint tomorrow?"

"We'll see."

I sigh, setting my lunch box aside. I pick up the last volume, determined to finish so I can paint tomorrow. Justin nudges me and I can't help but nudge him back. He smiles before grabbing the book from my hands. "Eat," he says.

"Fine." I pull my sandwich out and take a bite. "Is

that better?"

"Much." He grabs one of the pillows and puts it behind his head, closing his eyes.

"Umm, shouldn't you be painting?"

"No, actually."

"Oh? Well Troy looks like he's about to kill you." Justin peeks out of the corner of his eye and gives Troy a wave.

"He'll get over it." He rolls over, resting his head on his hand, leaning in toward me. My heart does acrobatics. I bite my lower lip in an attempt to breathe steadily.

"So, why aren't you painting?" I ask, trying not to lean in toward him too.

"Because I need to learn to relax. In fact, no one should be painting." Justin turns around and yells, "Call it."

Troy turns toward Justin, throwing up his arms and pointing to his watch. The other guys check their own watches before hesitantly climbing down from their ladders. Justin waves them over.

"So guys, after last week's debacle," Justin nods toward my hands, "I've decided that maybe I need to relax on our deadlines a bit."

Troy interjects. "No way. We're a week ahead. We can make gold this summer if we keep this up."

Justin shrugs. "True, but come on, a couple games of basketball won't ruin much."

"Ball?" Troy smiles.

Justin peers over his shoulder. "There's a court on the other side of the hill. Let's try to play every day after work." He looks around the group. "Unless you have plans?"

Troy looks at me. I avert my eyes. "Nope. Let's do it," he says.

"Seriously?" Alex actually bounces.

"I knew I liked you." Emmanuel extends his hand, pulling Justin off the ground.

"Alex, go get the ball," Justin says.

"I'm not a dog, man."

"Alex, do you want to play or not?"

Alex rolls his eyes before running off to the truck to retrieve the ball. The guys follow, picking up their ladders and supplies off the association's grounds. Justin turns toward me, "So, you're in?"

Basketball? I haven't played since the state final. My gut squeezes. No. I'm not ready yet.

I hold up my hands, "If I can't paint, I can't exactly play ball."

"Right, maybe tomorrow?"

I shrug, "We'll see." He smiles at me. I pull the book back on my lap.

"No way. You may not be playing but you're not sitting up here reading like a loner." He grabs me under my arms, pulling me up off the ground. "You'll at least watch."

"But I'm almost done."

"Fine, you can bring the books." He nudges me. This time I manage not to nudge him back. I don't like this. It makes my eye twitch to be so close to a game.

There's a picnic table away from the court where I sit and pour myself into my final outline. I write feverishly, trying not to notice how Troy predictably drives the baseline but hits the boards hard on defense. Or how Jake's follow through always falls to the left and he spends most of the game purposely pissing off Alex. Alex plays naturally but spends too much time seeking revenge on Jake to be a consistent player. Luke is solid on defense but he sets weak picks. Emmanuel always drives to the left. And, Justin, playing more effortlessly than Alex, always sinks the outside, baseline shot.

My heart aches more with every beat of the basketball and every *swish* through the net. I look at the court. Why can't I just let myself play? My heart gallops.

No. Stop it.

But no harm could come from taking a few shots or holding the ball. Our school was too big for them to know my history. They wouldn't ask any questions. This is no big deal. I can do this.

I finish tearing out one last swatch of color, placing it behind the last page of my outline. I swing my legs over the edge of the bench, watching Justin make a quick pass to Jake.

This is happening. I stand up, ready to play. My heart rattles my rib cage. Jake squares up and sinks a three-point shot. "Game," he shouts.

Relief, my best friend.

Game over. The net still sways from the last shot.

It's better this way. I grab the books and my outline off the table and walk over to Justin, who is still throwing up shots.

"I'm done," I say, holding my outline out to him.

He shoots a three pointer before turning toward me. The sound of a swish inevitably follows. "Let's see." He scans the material. "Thirty-eight pages?" He laughs. "I can't really argue with that."

"So, can I paint tomorrow?"

He shakes his head. "Not happening. If your hands

aren't up to a little game of ball, there's no way I'm letting you hold a paintbrush all day."

I frown at him. "What if I don't want to play?" I sound a bit like Eric but it's better than letting on how panicked it makes me.

"Then you'll be doing more research." He turns away from me. I pull on his arm, turning him back around.

"That's not fair."

"You're part of this crew, right, Lucy?" His smile disappears. "This is all about team building."

"So?" I'm agitated. No one can force me to play basketball. It doesn't matter that I had almost done it on my own.

Almost.

"Playing is not optional. It'll help our performance." He nods down toward my hands before continuing in an authoritative voice, "If you're injured, you can sit out. Otherwise, I expect your participation or you can consider not working." Justin doesn't hesitate to remind me he's boss.

I bite my tongue before giving him a polite smile. "Then what time do you want me here?"

"Same time."

"And what will I be doing?"

Justin shrugs. "I'll figure something out." He turns again to walk away. This time I let him.

I stay behind the group, pretending to organize the research materials. They climb up the hill together before I turn around to stare at the empty basketball court.

My feet find the top of the key. Has it really been nearly two years since I stepped on a real court? I look at the basket, wondering what my body remembers. I square up and take a shot. The imaginary ball leaves my hands and I shake my head. Its trajectory would have hit the board too far to the right.

I square up for another. This time my follow through is midline. The trajectory would have arched gracefully. *Swish.*

Yes. I still have it, somewhere.

I grab the books and climb up the hill to my car. The lot is empty. I drive home contemplating how much this job is worth to me. I've fainted, hung off a roof, been forced to watch and maybe play basketball, and I've spent hours agonizing about my weird relationship with Justin. Maybe it would be best to stop?

But *Pride and Prejudice* is not an endless novel. I think of Alex and how he makes me laugh. I think of the banter I've learned to love while driving with Justin. Or how satisfied I feel every time I watch new paint cover up the old. Plus, what would I do without the job? I need it. I'll ride the basketball phase out. Justin seemed a bit off today. Maybe he's just in a bad mood.

The next day is worse than the day before. Justin hands me his accounting books and a calculator. I spend the entire day checking his books and receipts. The work is mindless and slow, the time crawling along with it. I approach Justin twice about painting again but his answer remains the same, "No." My stiff legs envy the guys climbing up and down the ladders. I'd have been in tears at the end of the day if it wasn't for how pissed I've become at Justin.

He rarely speaks to me now. When he does, it is only to check my work. He never smiles while we talk and, even worse, doesn't even attempt to tease me. He has no problem joking with the other guys but around me he acts like stone.

He's pushing me away. I don't understand. Yes, I freak out internally with every smile or nod that comes my way. But not once have I acted like Troy or, worse, like Marissa. I'm not throwing myself at him or trying to destroy his life.

But he seems determined to distance himself from me.

It hurts me in a way I hadn't expected or experienced before, a new level of loss. I'm losing a friend and, with him, a piece of myself. Whether I want to admit it or not, I trusted part of myself to Justin. I'd been more honest with him than I have been with anyone in years.

The next day brings more hurt, frustration, and isolation as the day wears on. Justin's completely lost all interest in our friendship. Not even saying hello.

I finish the accounting books during lunch break. I take off my bandages, easily flexing my fingers without pain. My stitches are nearly dissolved and the cuts are healing well.

There isn't any good reason I can't paint.

Justin leans against the shady side of his truck listening to his iPhone while eating chocolate pudding. At ease, he's oblivious to the agitation that surges through my system as I walk past him. I climb into the truck bed, grab my ladder and an empty bucket with a paintbrush and rag. Justin clears his throat. "And what do you think you're doing?"

"I'm done." I climb out, pulling the ladder behind me and throwing it over my shoulder. My palms protest a bit but I don't care.

As I walk away, I expect Justin's refusal. It doesn't

come. I'm victorious. Ready to work and he can't stop me.

Suddenly, the weight on my shoulder lifts. "What?" I snap.

"You aren't painting." His voice is stern.

I throw down the bucket and tear off my bandages. I wiggle my fingers and flex my palms. "They work fine."

Justin shrugs. "I see that."

"I've finished all of your busy work. I'm working." I glare back at him. I watch him take a deep breath before he answers.

"Fine. You can work. But not with these." He nods toward the ladder that now rests on his shoulder and my bucket on the ground. "You can go back to yesterday's house and check the trim lines."

"Isn't that your job?"

"Technically, yes." He won't meet my eyes. I want to shake him. I can't keep my anger in check any longer.

"So, is that my role now? Anything that keeps me away?" He won't look at me. "Justin, am I that bad to be around?" I bite my lower lip, fearing the answer to the question.

"I don't know what you're talking about."

I grab his arm. He glares down at me. "What did I do?" The words slip out before I can stop them. I sound desperate. Justin's face grows momentarily sorrowful. My stomach violently flips. It scares me.

"Nothing," he says, looking into my eyes. The depths of their green startle me. Gorgeous.

I try to recover my argumentative momentum but my desire for the truth wins out. "So what's with the shut out?" I take a step closer to him. My brain screams at me to run away.

He purses his lips before shaking his head. "I have no idea what you're talking about." He nods toward the green house's front door. "Check the trim around the door and porch windows. If you need something, let me know." His words are cold.

He leaves me standing alone on the porch, watching him walk away. He has no idea what I was talking about. Have I imagined the whole thing? In desperation to deal with Marissa and Zach, have I concocted a bond of friendship out of nothing?

I face the trim, pretending to review it.

No. I haven't made up my connection with Justin. We had a unique relationship before I discovered Zach and Marissa. I admit that it stemmed from frustration and annoyance. It was not a romantic bond. But we have a bond. Normally people become closer after a tornado runs them down. Instead, everything changed. I will my heart to harden toward him. I can't deal with any more loss.

***

Troy calls the day's end as I'm finishing my review of Justin's work. Of course it is flawless. No wonder he owns this stupid company.

I walk to my car, avoiding Alex's attempt to catch my eye. I'm going home.

"Lucy," Troy yells from behind me. "Don't forget court time." That's exactly what I was *forgetting*.

"Yeah, come on. Best time of the day." Alex's voice makes me stop. I can't blow him off. I explore my mind for excuses. I don't feel well. I have to take care of Eric. My parents need me home. I am moving to Utah.

Justin pulls the ball out of his truck. He turns toward me and shakes his head. "Lucy doesn't play. Let her go home."

I glare back at him. I've had it with him ordering me around. I don't care that he is my *boss*. I can't take any more of his crap. "No." I grab the basketball out of his hands and my palms spark with excitement. "Actually, I think I will play." We glare at one another. My challenge hangs thick in the air.

"Oooo. You think you got it, huh, Lucy?" Alex whoops in the background. "You think you can handle me?"

"Yeah," I shout back to him as I turn away from Justin. "I'm pretty sure I can keep up."

Troy claps his hands, ready to take charge. "Okay, Lucy you're with me and Jake. Emmanuel, you ref. And Justin, Alex, and Luke — Good luck!" Troy's hand lingers on my upper back, leading me down the hill and to the court. "Lucy, be careful. They play a bit rough sometimes under the boards." I try not to roll my eyes. They didn't even box-out. "I'm going to take Luke because I'm great under the boards and he's our only threat there. Jake always takes Alex because, well, they have their love affair thing going on." I nod, understanding. "That leaves Justin for you."

Perfect.

Troy continues, "Now, Justin is good. … No, he's the best. Watch for his outside shots. He's quick on his feet so stay low. He prefers the—"

"Left, baseline shot. Yeah, I know. I've been watching you guys, remember?"

Troy smiles. "You've been watching us?"

"Well, you know. It's kind of part of the job." I echo Justin's requirement.

Troy nods before pulling me close, blocking my view of the court. Good, I don't need to see it until I get on it. I can do this. Anger is my fuel. Justin is going down.

Troy leans in and whispers, "Just keep Justin off the left side and Jake and I will do the rest. Don't worry about it." I gently push him away but he keeps standing in front of me like an oaf.

I bat my eyelashes at him. "The game?" My ankles dance. No fear. Just delicious adrenaline.

"Oh right. Let's do this!" Troy hands me the ball. "Take your time getting us *the rock*," he nods down toward the ball in an informative way. "We can win this."

Somehow, I get to the top of the key. Justin walks forward to meet me. "You're really going to play?" He offers me an out. My gut wants to dash but my feet hold firm.

"Yes," I say. "I'm done with all of this. I'm playing, now." My soul speaks. Justin backs away. Totally freaked him out. Good. All for my advantage. He's going down.

"So Troy, I pass it to him, checking it? Right?" I say.

Troy glows. "Right, Lucy. Check it to Justin and then the game starts."

"Oh, alright." I put on a clueless face.

This is going to be awesome.

"Okay." I toss the ball feebly to Justin. "Check."

Justin smiles back at me but my heart does not sway.

I am unshakable now.

"Okay, Lucy. Now the game is on." Troy informs me from below the hoop.

I smile back at Justin while I give the ball a few clumsy dribbles to the right.

"Good job. Now pass it," Troy instructs again.

I ignore him, allowing my brain to assess the game. Luke is keeping Troy out of the lane, which is easy because Troy only shuffles back and forth on the right side. Jake and Alex are shoving each other on the baseline. This allows the left side of the lane for driving. As I'm looking down at the ball, fake dribbling, I notice that Justin is at complete ease.

That lady after the tornado was right; he severely underestimates me.

I look up at him while dribbling like a klutz. "Ready?" I ask with a wink.

He pulls up, confused, giving me an opening to drive the lane.

I push the ball down close to the ground, going in quickly on the right. He follows a step behind. Crossing the ball behind my back, I turn with my left leg forward, using my back to force Justin to my outside. I redirect, finishing my drive down the left side of the lane before passing underneath the basket and throwing up a reverse lay-up.

Swish. HELL YES. I want to sing. It's like being ripped open and all the past comes flying out of my chest. I'm free.

Everyone stops moving, mouths dangling.

I turn toward Troy, "Umm, Troy, is that what you had in mind?" He nods with large eyes.

"WHA', WHAAAAAAAAAT?!" Alex shouts from the top of the key. "Justin just got schooled!"

Justin's mouth hangs open. I glare at him, giving him a few moments to take it in before I walk up to him, ball in hand.

"You play?" he asks.

"Oh. I play. Do you?" I hold out the ball to him. Challenge made.

He closes his mouth. His green eyes grow more intense. He takes the ball from me and smiles. "Be careful, Lucy."

I roll my eyes. "I can handle it. Trust me."

And so it begins. I fly off my adrenaline. I move effortlessly with the ball around the top of the key. I thrive on defense, stealing the ball from Alex anytime he mocks Jake. I keep Justin off the baseline, enjoying his surmounting frustration. I show off. Justin needs to feel the sting of defeat with every shot I make. There's no way I'm losing this. Not to him.

The game ends quickly. I clearly have the advantage because no one has ever seen me play. In the end, we win twenty-one to thirteen. I score fifteen from drives alone.

Justin only scores eight.

Jake sinks our winning shot. It's the first time that Troy and Jake have won. Troy runs toward me, with his arms open. He suddenly scoops me up and throws me over his shoulder. He runs with me around the court, circling Justin, Alex and Luke while yelling, "She's ours. Look who's the star now Justin." I can't help but smile. Troy says everything I want to say. After a few circles of the court, I get dizzy. I pound on his shoulders. He finally swings me down as he continues to swagger.

I walk off the court without a word.

My work is done.

CHAPTER SEVENTEEN

I arrive home in time for dinner. The smell in the kitchen is intoxicating. Roasted rosemary chicken, garlic mashed potatoes, and green beans—Dad, always the culinary genius. I can't resist. I grab a glass of water and sit down in my spot at the table. I love this place in the corner, on an old wooden bench near the window where I can watch the pond. My pond. It is the only thing I initially liked about our new house. When we moved here, I imagined it was whispering life's secrets to me but I just couldn't hear them yet. So I'd sit and wait patiently, hoping the ripples would reveal something magical about my future. This was before I started my horrendous freshman year. I look out onto the water, shamefully surprised that that same gullible hope remains. The sun bounces crystals off the ripples on the surface. I listen but don't hear any secrets. No surprise there.

It takes me a moment to escape my nostalgia. I blink and really look at the actual scene. The pond has changed a lot. Our neighbors have landscaped a waterfall into it. How did I miss that? Has it really been that long since I have sat in this corner, waiting and listening?

The kitchen door swings open and the air in the room becomes thicker. Mom has joined us. For a brief second her eyes pass over where I sit and then she doubles back. She blinks as if I am a dream and then settles her face into a blank expression.

"Lucinda." Her tone is low and her speech slow. I take a deep breath, bracing myself for impact. Mom stands in silence, a rarity. I take a second to look at her. Like the pond, she has also changed. Her eyes are deeper, making her crow's feet more pronounced. Her favorite pink shirt hangs more loosely off her shoulders. She takes a breath as if to speak, but no words follow.

She is exhausted.

All of the adrenaline from the game quickly drains from my body into the floor. My heart follows, sinking below, where it belongs. I look into her eyes, looking for some sparkle of life. I see her blue eyes, the same as mine, except they are empty. It's gone, like before she got well.

I don't know how long we look at one another. Dad coughs so I look away, refocusing on the water. I don't know how to begin a real conversation so it is easier not to. Our silence remains, only interrupted with a few bumps of glasses and plates while Mom prepares the table. The kitchen door flies open as Eric plows through it with his new truck. The moment he sees me in my spot his lips part into his huge, toothy smile.

"Lucy." Eric's speech whistles through a hole in his smile. He claps his little hands together. "You're eating tonight?" Not waiting for a response, he pulls Dad toward the table. "I want to sit here. Please?" He points to Dad's spot, which is right next to mine.

"Sure, kid. I'm sure Lucy would love to sit with you."

"Lucy, I can sit here." He runs to my side, using his hands to try to hoist himself up. I grab the back of his jeans, helping him up with a quick tug. He's a little guy.

Dad walks up behind Mom at the kitchen island, giving her a kiss on the cheek. Mom continues mashing the potatoes. Her eyes swollen. She seems close to broken, stress written in the lines on her face. I cringe, knowing exactly who the stress is from. Dad stands behind her, his hands hugging her tiny waist, holding her together. I struggle to keep composed.

How have I missed so much?

Eric finally settles himself next to me. His small legs touch mine. He looks up at me with the goofiest grin. "Hey, buddy," I say as I give him a side hug. His mouth opens up into an even larger smile. My heart tweaks in pain—obviously I have neglected him too.

Eric starts swinging his legs. I copy him. It seems like the only appropriate thing to do.

"Lucy." He grabs my face between his hands, pulling my head toward his seriously.

I laugh. "Yes?"

He pauses a moment, as if searching for the right words. "What did you do at work today, Lucy?" Perfect sentence. He looks back toward Mom and smiles. Clearly, they have worked on this today.

"Well, Eric, I painted."

"And?" He grabs my hand, studying the bandages.

I sigh; he is never satisfied with one answer. "I got to stand on a big front patio." I pretend it is much more exciting than it was. His eyes widen like I have discovered a dinosaur or something. My heart melts for him. I want to give him more. "And, Eric. Guess what else I did today?"

"What?" he whispers in amazement. He puts his pudgy hands back on my face in anticipation.

I can't turn back now.

I exhale, looking down into his eyes and say, "I played basketball."

Crack. A plate hits the floor. I don't need to look to know who'd dropped it. Eric's body startles, though he doesn't seem to be aware of it. He doesn't miss a beat.

"Did you make a basket? Did you win?"

I nod in the exaggerated way you say "yes" to a five-year-old. He squeals with delight. He loves watching me play basketball, cheering from the sidelines louder than anyone I know. He went to every game he could. Until I quit.

He misses it.

I hate myself for taking that away from him. I rub my eyes. I am a crappy sister.

Before Eric can ask more questions, Dad puts the food out onto the table and Mom slides into her chair next to me. Eric spreads both his hands wide, waiting for us to grasp them so we can say grace. I grab his hand. Out of the corner of my eye I can tell Mom is about to crumble. I'm sure she is overwhelmed. I can't blame her. I was talking about playing basketball, I'm eating dinner with the family, and I'm not being overly sensitive.

Even I'm shocked.

I contemplate Mom's hand. This would be the perfect opportunity to blow her off again, refusing to take it. But I can't do it. Not this time. How can I drive in the knife when I know I am in control? She's too broken to deal with it.

I extend my hand, laying my palm open on the table. She grabs it quickly as if she is worried I will change my mind. Her quickness startles me. She chokes back a sound. I study the birds etched on the white plate.

"Mom, why are you crying?" The ever-observant five-year-old. Mom's attempt to stifle the noise in her throat is fading.

Dad intervenes. "Lord, thank you for this opportunity to dine as a family. Please bless this food to our bodies and bless our conversation. Amen."

"Amen," Eric chimes in loudly.

I look up at Dad, thanking him with a soft smile for his quick prayer. He nods back ever so slightly then he claps his hands together and begins telling us all about his day. He over-describes every detail to safely monopolize the conversation. I concentrate on eating. The food is delicious. I'd eaten too many processed meals from under my bed. When the meal ends, I sit awkwardly not knowing if I should ask to be excused. Suddenly, Mom's hand rests on my arm.

Dad stands up and takes Eric to help him fix the lawn mower's engine. Before Eric leaves he asks me if I would play basketball with him sometime soon. I say yes. When the squeak of the kitchen door stops after their exit, I turn back toward Mom. I tense as I wait for her to begin.

"So, you played basketball today?"

"Yup." I poke at the extra chicken fat I've chosen not to eat.

"I'm glad." She opens her mouth, as if to say more about the subject but doesn't. "Have you made friends at your new job?"

I pause, wondering this myself. "Sort of," is the most honest answer I can give.

"Well, that's good."

I nod some more. I've become really good at nodding.

"Lucy, I just want you to know," I clutch the side of the table, bracing myself. She notices and stops speaking.

We sit in silence for a bit more, trying to cope with everything unsaid between us. I focus on the second hand of the clock, thinking of *Pride and Prejudice*. "Well, I have some homework to do."

Mom nods, not remembering it's summer and homework shouldn't be on my radar. I get up from the table, crossing the room to leave. As I reach out my hand to push the swinging door open, Mom says, "Lucy. Please remember what you just promised."

I swing around. I can taste that this is going to sting. "What are you talking about?" I can't believe she is going to force a fight now. It's like she wants us to be miserable.

"You promised Eric you would play basketball with him."

I nod, and my eyes widen. This is no news to me.

Mom stands up and walks toward me. Her face is serious. "Lucy. I intend on you keeping this promise. I do not want to have to explain to him all over again why you won't play with him anymore. Not to mention teaching him what promises mean despite your example."

There it is.

I glare back at Mom with the deadliest look I can muster. I lock my target and go in for the kill. "Thanks Mom," I begin sarcastically. "I was totally excited to play with Eric until now. Way to turn it into an order."

"If you make a commitment, you do it, Lucy!"

My blood pressure doubles while she continues to speak, her voice becoming more shrill.

"You can't treat Eric like you do school, basketball, or me. When you don't follow through, I'm the one explaining why he can't follow your examples."

My examples? I feel like she has punched me in the face. Spiteful energy surges through my system.

"Fine. I'll save you the trouble." I walk toward the garage door, pulling it open and shouting out, "Sorry Eric. I was lying. I will NEVER play basketball with you because I'm a witch." Dad looks back, stunned. Eric's lower lip quivers before he starts to wail.

My heart breaks into a million pieces.

"There, Mom. Now you won't have to."

I swing open the kitchen door and storm out. Eric continues to wail in the garage while Mom follows me with heavy footsteps. I grab my purse, slam the front door in Mom's face, and climb into Dad's car in the driveway. I am surprised the front door didn't fly open and Mom didn't run out and throw herself on the car. I can't believe her. I actually was myself and she ruined it, forcing me to become a horrible person. Of course I wanted to play with Eric. I remembered how happy it made him. I wanted to make him happy again.

I turn the dial of the radio, fumbling in my purse for my keys. I can't get out of there quick enough. I throw the car into reverse, ready to peal out of the driveway. But Eric's intense sobs pouring from behind the garage door stop me. Did I really just hurt my five-year-old brother in a backwards attempt to hurt Mom? I stare at the garage; he sobs so uncontrollably he starts choking.

I bite my tongue. Who have I become?

I have a choice. I can get out of the car and do the hard thing, go back inside and apologize to Eric or I can drive away and leave a huge knife in Mom's back and give Eric reason to hate me forever. I take deep breaths, trying to force myself to reason. Mom was trying to protect Eric. I'd have done the same thing had Eric needed protecting from me. My heart sinks. Wait, he did need protection from me.

I turn off the ignition and, before I can change my mind, I click the garage door opener. I step out of the car as it retracts up. My parents glare back at me, daggers of disappointment thrown my way. Eric stops crying, turning toward the noise of the garage door. He takes a moment to look at me before reburying his head in Mom's lap with further sobs.

They hate me and I can't blame them.

I take a step toward them. "Can I speak with Eric?" Eric, ever trusting, turns around. He nods.

Mom stands up, red-faced. "No. Absolutely not. You're done."

Dad cuts her off. He puts his hand on her shoulder and squeezes. "Sarah, let me have a word with her and then she can speak with Eric." He looks in my direction, his eyes piercing mine, "And then Lucy will speak with us."

Mom relents, taking Eric by the hand into the house. Dad motions for me to join him next to the lawn mower. He busily bends over it, moving parts and playing with wires. I stand next to him watching and waiting. He usually plays mediator not direct discipliner. I wonder how many weeks of grounding this conversation will send my way.

"Lucy." Dad continues to tinker with the motor as he talks. "Do you have any idea how cruel your choices and words are to this family?" His bluntness feels like ice cold water.

I can't answer. Of course I knew how cruel I'd been. That's why I came back. Apparently, I'd become an expert in cruelty. I hated it. I hated myself for it. Tears well in my eyes. I wipe them away—I don't deserve to cry. Thankfully, Dad keeps on tinkering with the motor, not noticing.

"You've come to a point in your life where you're old enough to make choices that define yourself and your future. If you continue down this path, do you think you will have a relationship with your brother when you are away at college? Or how about a mother to call and talk to when your heart breaks? Or even farther than that, dear— what about your children? Do you want them to be able to have a relationship with their grandparents? A relationship with you?" He pauses, looking up from the mower.

I stand there, finally allowing my tears to spill down my cheeks. Of course I want all of that.

No. I need it.

Have I already jeopardized this? How did I get this way? How could I intentionally hurt Mom, over and over, when I know how fragile she really is? Why am I so evil?

I swallow.

That is the truth.

I am evil.

My chest is hit with a sudden pressure, like I'm roped to cement blocks.

My throat thickens. It's hard to breathe. The usual tense air that hangs between my parents and me has solidified. Too thick to inhale. What I can get in, exits in quick sobs.

My hands shake and my heart races out of control. What is happening? The room spins. I watch Dad stand up from the motor, extending a hand which I grab. He lowers me to the ground.

I hug my knees, sobbing, trying to take in a deep breath. I rock back and forth. My ears are ringing.

I am evil.

It is the saddest thing I've ever known.

"Sarah, come quick." Dad's voice echoes behind the loud ringing.

My crying turns into a wail. I rock back and forth.

I am evil.

About to break Mom for the second time.

Evil.

The room spins.

No wonder Mom was depressed after I was born.

Somehow, she had always known I was evil.

I feel a hand on my shoulder.

A warm body sitting behind me, arms wrapped around me.

Rocking with me.

Was I seriously born to be so cruel?

The body rocks me back and forth, changing my rhythm.

I take deeper breaths. The ringing stops.

My sobs turns into normal breaths and tears.

I rock.

We rock.

Back and forth, in the corner on the sweaty, concrete floor of the garage.

Rocking.

I don't know how long we rock. I feel her arms around me.

Mom.

When I turn around to look at her, her face is red, tears running down them.

I take a deep breath, "I'm so sorry, Mom."

I start sobbing again, falling into her arms. She holds me. She sobs too.

We rock and sob.

"I love you," she whispers in my ear.

I try to say "I love you" back but it's incoherent.

I don't deserve her love when I am so evil.

But she really does love me and that just makes me sob more.

She holds me tighter, rocking me back and forth and whispering her love for me.

It hurts to be loved so much.

Finally, my sobs get under control. Mom holds out her hand, helping me up to my feet. She keeps her hand on my back as she leads me into the house. We pass through the kitchen, where Dad sits, waiting. Mom whispers, "It's okay, Dan." When I see Dad's pale, concerned face, I start sobbing again. Mom leads me to my room. I crawl in bed. She sits next to me. We never speak, the tears falling from my eyes and an occasional sob escaping my chest seems to be enough.

I am pure evil.

I don't remember falling asleep. I do remember her stroking my hair.

CHAPTER EIGHTEEN

I wake up to the early morning light, when the air is fresh and slightly tinged blue. Five thirty-five a.m. It feels like I have been sleeping forever but I have a horrible headache behind my eyes. Why?

Crying. Last night's events resurface. I freeze, holding my breath. Did that all really happen? And to think Mom looked like she was about to crumble. Ironic. Apparently I'm the person one crack away from shattering.

And I cracked.

Evil.

I let out my breath. I need to get away. The house is quiet except for the occasional snore from Dad down the hall. I tiptoe around my room, digging through my drawers and closet for an old running tank and pair of running shoes. I throw my hair into a ponytail, creep down the stairs and out the front door.

My feet hit the driveway and I transition into a jog. I turn onto the running path that links a chain of parks, winding around a chain of ponds. The running-way is empty this morning, the pavement mine. My feet fall into a rhythm along with my breaths, four seconds in and four seconds out. Each breath of the morning air seems to launch my body into further hypnosis with its jogging rhythm. My body is in sync, now it's time to address my mind.

Evil. Wow. Did I really try to hurt my mom by hurting Eric? And why was I trying to hurt Mom?

The dark corner of my mind answers: Because she wants to control you.

I rebuke: But isn't she my mother? Doesn't that give her the responsibility to parent me?

I run faster. That answer is clear.

But I'm still evil. What about when I hid in the bathroom stall and listened to Marissa degrade Sally? When did I become the type of person who would stand by when someone hurts another?

Mom has reason for her need to control. Even if I don't like how she delivers it.

I sprint.

I used to be the one telling off my teammates the moment they started talking smack about a player on the other team. Now, I'm too weak to stand up for anyone, even myself. Why couldn't I see Marissa for what she really is? A selfish and manipulative person.

She is everything I have become.

I've adopted her way of life, using cruelty to control others. I intentionally hurt Mom, while Mom has never intentionally hurt me. Eric, another victim of my assault. Mom looks like she is going to break again. Do I really want to watch Mom suffer through more depression? My gut twists. No. I need her.

My feet fly beneath me. I need to run away from my guilt. I can't be cruel anymore.

I am different from Marissa. I have to be. I'm done following. And I'm not going to be afraid of her. It is time to face her. Matt's party provides the perfect opportunity. I have to show myself how she is the weak one.

That I am different.

Mom's constant reminder echoes in my mind, "You always have a choice, Lucy." I can choose to be strong again. I can choose to have values and stand for them. I can choose to be kind and loving.

I can choose to be different.

I stop running, panting alone on the path. I am going to try, for real this time. I can't be perfect but at least I can be me, the real me.

I hear the patter of feet behind me. I move off the path into a bordering garden as a group of women jog past. The smell of the daisies and sunflowers are overwhelmingly sweet. I inhale the smell over and over, hoping it'll help me remember this moment. I need its strength.

I feel lighter as I jog home. The heat from the rising sun beats down on my back. My favorite clouds, small white wisps, seem delicately placed in patches in the bright blue sky. I run past a man cutting his grass, the smell fresh to my senses. The neighborhood has come alive. People walking their dogs around the block, loading their cars for a day trip to the lake, or just laying out on their lawn and enjoying the sun before the heat index soars.

I arrive home filled with a strange combination of remorseful yet positive energy. I sit down on the front step, slowly taking off my shoes, hesitating to enter. I don't know where to begin. Should I pretend that nothing happened? Should I apologize? Say thank you?

Do I even acknowledge that I still need Mom to put me back together again?

I pull off my sweaty socks. No. I'm not going to allow pride to stand in the way of having a good relationship with Mom. I don't want any more fake relationships in my life. I rise to my feet and turn around to enter the house.

The door flings open, startling me. Mom stands behind it, wet streaks down her cheeks. We look at one another for a brief second. I decide to leap, without hesitation.

I rush into her arms.

Mom trembles as she hugs me, "Lucy," she begins. "I thought, I thought …"

I pull away from her gently and look her in the eye, "What? It's okay."

She nods, more tears. "When I woke up and you were gone, I thought that you were really gone. I thought I had lost you forever." I don't know if she's talking about me literally leaving or just our relationship but it doesn't matter. It is true. She nearly lost me forever. In fact, I nearly lost myself forever.

"Well, you didn't. Don't worry."

"I'm so sorry, baby. I know I have been horrid. I just don't know what I'm doing. No one prepares you for the day everything changes, and you don't know your daughter anymore."

"Mom, don't worry about it. I don't even know me anymore."

"That's the worst part. I let you lose yourself. If I would have paid more attention …"

"No, Mom. There was nothing you could have done. This was all me. And, trust me, more attention would have made it worse." I take a seat on the bench on our front porch.

"All the books say to fight to know what's happening. I'm fighting, I'm trying." She sits down next to me, her words so honest and full of exhaustion.

"Please know that I appreciate that you try. I know it's a good thing." I take a deep breath. I need to be honest. If this is going to be real, if this is going to be me, I need to tell the truth. "But, sometimes, you do overreact. Or you react in the wrong place, at the wrong time."

"Like the party …" She folds my hand into hers.

I nod.

"I'm sorry. I just lost it. I snapped. You weren't in your room. You left, snuck out. Not only was it disobedient, it was dangerous! What if something happened to you? We wouldn't have known you were gone until morning. I called everyone I knew to find you. My brain felt like it exploded. In that moment, I feared everything horrible had happened to you. When I found you had snuck out to go to a party, I lost it. And then, I got angry. More angry then I've ever felt before. You snuck out. You disobeyed your father and I. It was a punishment you deserved. I know you knew it, I could tell when we grounded you that night. But then you still left? All I could think was 'What's become of my girl?'"

Tears stream down my cheeks now. I never thought about how terrifying it must have been to find my room empty. It's not like I left a note. I wonder how long she looked for me.

"And then when I realized Marissa was involved, I was ashamed. Ashamed that I let you lose yourself to such a weak bully."

"Don't worry. I'm done being a Marissa clone. Trust me. It's way too much work. Much easier to be me, once I figure out who that is. I'm sorry I disappointed you, Mom." I reach, offering her a hug.

"I'm sorry I disappointed you too. Let's communicate more, and hopefully I can be a more reasonable parent. Deal?"

"Deal." She wipes a tear off my cheek. Her eyes are so blue and beautiful. She could have been a model. How have I never noticed her beauty before?

"You look pretty, Mom."

Mom's face breaks into a large smile. "Stop, please. You aren't grounded for yesterday." Ah, a joke. My heart relaxes, thankful for the transition. "No compliments needed."

"No, really, Mom. You're beautiful."

"Eh." She drops my hand. "You're crazy." I watch her face drop. She really doesn't believe me. I've been such a neglectful daughter. I swear to tell her she is beautiful more often.

"Oh, Justin's inside waiting for you," she says. I bite my lip as she studies my reaction.

What is he doing here? It's seven thirty in the morning. And during our breakdown? Crap.

"Uh, isn't it kind of early for visitors?"

"I don't think that can keep him away."

I roll my eyes. "It's not like that. Trust me. With Justin, there's always a business agenda. Don't even go there." I sit down on the front porch. "Can you just send him out here? I don't really want to deal with him inside. Not after last night." My home is for once cleansed of emotional confusion. I want to keep it that way.

The door squeaks. I don't turn around. Justin can do the talking, if he finally wants to.

"Hey, Lady."

"Isn't it a bit early for this?"

"For what?"

"I don't know, whatever you're here for." Of course, after days of shutting me out, he chooses now to talk. Puffy red eyes, no makeup, emotionally drained, and my sweaty running glow. Awesome. He sits down next to me. I pray that the tears I've just cried are the healthy, non-blotching sort. "Well?" I want to get this over with.

"Well?" His knee bumps mine. I can feel his crooked smile but I refuse to look. What is he doing?

"What do you want?"

"Come play ball with me."

"Now?" My heart does back flips.

"Yup."

"Why?"

"Because I don't believe it."

"It?"

"You."

"Well, you already saw it. Believe it."

Was I just some game to him?

He grabs my hand. "Come on."

I didn't know basketball could be so frustrating. We move in sync and everything feels so electrified. Justin's hand on my shoulder or the small of my back, my skin tingling out of control. My heart freaking out when he smiles at me. *Swish*, each time I shoot. My game is on. I couldn't miss a shot if I tried. Justin, on the other hand, is not trying at all.

It pisses me off.

"Why did you drag me out here if you aren't gonna play?" I ask after I reject a lazy lay-up. I sink a three pointer. "This isn't even a game."

He chuckles and my butterflies zoom.

"I'm just getting an idea of what you're made of."

"Oh?" I toss him the ball. He squares up, waiting for me to reject him. I do. "And what have you discovered?"

He steps closer to me.

Perfect jaw. Perfect shoulders. Perfect collarbone. Perfect everything.

"A lot," he says with another step. We stand together then under the hoop, the ball bouncing away. I know I should look away but I can't. I shiver. I can get lost in his green eyes forever.

Time stands still. My heart does not.

He leans in toward me.

Is he going to kiss me?

My whole world turns over.

Yes.

No, wait.

No.

Jennifer.

I eye Justin, he smiles playfully, brushing my side-swept bangs out of my eye.

No. I'm not evil. I won't be a Marissa. He's with Jennifer. I can't let this happen.

He leans in closer.

I lean away.

"Your cross-over," he says. Picking up the ball and showing me a cross-over dribble, low to the ground.

"What?"

"It's sloppy." He shrugs, tossing me the ball. "That's what I learned."

I stand frozen, ball in hand. What just happened? My face heats. He was only taunting me. I'd totally imagined that whole moment. Of course he wasn't going to kiss me.

I fake confidence, "Shut up. My cross-over is solid."

"Suit yourself." He grabs the ball. "Well, I've got to run. Thanks for the game."

"You call that a game?"

"Okay, insight then." He waves, climbing into his truck.

Yes, wonderful insight into my heart.

A kiss? How stupid can I be?

I try to avoid myself all morning. I'm too embarrassed to live. Thankfully, no one else knows. I don't even think Justin knew that I, for just a second, thought he was going to kiss me. The moment will go with me to my grave. He is so out of my league.

A text from Matt forces my head out from under my blanket.

Matt: Party tonight. You promised. 7.

Right. Birthday party. Matt. Marissa. Zach. Confrontation.

Am I ready?

No, but that doesn't matter. If it was up to me, I'd never be ready. I'd be happy avoiding Marissa and Zach for the rest of my life. But realistically, that is impossible. I'm sick of being passive and part of people's games. It is time to take control.

I'm going to that party. Marissa and Zach can shove it.

I'll walk in confidently. They'll never know what hit them.

I'm fine. No, I am terrified. I've never been to a party alone and without Marissa's connections, I barely know anyone.

That needs to change. I glance toward *Pride and Prejudice*, my bookmarker almost three fourths of the way through. It's time to make some real friends.

I empty my closet onto my bed, hoping to find something that will make me feel confident and real. Most of my dresses are earth tones with an empire waist. I put one on. It hangs loosely and gives me little shape. Yuck, ugly.

Marissa always disagreed with me, explaining how the style was perfect for hiding my curvy hips, which just weren't fashionable. I turn around in front of the mirror. It looks like I'm wearing a peasant frock. I was crazy to listen to her.

I sort my clothes, throwing everything Marissa approved to the side. My remaining wardrobe is pathetic: a few pairs of yoga pants, my maxi skirt, some tank tops, a pair of leggings, and an old, favorite pair of jeans. I return to my closet, not willing to admit defeat. Even if I have to run out to buy something, I am going to this party. If I don't, I fear I'll live in a hole forever.

My eye falls on a dark plastic bag stuffed behind my shoe rack. I peer in, hoping for at least a fitted t-shirt to pair with my jeans. A green wad of gingham material is shoved inside.

I pull it out slowly, examining my discovery. A casual sun dress with a heart shaped neckline and halter ties. This is the dress I bought for my first high school party. Marissa's opinion echoes in my ears, "Girl. Take that off. It makes you look ghastly." She let me wear one of her strapless bubble dresses instead.

I iron the dress before trying it on. This better work.

The dress fits me perfectly. It hugs my chest without showing too much cleavage and accents the small size of my waist between my curves. I shift uncomfortably in the mirror, pulling my hands through my auburn hair. The dress color makes my hair look rich and dynamic. Also, with my curves highlighted, I don't look so bulky. What was Marissa thinking?

That's when it hits me. Marissa knew exactly what she was doing. She played my features down so she could be the hot one. That's all I was to her; an accessory that helped highlight her looks and made guys turn her way.

I smile at myself. I can't wait to see Marissa's expression tonight.

CHAPTER NINETEEN

Matt lives in the development next to mine. I walk to the party, needing the exercise to steady my mind. I focus on the truth: Marissa degraded me to help her feel beautiful and confident and Marissa and Zach know nothing about commitment, truth and kindness. They are weak. I will be the strong and compassionate individual.

At least, that's what I hope.

I stall outside of Matt's backyard fence for a brief moment. It's time to do this or I'll hate myself forever. With a smile plastered to my face, I push open the gate. The yard is more crowded than I expected, putting me at ease. I can easily lose myself in the mix. I won't have to stay long. Just long enough for Marissa to see me.

Matt waves as I step through the threshold. He motions for me to join him near the grill.

"Wow, big turn out." I say with too much nervous energy.

"I know. Weird, right? People must be getting bored early this summer." He turns a row of beef patties. Olive, the petite red-head from our advanced math class, holds out a plate of cheese for him.

"It's not weird," she says in her quiet voice. "It's your birthday. People like you. It makes sense." She shrugs and smiles at me. "Hi, I'm—"

"Olive. We were in math together."

Her nose scrunches up a bit, "We were?"

"Yeah, I sat in back."

"Oh, I'm sorry. I swear I would have remembered you." Olive's eyes dart away from mine. I can feel her embarrassment. Matt places his hand on her shoulder. I watch that side of her body gently relax. I smile. There is definitely something going on there.

"Please don't worry about it. I kept to myself." I explain to her. She studies my face for a while.

"Oh, you're that Lucy girl." My heart sinks. How does she suddenly know that? "Everyone knows about Marissa and Zach, which means everyone knows about you." Olive nods toward a group hanging out in the corner. Marissa is sitting on Zach's lap, giggling loudly at someone's joke. "They've been super obvious and super annoying." Marissa squeals in the background. Olive covers her ears. "I swear. That's the worst noise in the world."

"You have no idea." My stomach churns at the sound.

"I'm sorry. This is probably hard on you." Olive fidgets. I like her. She is honest and awkward. She stares at me for a long time, waiting for my answer.

"Well." I look back at them. Zach's arms are wrapped

around Marissa's waist. She squeals again. My stomach relaxes. I mostly just feel humiliated that I ever dated him and was friends with Marissa. "Actually, it's not that bad. I mean, I'm pissed but, honestly, I don't really care about them anymore."

"Wasn't she your best friend?"

I shake my head. "She just used me."

"I'm sorry."

"Eh. It sucked." Zach nibbles Marissa's ear. The little hairs on my arms stand on end. Creepy. "I'm glad it happened. I'm way better for it." I echo Justin's opinion, which I realize I totally agree with.

Olive pats my back. "Good for you."

"Thanks."

Matt rejoins us. Olive naturally leans toward him and he leans back in response. Neither one seems to notice their slight shift in position. Olive eyes the food and drink tables. I sense she wants to return the situation to just being her and Matt.

I take her unintentional hint. She deserves the chance. "Well, Matt, those burgers look amazing. I'm starved. I hope you have a happy birthday. Thanks for the invite."

"Sure. Have a good time."

I grab a water and fiddle with the lid. The backyard is more crowded than before. I only catch occasional glimpses of Zach and Marissa between bodies. I just have to let them see I'm here so Marissa will know I'm not scared of her. And then I can pretend to mingle a bit longer before I walk home.

I take a deep breath. I can do this.

I catch a familiar head of blond hair out of the corner of my eye. Luke. We never really hung out much at work. I scan the crowd for someone else I know. My eyes fall back to Luke. He's playing soccer.

What is wrong with me? I know Luke. Yes, we barely speak. But it would be weird of me if I didn't say hello. It's time to stop being passive, for good.

I take advantage of my brief moment of bravery, crossing the lawn and waving to Luke. He immediately waves back with a smile. Good. This isn't going to be weird.

"Awesome. We're getting killed, Lucy. Are you half as decent at soccer as you are at basketball?"

"Ummm, maybe a sixteenth?" I was on a soccer team for a few summers in elementary school. I remember the basics.

"That'll have to do. Come on." He grabs my hand and pulls me out onto their makeshift field. The boundaries and goal posts are marked with Pepsi cans.

My nerves settle as I focus on the game. Laura, Luke's girlfriend, befriends me immediately. She's a bubbly brunette with a Southern accent. She chats with me the entire game about how she moved from Georgia and how lonely she was until she met Luke.

"Did you grow up here?" she asks after telling me her life story.

"In Minnesota, yeah. But I moved to this district when I was a freshman."

She shrugs, "Same situation then. You still had to move in high school." She lowers her voice. "Did you find it difficult to make friends here?"

I think of my horrible freshman year and hear Marissa's squeal in the background. "It was horrible. To be honest, it still is."

"Oh thank gawd. I thought there was something wrong with me." She nods toward the group of senior girls that call themselves "The Lunch Buddies" huddled in the corner. "They stared at me like I was insane when I asked if I could eat with them in the cafeteria." She pretends to pout. "I had to eat alone in math that day."

I laugh. "I ate a lot of lunches in the janitor's closet."

"Yeah, the girls here are cliquey." She pulls her hair back into a French braid. She sighs, looking at Luke, "But the guys. Oh, they are so much better here. Back home they just want to charm their way into your pants. Luke's not like that." She nods over my shoulder. "Neither is he."

I turn to look. Her eyes rest on Justin who's standing near the gate. My heart twists. I force myself to look away.

"He showed up early to our Pre Calc class and found me eating lunch alone. He invited me to eat with him the next day. I didn't believe him so I went back to eat in math the next afternoon. But, there he stood with his Jennifer, waiting for me. He was actually the one who introduced me to Luke." She clicks her tongue. "Sad thing about him and Jennifer, though. I really thought they'd make it."

What?

I furrow my brow, looking back at Justin, who laughs with some guys at the gate. Jennifer isn't at his side.

"Jennifer broke up with him last night. I'm sure they'd prefer if the world didn't know so quickly." She taps her cell phone. "But word travels fast with these. I'm surprised he's here." Laura nods back toward the drink table. Jennifer stands smiling and chatting with a group of friends.

Why didn't he say something to me this morning?

My eyes travel back to Justin. He moves toward

Jennifer, occasionally stopping to laugh and greet people along the way. He approaches her from behind, reaching out to tap her shoulder. I hold my breath. Jennifer turns around and smiles. They hug briefly and I swear a hush falls through the crowd. Justin steps back from her and hugs her friends as well. He chats briefly before he moves on to his next group of friends.

"Well, that doesn't surprise me. They had the best relationship. Why not have the best break-up too?" Laura shrugs.

I nod, turning my attention back toward her. She asks me questions about my dress while I track Justin in my peripheral. He grabs a burger with another guy from the basketball team. He laughs, pulling his hand through his hair and my heart flies into a frenzy.

Laura giggles. "Ooo!" She points at Justin who is sitting down to eat his burger. "This will be fun. Watch them gather." Within a moment, random girls start approaching him. They all lean in, flip their hair, and let out loud, flirtatious giggles. "We need a seat for the show." We abandon the soccer game, which we weren't really playing anyway. Laura leads me over to a high table. "Let the games begin," she jokes.

Laura calls the game. "Here comes the tall, leggy volleyball captain. Look at those tight shorts! She's going in for the kill, bending over to pick up her napkin and showing off her main *asset*." Justin briefly looks at her bum, and smiles before looking away. "No ace; sorry sweetheart."

I bite my lip. The thought of him being with Jennifer seems natural but knowing he's checking out other girls makes me feel so unnoticed. I take a deep breath. No. I need to feel good about myself tonight. I won't let my mind go there.

Laura pretends to gasp. "Oh no. Is this really happening? Too soon girl; too soon. Allison approaches, one of Jen's closest friends." Allison sits down on the end of Justin's lounger, crossing her legs. Justin responds to her with his genuine smile and brushes something off her shoulder. Once, he looks over her shoulder and rolls his eyes at Jennifer.

Maybe they haven't broken up after all? He seems too relaxed and happy. Jennifer bats her eyelashes and rolls her eyes at him before she returns to her conversation with her friend. They seem okay. I push my disappointment aside. Maybe it was a fake break-up? I want Justin to be happy. He deserves it.

My thoughts and Laura's play-by-play are interrupted with a loud clearing of the throat. We turn around. My stomach jolts. Marissa stands behind us, hands on her hips.

"And what do you think you're doing here?" Her face is scrunched up into what she uses as her intimidating expression. I never noticed how much it really makes her look like a pig. I stifle a laugh. I can do this.

"Hi, Marissa. Matt invited me," I say in a relaxed, unbothered tone. I refuse to stoop to her dramatic level of life.

"But you knew we'd be here." Marissa speaks loudly, trying to draw attention. People turn around to stare at us. Laura whistles lowly. Marissa glares at her.

I shrug. "I thought you might. But, no big deal." I turn back toward Laura. Marissa shifts behind me. It's driving her crazy that I'm not playing her game.

"Nice dress," she spits out.

I turn back around and tug on the dress's side. "Really? Thanks. Maybe you remember it?"

"How can I forget such a rag?"

Laura stands up next to me, not having enough experience with Marissa to avoid her drama. "Are you crazy? The dress rocks." She spins me around. "Look at her!"

Marissa pretends to gag. "Yeah, without me to dress her she looks—"

"Beautiful." A comforting low voice interrupts Marissa from behind us. I turn around.

Justin.

My face grows hot. He walks forward, stopping at my side. I hope he can't hear my heart pounding against my chest.

"Oh Justin, just because Jennifer dumped you doesn't mean you have to lower your standards." Marissa looks me up and down. She leans in toward Justin. "You can do much better than that."

I speak quickly. "Listen, Marissa. You've had your fun." I nod toward the crowd. "Everyone's watching; that's what you wanted, right?" I whisper so only Marissa, Justin, and Laura can hear. "Now, how about we end this before you end up looking bad?"

Marissa laughs. "What's that? You want Zach back?" Her words slur together. My mouth flies open to protest. Justin's hand rests on my shoulder. Laura grabs my other hand. I take a breath, steadying myself.

Marissa takes a step toward me. Her breath smells of alcohol. "I'm sorry, babe. Zach was only with you to get to me. You'll have to learn to understand." People snicker.

I force myself to stand up straighter. "Honestly,

Marissa. I don't really care." I nod toward Zach who has come to watch. "You can have one another. I'm good." Marissa purses her lips, reaching out and pulling Zach toward her. I feel Zach's eyes fall on me. His eyes survey me and my skin crawls. My eyes dart away.

"Well, good." Marissa snaps. Her frustration is palpable. She pulls Zach's arms around her. "I hope you can find someone like Zach someday."

"I did, remember? Turns out, he's not my type."

"Exactly. He's mine." Zach kisses her neck and she forces out her high-pitched giggle.

"Aw gawd!" Laura adds. "Go get a room."

"Good idea," Zach adds. Marissa giggles again. The crowd groans.

"Have fun." I wave goodbye, turning away from them and willing them to leave. The crowd thins.

I welcome the relief. They are gone. I did it.

Laura is the first to speak. "Nice entrance, Justin. Very smooth. Very heroic."

"Yeah, thanks for that." I add. He looks down at me, his green eyes smoldering. I would be lost there forever if it wasn't for Laura's cough. I immediately take a step back.

No. It doesn't matter that he is available. I'm not like the rest of those girls. I know where I stand with Justin. Friendship. That's all he wants. I wouldn't dare ruin that.

He shrugs, removing his hand from my shoulder. "No problem," he says casually. He nods toward his friends eating on the lawn chairs. "I'll see you later."

"Wow. What was that about?" Luke says as he hands Laura a burger.

"Lucy just made Marissa look like a fool," Laura bubbles.

"Really? About time."

"Yup. It was effortless. It was collected. It was … confident."

"Really?" Thank God. I can't believe I pulled it off.

"Yeah, she won't mess with you again. Trust me."

"Thanks." My post-confrontation adrenaline begins to rise, but it isn't the good type of adrenaline. It is the type that makes me freak out. My mind and emotions are on overload. I need to get out of here. I nod toward their burgers. "That looks good. I think I'll go get one."

"Do you want me to grab you one?" Luke offers.

"No. I'm good. You guys enjoy. Laura, it was great to meet you. We should hang out."

"Oh, don't worry." She hands me my cell. "I already added my number. Hope ya don't mind."

"Not at all. I'll send you my number later."

"I kind of already did that too. What can I say? I'm desperate for some girl talk." She glances sideways at Luke, "No offense, babe."

Luke grabs my wrist dramatically. "Call her, please. It will save me."

I force myself to laugh appropriately. I grasp my hands. They are beginning to shake. I wave goodbye before disappearing into the crowd and slipping out the fence gate without further confrontation. The side yard is empty. I toss my purse on the grass and lean back against the fence. My whole body feels jittery.

I don't know where to start. I'd successfully stood up to Marissa and Zach. Marissa looked like a drunken fool in front of everyone. It went better than I could have hoped. So why did I feel so disappointed?

I remember Justin's voice uttering "beautiful." My face

warms with a fresh blush. Did he really mean it? I start to ache. No. He can't have. How can he return to being so stand-offish if he did? He was just sticking up for me, saying whatever would make Marissa upset. I have to hand it to him. It worked.

I bend down to pick up my purse. I'm ready to go home.

"Lucy, you look amazing tonight." My stomach turns over. I don't even need to look up to know that voice.

CHAPTER TWENTY

"Uh, thanks." I push past Zach as he grabs my arm.

"Where ya going?"

"Home, Zach." I shake my arm. "Let me go, now!"

His grip tightens. "Oh come on. I think we can make up. Don't you?" He pushes me against the fence. He smells like whisky.

"Leave me alone." He steps toward me. My flight response soars. I try to run past him. He grabs me and slams me back into the fence. "I'll scream."

He laughs. "No one will hear you over the music." I scream anyway.

He leans toward me.

"Don't." I push him away.

"You know you want me." He slips his finger under my dress's strap. I shove his chest with all my weight. He replaces his hand against the fence, positioning himself so close I can taste his whisky breath.

"Why else would you dress like that? Marissa would never have to know."

"Not happening." I duck under his arm, screaming as I bolt.

Even drunk, his reflexes are still supreme. He grabs my arm and throws me back against the fence. The back of my head makes a loud thud. The sound startles Zach. He steps away from me with a conflicting look on his face.

I meet his eyes. "Zach, stop."

"Youwantthis," he slurs. I scream but it only seems to entice him. He forces his lips against mine. My mouth fills with bile. I don't swallow it in case I need to spit it in his face. I close my eyes as his body pushes against mine. He is so heavy. It's hard to breath. His hand goes straight to my chest.

I spit the bile at his face and knee him in the balls.

"That means 'no,'" says a deep voice.

My eyes fling open. An older man grabs Zach's arm and flings him to the ground. I suck in new air. Matt rushes to my side. The older man effortlessly picks Zach up and throws him against the fence. His strength surprises me. Zach's body slumps to the ground.

"That's not how you treat women, son."

Zach nods, sleepily. The older man spins around to Matt. "Did you serve alcohol?" His voice is thick with accusation.

"No. He brought it." The man studies Zach, then Matt. "Come on, Dad. Is it really that hard to believe?"

Matt's dad returns his attention to Zach. "Get off the ground. You're coming with me." Zach shakes his head in refusal before he retches. The smell of his whisky vomit overpowers me. I duck my head behind a bush and do the same. Mr. Johnson reaches down and yanks Zach up by his collar. "Either come now or I'll call the police." Zach swears but relents. Mr. Johnson nods to Matt, "Sorry, son. The party's over."

Matt doesn't protest. He opens the gate to slip in back and end the party. Justin is on the other side talking with some volleyball players. He glances at me, Zach, and Matt's dad. His jaw drops. He drops his conversation and steps to my side of the fence. He closes the gate behind him.

"What happened?" He touches the back of my arm.

I can't answer. My heart spins out of control. I want to close my eyes, curl up on the ground, and make all the feelings stop. I can't make eye contact with him. Mr. Johnson starts explaining that he thought he heard a scream from inside. I can't take anymore.

I walk away. I'm done.

A rough hand touches my shoulder. I flinch. "Lucy," says Mr. Johnson. "I don't think you should walk home right now. I'll take you home after I call Zach's parents." He leads me to the front porch. "Have a seat, okay?" I nod, totally numb now.

"Justin, why don't you wait with her?" Mr. Johnson suggests. I shake my head but he doesn't notice.

"Of course," Justin answers. I can't meet his eyes. I just walk away from him and curl my knees up to my chest on the porch swing. He pulls up a chair next to me. "I'm sorry, Lucy." His voice is warm and tender. Every nerve in my body jolts in confusion.

It hurts.

"Why do you do that?" I snap.

"Do what?"

"You really don't know?"

"No. What is it?" He reaches out and places his hand on mine. It sends me reeling.

"That!" I pull my hand away. "One second you act like you care about me, as friends," I clarify, "and the next second you push me away. And now, today, you care again?"

"I have no idea what you are talking about," he says in a cool tone.

"See, right there!"

"What?" he snaps.

I glare at him. "You waltz into my life annoying me to death when really you are trying to *save* me. I become enlightened, not through any of your help," I add, "and we decide to be friends. Then a tornado runs us down and suddenly I'm not worth any of your time."

Justin rolls his eyes. I continue. "You barely say hello. When you do talk to me, it is only about business."

"Well, I'm your boss!"

"And then today you show up to play basketball? And then left, just like that. If you wanted to talk about Jennif—"

"That's not why I was there."

"You could have told me. I wasn't going to text the world."

"Well, I thought better of it."

"And why is that, wise man?"

Justin shrugs nonchalantly.

My blood boils. "So that's it?" I demand.

He sits back down and pulls his cell phone out of his

pocket. He opens up some sort of Tetris app.

"Fine." I walk past him down the steps. My heart stings. "I'm sorry I'm such a bother."

"Where are you going?" he demands.

"Home."

"But Matt's dad is driving you."

"Obviously, he isn't."

"Lucy." He crosses his arms over his chest. The veins in his forearms are pulsing and his muscles are twitching.

My heart is fried. "Justin, you are so—"

"Impossible," a light voice interrupts. Jennifer steps out from around the house.

"Precisely." I exhale, pulling my fingers back through my hair.

Jennifer approaches me. "I'm sorry. I didn't mean to eavesdrop. I was just helping Matt clean up in back. He told me what happened with Zach." She rests her hand on my forearm. "That must have been terrifying." She turns toward Justin, not expecting me to answer.

"Justin, I'll walk her home. Tell Mr. Johnson she just needed some girl time." She nods toward the front window where Mr. Johnson is yelling into the phone, presumably to Zach's parents. "I've got this."

"Fine." Justin flings his hands in the air in defeat. He storms into Matt's house, slamming the door behind him.

I let out a long breath.

"Thanks," I mutter. I start walking away, hoping Jennifer isn't really intending to follow.

"Wait." She catches up to me. "You seriously can't walk home alone after what just happened."

"I don't even know what just happened."

Her voice is tender. "With Zach or Justin?"

"Both, I guess," I say honestly, exhausted from hiding my emotions.

We turn onto the walkway connecting the developments. Light from the full moon bounces off the black asphalt. "Justin can be intense." She takes a spot at my side. She walks with me comfortably in silence. I concentrate on inhaling the cool night air, willing it to calm me down. Occasionally, she places her hand on my back. Jennifer is being so nice and she doesn't even know me.

No wonder Justin likes her.

"Thanks." I stop walking. I want her to know I really mean it. "I'm sorry about you and Justin."

She smiles. "No problem. As far as Justin goes, it really isn't a big deal." She doesn't seem shaken at all.

"Oh. Are you guys still dating?" Jennifer's eyes widen in surprise. "I'm sorry. That was rude. I just noticed at the party you guys still seem …" I search for the right word.

"The same?" she offers.

"Yeah."

"That's because we are."

I nod and continue walking. I try to hide my disappointment. "That makes sense. I guess I'd try to keep everyone out of my relationship if I were you too."

"No, no." She smiles at me. "We aren't together anymore."

"But?" I stop. I don't know why I'm arguing with her.

"Justin and I are great friends." She stops walking for emphasis this time. "He's a great guy."

"I know. He's everyone's favorite." My eyes roll before I can stop them. "If he's so great, why did you break up with him?" I clasp my hand to my mouth. I can't believe I just asked that.

Jennifer laughs. "He's right. You are funny."

I don't know what to say to that. I'm still hoping she'll answer my blunt question.

"That was his idea actually," she adds calmly.

"To break up?"

"No. That we tell everyone I broke up with him. It was mutual." She nods toward the bench on the side of the walkway. I sit down with her.

"We actually haven't been dating very long."

"You were together over a year."

"Yeah but," she sighs. "We only really dated a few months before we realized that we weren't that into each other."

"So you pretended?"

"We really liked each other as friends. Pretending meant we wouldn't have to deal with people hitting on us all the time." She shrugs. "Being together was a built-in excuse. I always have a date for the dances without the drama." She smiles. "You saw those girls at the party, right? Imagine that happening all the time." She pulls her hair back into a tight pony tail.

I smile back at her. "Somehow I don't think Justin minded it much."

"No. Tonight he found it amusing. But trust me. He really does hate it." Jennifer starts picking at her fingernail polish. Her leg bounces. I'm surprised she's a fidget-er.

"So then why did you choose to end it?"

"I met someone," she says with slow intensity.

"Who?"

She turns toward me, her face serious. "I'm going to tell you because Justin says you are a good person. I trust him so I trust you to keep this secret. Okay?"

"I promise." I am surprised at the magnitude she puts on the moment. Her leg bounces up and down. I put my hand on her shoulder, helping her calm her nerves. She smiles at me and takes a deep breath.

"Her name is Trish."

I process what she says for a second. The second seems too long, making me feel rude. "Oh, awesome!" I sound overly enthusiastic trying to cover up for my paused second. I slap my hand against my forehead and she laughs. "No, I mean. Seriously, that's good for you." I place my hand on her arm. I hope she feels my sincerity. "How'd you meet her?"

She squeezes my hand back in understanding. "At a track meet this past spring. We've been seeing each other for a while. Justin covered for me. But I don't want to hide anymore. I need to be myself, you know?"

I nod. I totally get that. "Who else knows?" I ask as she starts picking her nail polish again.

"Justin, our families, and, now, you." She assesses me out of the corner of her eye while she refocuses on her nail polish. "Justin, of course, was the first to know. In fact, I think he knew I was a lesbian from the start. He actually helped me realize it." She giggles. "Don't tell him I said this but, seriously, if making out with a guy like Justin doesn't do it for you, no guy would." I smile back. I can't imagine a better test.

"I had to be honest with Justin. We'd grown so close. It was hard at first but he wanted to be my protector."

"From what?"

"Oh, come on, Lucy. Our school is a deadly judgmental social system. If I came out at the wrong time, they'd eat me alive. I wasn't strong enough before." She stands up, ready to walk again. "But I am now. Maybe I can even change things?" She forces a laugh. "A lesbian head cheerleader and class president—I'll be big news!"

"When do you plan on sharing your relationship with everyone?" I ask gently. I shy away from the traditional *coming out of the closet* phrase. It sounds too cliché.

"Well, it's still pretty fresh with Trish. I don't really want to drag her into it yet. Maybe after winter break at the Snow Ball?" she lifts her eyebrows mischievously.

"Wow," I imagine Jennifer and her mystery girl entering through the grand archway of the country club's ballroom. "That would definitely make an impression."

"Exactly."

We walk a bit longer, fantasizing about people's reactions. I point out my house a block away. "Do you want a ride home?" I offer.

She pulls out her phone. "No. I'm good. Justin will come get me." After texting him, she turns to me. "Justin really is a good guy. Give him a break. He just needs to figure out how to be around a girl that isn't me. He wants to be your friend."

"Only if you do me a favor?" We sit down on my front step, waiting for Justin.

"Sure."

"Will you please lecture him about being consistent?" I groan. "I don't think I can take any more of his oscillation."

She laughs. "Oh, trust me. After listening to your little brawl, I've got a lot of pointers for him."

We hear the clanking sound of Justin's truck before it turns the corner. Jennifer laughs, "That's so Justin. That drive should have been at least five minutes. I bet he was waiting down the street."

The truck sputters loudly. "Why doesn't he buy himself something nice?"

"Because he's Justin." She rolls her eyes dramatically. "He thinks the whole BMW for your sweet sixteen is absurd. He loves driving a clunker for stories to tell his kids." The truck sputters to a stop in the driveway. She shakes her head. "I can't believe I let him take me to prom in that thing."

"Thanks for walking me home." I help her up off the stairs.

"No problem. Thanks for listening. We should hang out, okay?" She smiles genuinely before nodding toward Justin. "I'm sure I'll see you soon." I wave as she walks away. She stops briefly to greet Justin before crawling into his truck. Justin continues up the walk toward me. I lean against the porch rail, waiting with my heart on guard.

"Lucy," he begins. His tone is neutral. "I was out of line." He stands next to me with his hands in his pockets. "I'm sorry for how I behaved, both tonight and this past week." His bold green eyes look down at me tenderly.

Jennifer gives me thumbs-up from the car. I sigh. "It's okay," is all I can manage.

He shakes his head. "No. Trust me. It's not. For me to act that way after all you've been through …"

"The fainting, heartbreak, tornado, or assault?" I try to ease the mood.

He sighs, and my eyes rest on his lips. My knees go weak so I lock them.

"I guess all of it." He shakes his head. "What I'm trying to say is this. I really do want to be friends, okay?"

"Alright." We stare at each other for a moment. My

home phone rings inside. I motion toward the door. "I should probably go. That's probably Matt's dad. My folks are going to have a lot of questions."

"Good luck with that." Justin nods while stepping away. "I'll see you soon then, okay?"

"Yup."

He climbs back into his truck. He leans over in the cab and gives Jennifer a hug. Jennifer waves as they pull out of the driveway.

I yawn. I feel like I've lived through a weird, confusing dream. I push open the front door. The kitchen door muffles Dad's harsh voice. I fight back another yawn before pushing the door open. My parents' eyes are wide with worry.

This is going to be a long night.

CHAPTER TWENTY-ONE

Dad is livid. He keeps asking me to recount what Zach did and how I reacted. He writes it all down. I try to emphasize that Zach was drunk and confused. Dad keeps throwing around the terms "attempted rape" and "assault." He relays my story to the cops, the principal, really anyone who will listen while I sit humiliated at our kitchen table. Zach's parents refuse to believe it. Zach has assured them that I'd thrown myself at him in desperation.

Dad spends all Sunday orchestrating phone calls with Mr. Johnson, the police, our school principal, and Zach's parents. But none of his work gets him anywhere. Other than Zach's clear underage drinking, Zach's actions are lost in a grey area.

None of the conversations make me feel any better. I don't know if I want Zach arrested. Yes, he was an ass but

I didn't think he'd really rape me. Dad laughs when I say that. I'm apparently naïve. That's when I quit. Dad has what he needs from me. I can't do this any longer.

I escape to my room and pour myself back into the world of *Pride and Prejudice*. I finish the book at sunset. I'm not ready to surface to reality so I go straight from my bed to my computer where I open a blank document to begin my essay.

I write about the themes of love and social forces. It seems I can't escape them if I try. So, I don't. I pour myself into my essay, allowing it to speak the words I so desperately want to hear.

My fingers hit save just before midnight. I'll drive the finished essay into school tomorrow. I'm not expecting a changed grade. I just want Mr. Taden to know I finally tried.

I sleep fitfully. My dreams tangle Mr. Darcy and myself in the tornado. I swear to him that I will find his Lizzy and tell her that he survived. I can't remember why Mr. Darcy can't find her himself, but the urgency all weighs on me. My search throws me into a panic, and Zach is always my obstacle. Occasionally I catch glimpses of Marissa making out with Mr. Collins in an attempt to aggravate Lizzy. I search the countryside for her but Lizzy can't be found. I return to Mr. Darcy with no news of his Lizzy. He shakes his head and laughs at me. "Lucy, you're funny," he says with Justin's voice.

The change in Mr. Darcy's voice jolts me awake. My heart eagerly anticipates what he'll say next. I remain still and hold my breath, hoping to hear him speak again. A few moments pass before I realize I'm in my bedroom, alone. I rub my face. This isn't the way to start the day. I need to guard my heart. I am already swooning, and Justin hasn't even made an appearance.

The grandfather clock downstairs chimes six times. I can sleep more or get up to meet the guys at the seven a.m. start time. I swing my legs out of bed. Justin will just have to deal with me painting today. Dad's footsteps shuffle loudly below in the kitchen. I wonder if he slept at all.

When I push open the kitchen door, Dad sits at the table with a cup of coffee and a case of bed head worse than Eric's. "Hey, Dad," I try to say casually. I cross in front of him to the fridge, flinging my backpack on top of the counter along the way.

"Hi, honey," his voice is still filled with concern. The swinging door squeaks and Mom walks in.

Mom had been unusually quiet the day before. She let Dad do his thing and me do mine. She offered us silent support as she distracted Eric most of the day. That night, when she saw me she just held me and let me cry. She knew exactly what I needed. I love her for it. It's yet another moment of miraculous mothering all because I am willing to receive it. I smile at her while wondering what other moments she offered but I pushed away.

I quietly make a few turkey sandwiches and stuff a bag of chips in my backpack. Dad eyes me questionably as I cross the kitchen and grab his keys off the hook. "Lucy, I don't know if that's a good idea."

My heart sinks. I knew this would happen. "Dad, I'm ready, though. Look." I point to my painting clothes and my packed bag like a toddler.

"I'm not comfortable with it."

I groan. "Zach's not going to be there, Dad. None of those guys are friends with him."

"I know but still. It's too soon. Don't you think?"

I bite my lower lip, trying to control my brewing temper. "Dad, seriously, there's no reason for me to stay home. I made a commitment to this job." I eye him and Mom. "Actually, you made a commitment for me to this job," I add for emphasis.

"That's true," Dad says. "But that also means I have the ability to break the commitment."

"Come on, Dad." I whine. My hand flies to my mouth in surprise. I hate whining, it instantly discredits me. "I'll call home during all of my breaks. I promise."

Dad shakes his head. I look to Mom, hoping she'll help.

"Charlie," she says while crossing the room and resting her hand on his shoulder. "You know she's right. Those guys are her friends." I hold my breath. Mom rarely if ever presents an opinion contrary to Dad's. "You can't keep her locked inside forever."

Dad looks down at Mom and I see them as a couple, not my parents. He gazes at her and she fixes his hair. He closes his eyes, enjoying the feeling. It is sweet but weird. I fidget with my backpack straps. I normally would have coughed or left the room but I hold out, hoping their moment would end in my favor.

Dad sighs, "Okay." He turns to me. "Lucy, call home during every break. Also, what's Justin's number? I need another way of getting ahold of you if I need to." He glances at the red phone tethered to the wall. "You never know, maybe I'll get somewhere with the police today?" he grumbles.

"Sure. No problem." I pull out my cell and write Justin's number on the white board on the fridge. "I promise I'll call. I'm going to be just fine. Trust me." Dad squeezes Mom's hand.

The doorbell rings. "UPS." Dad stands up and pushes open the kitchen door. "Probably Eric's birthday gift."

Mom walks over to me and I hug her. "Thanks. I can't stand to not be doing anything today."

"Yeah, I know. That's why I had to start my garden." I look out the window at our unusually beautiful backyard. It is a constant reminder of how sad I've made her. She pulls away from me and I plaster a smile on my face. "We'll be expecting your calls, do you understand?"

"I won't forget."

Squeak. The kitchen door flies open. Dad walks back in shaking his head. Justin follows.

Justin hasn't shaved this morning so his stubble is extra thick. His shirt hangs perfectly from his broad shoulders. He looks like he stepped out of a romantic comedy. I am completely caught off guard and mumble some sort of greeting. I glance at my parents, both dressed in robes, and I shift uncomfortably. The last thing I want is Justin to see my parents in pajamas. Somehow that's worse than him seeing me in pajamas.

"Hey, I thought I'd stop over on the way to work and offer you a ride."

Dad rolls his eyes at Mom and she smiles. I pretend I don't notice.

"Sure. Is that okay, Dad?"

"Well," he grunts, "It seems that I can't keep you here or keep them away. So go."

I glare at Dad. I expect that from Mom, not him.

Justin's face slowly processes Dad's words. He opens his mouth to re-explain his motives but I intervene.

"Come on, Justin. Let's go." There's no way I'm letting Justin's sass ruin this for me. I open the swinging door. "I'll call during breaks," I emphasize as I hold the door open for Justin. We are not going down that road with my parents. Not today.

Justin raises his eyebrows at me. He clearly understands the awkwardness of the situation. I motion for him to walk through the door, urging him to drop it, for once. He smiles, turning back toward my parents. "Thank you, sir. I'll have her back before dinner. I promise." I groan. He couldn't have made that sound more like a date if he tried. Dad glares daggers at Justin. Mom laughs as I grab Justin and pull him through the door.

I pull the door shut behind me. "Cut that out. They can still change their minds."

Justin laughs as he steps onto the front porch. "It was too hard to resist. That room was thick with Daddy's little girl sentiment."

"Of course it was." I heave myself into the passenger seat. "You'd feel the same way if it was your daughter."

Justin laughs. "Oh, no, trust me. If it was my daughter, I wouldn't have let another guy into the house. Let alone let you leave the house with him." Justin pulls out of the driveway.

"Really?"

"Yup," Justin smiles mischievously. "No guy can be trusted. Your dad knows that. Did you see his eyes? If looks could kill."

"Then I'd be a very happy person right now."

He grins. "Well I'm glad to see you didn't lose your fire."

"And I'm glad to see you are still my consistent,

annoying and egotistical friend."

"You know it," he says with unknowing charm. I refuse to let my grin creep across my face. "So, how did yesterday go?" he asks.

"Fine, I guess. Zach really can't be held accountable. It's driving my dad nuts."

"That sucks."

I shift in my seat. "I don't think Zach would have done anything more, though." I watch, but his expression doesn't give anything away. "Do you?"

"I thought about it all day yesterday. I want to say no but I just don't know. He's not himself when he's wasted."

"He always listened to me before."

Justin clenches his jaw. "You had to say no before?"

I shrug like it was no big deal. The vein in Justin's neck throbs. "No guy should ever push a girl so far she has to say no."

I roll my eyes at him and laugh. "Come on, Justin. How else are they going to know?"

"That's not how it is supposed to work."

"Oh? Then how does it?" I mock him.

Justin shrugs. "First comes love, then comes marriage, then comes the baby in the baby carriage." I laugh, thinking he is joking. He doesn't smile. He turns to me. "Guys shouldn't operate like Zach. There should never be a question when you get to that point."

I don't know how to respond. Justin's reasoning astounds me. I didn't know there were guys left that actually felt that way. "So you're saying?" I need clarification.

"I will never force myself on a girl."

"And?"

He sighs, "Yeah. It sounds stupid. But I want to be married first." He shrugs. "I've seen too many people heartbroken over what they didn't need to give away. That's not going to be me." He smiles softly and my heart breaks free of my guard. It does cartwheels. "And I definitely refuse to risk the heart of a girl I like. I've waited seventeen years. I can wait longer."

"But what if you don't get married until you're thirty-five?"

"Then I am in for a very long and frustrating wait."

"You'd really want to wait?"

"Well, I'm hoping I won't have to wait that long." He leans over and flips on NPR. "Do you mind?"

I shake my head and watch him settle into our old morning routine. I pretend to gaze out the window, processing everything he said.

I've never realistically contemplated waiting until marriage. I wrote it off somewhere between watching MTV's Spring Break and my friendship with Marissa. It didn't seem possible. Could a relationship even work out if your first time having sex was on your wedding night? How can you know if you're marrying the right guy?

My grandparent's marriage comes to mind. Grandma told me all about their honeymoon last summer while she sipped a mimosa on the deck with Mom. Mom left but I stayed for the details. Somehow it wasn't that weird coming from Grandma. That's how their marriage worked. She assured me it was worth the wait. And, here they are today, fifty-five years married. Today, the divorce rate is over fifty percent. I have no idea if Mom or Dad had sex before their wedding night and, honestly, I don't want to know. That's one conversation I've successfully avoided.

"Do you think I'm ridiculous?" Justin teases, interrupting my thoughts.

"Oh no. I just," I sigh. "I've never met anyone like you. That's all." My heart swoons with the truth of my words. Somehow Justin's commitment makes me want to be his girlfriend even more. It feels counterintuitive.

Justin chuckles. I can't help but let out a small sigh of delight. Crap.

"Well," he smiles, "I'm glad you've met me then."

I nod and force myself to turn back toward the window. My defenses have given up and my heart can't be trusted on its own. I focus out the window, expecting to watch the bushes that hide the low wired fence of the Cross-Town Highway. My eyes fall on a high noise barrier instead.

"Wait. Where are we going?"

"It took you a while."

"We aren't painting?"

He shakes his head and nods toward my hands. "You've got to be kidding me." I stretch my fingers and bend my palms. They aren't even bandaged anymore. Minnesota's white, domed capital rises in the distance. "Why are we going to St. Paul?"

"Finishing that research project." He pulls off the highway onto Grand Ave. I eye Summit Hill, a steep, small road that cuts straight up the natural cliff of the river valley. "You aren't going to try to drive this thing up that are you?"

"Yup. She can handle it." He pats the steering wheel in encouragement. The light turns green and I grasp the bottom of my seat. The motor huffs and sputters as we climb. We no longer face forward but up. I am certain we are going to flip over backwards. I close my eyes and brace myself. Every other calamity seems to happen in my life. Why not this too?

Justin laughs as the truck makes a choking noise. "Lucy, you can stop white-knuckling it. We made it." I open my eyes. "Aw, come on! Eyes closed? You missed all the fun." He nods back down the hill. "We can do it again if you'd like?"

"Never again." I glare at him in response. "Not in this junker."

"Shhh. You'll hurt Thelma's feelings." The truck sputters as he pulls up to Summit Avenue's stop sign. I decide not to humor him with asking about the truck's name.

We drive a bit before parking along the street. I climb out of the truck, recognizing a few of the homes from the Victorian volumes I studied. Justin follows me with my notes from last week.

"Where are we going?"

He nods as he puts his hand on my shoulder, turning me around and away from him. "There."

CHAPTER TWENTY-TWO

I stare at the massive stone structure of the James J. Hill House. The mansion with the striking carriage entrance looks stunning against the lavender morning sun. The grand chimneys that split through the aged roof have a beautiful green tone to them. Graceful arches of brick protect the entrance. The mansion is beautiful.

"I'm bidding to paint it," Justin explains. "It's a huge job, a hard job. But it'd be an awesome job."

"It's stone," I point out the obvious.

Justin laughs at me, putting his hand on my back as he leads me across the street toward the mansion. "Look closer. There are hundreds of windows to trim and other small nooks. The exterior is all about the details. Plus," he nods toward the entrance and smiles, "the inside has lots of walls to paint."

"That would take all year."

"A couple, actually. If we got the job, we'd start next fall."

"But won't you be away at school?"

He shrugs. "I got into the Carlson School of Management at the University of Minnesota. It's ten minutes away. I should be able to swing it."

"But how will you have time to paint?"

"I'll paint a bit but mostly Troy will hire appropriately."

"He's not going to college?"

"He's going to pick up an associate in business during the evenings. He's never been big on school. He loves to paint and he really is a great manager. If I snag this gig, the experience will set Troy up for a successful career."

"And you?"

"Well," he laughs. "I'll be able to afford college."

He opens the notebook to a blank page. "We need to gather notes so I can build a realistic proposal." He walks up to the door of the carriage entrance.

"I don't think if you knock they're going to let you in."

"Oh yeah?" Justin knocks loudly. Moments later, the door swings open. "Hi, Mason," Justin says as he steps into the mansion. "This is Lucy." I follow him through the door. The woodwork is dark and stunning. I remember it vaguely from my tour in second grade.

"Nice to meet you." A middle-aged gentleman extends his hand. I shake it and he grasps the back of my hand with his other hand in an old-fashioned shake. "I'm Mason. I have the honor of being the groundskeeper here and," he eyes Justin, "your personal tour guide." He weaves my arm through his as he walks me out of the entryway and into the grand entrance. I gasp at the staircase looming before me. I turn back to Justin. "How did you get us in before hours?"

He shrugs. "They like me."

"We're old family friends," Mason explains. Justin walks past us, examining cracks in the paint near the baseboards. Mason drops his voice, "Also, it helps when your dad's the governor."

"He's not the governor, Mason," Justin insists as he sits down on the ground to get a closer look.

"Not yet," Mason playfully taunts. Justin ignores him.

Mason proves to be a delightful tour guide. Justin surveys every room, jotting notes as he examines the trim, fireplaces, walls, and wallpaper. I, on the other hand, can't even think about painting. I allow myself to get lost in the grandeur of the space and swept up in Mason's captivating story-telling of the mansion's rich railroad history.

Mason shows us every nook and cranny of the house. Most people only see a few rooms, never the offices and certainly never the rooms that aren't safe for large touring groups, like the children's theatre and schoolroom.

Our tour ends at the top of the grand stairway. Mason drags Justin away from the wallpaper. He nods to me and the steps. "You aren't going to let this lovely girl walk down these stairs alone, are you?" I open my mouth to protest but Mason shakes his head at me. "Don't be so modern." He slips my arm through Justin's. The butterflies that I have worked so hard to keep dormant spring to life. "You can't miss this opportunity."

Justin nods down the stairs. "Shall we?" he asks with a proper voice and a joking smile.

"We shall." I force myself to stand up straight and play the part. It is the only way I'm getting through this without falling deeply in love. I nod toward the steps and we start descending.

Mason's voice echoes behind us as we arrive at the first landing, turning down toward the grand room. "Now Lucy, just imagine a crowd of people. All eyes are on you as you descend gracefully to greet them below." Justin stifles a laugh as Mason speaks gracefully. I elbow him. "They look at you in awe and you know you are the most beautiful girl in the room," Mason adds.

Justin doesn't say anything this time. He leads me down the stairs. My heart flutters with my arm in his. I need this to end, soon. I lean forward, trying to quicken our pace. Justin feels my cue so, naturally, he goes even slower. He snickers at me when we finally reach the bottom.

"Beautifully done." Mason tromps down the stairs behind us. "Now to the exterior."

The exterior tour is brief. He points out the wooden trim and siding up high in the window eves. I don't even try to strain my eyes against the sun to see the spaces. Instead I wander over to the side of the mansion and place my hand on the stone work. Each stone is rugged and cool beneath my touch. I respectfully step away from the mansion.

"I see you're in love," Mason offers. My stomach flips over as I glance at Justin who is shielding his eyes from the sun. Mason smiles at me and nods toward the mansion, "The house has that effect on people."

"Yes, it's beautiful. Thank you for this opportunity. I'll never forget it."

Mason laughs and eyes Justin. I blush. "No one ever does." He winks at me as he walks away. "Justin. I've got to get to work. Can you see yourself around front?"

"Absolutely. Thanks, Mason." Justin walks toward me, still shielding his eyes from the sun as he examines the upper windows. I wave goodbye to Mason.

Justin jots down one last note before shutting the notebook and turning toward me. "So, wasn't that better than painting?"

"That was incredible."

"I know. I've been in love with this place forever. Mason used to let us play lawn games here on the Fourth of July when we were little. I can't believe I might get the chance to work here. Let's go grab breakfast. I need to pick your brain." He hands me the notebook. "Over the research." He pulls out his phone and hands it to me. "You should check in with your folks. I'll wait in the car."

I slide the screen to unlock his iPhone. He has three missed texts, two from Allison and one from a girl named Hannah. I sigh. It is only nine a.m. Jennifer was right. He doesn't get a break.

***

We return to the association as the crew's breakfast break ends. Justin rounds up Troy and shows him the notes. He doesn't notice me climb into the truck to grab my supplies. I find Alex and get right to work. I immediately find my rhythm, brushing the blue primer over a faded brown.

The rest of the day is everything I need. It is normal. Troy even manages to keep his distance. Other than Alex's guidance, Luke is my only interrupter. He begs me to call Laura because she's going to drag him jeans shopping with her. He swears it's his living nightmare. He makes sure I dial before he leaves.

Laura answers on the first ring. "Oh, thank the lawd," she says with her Southern twang. "I think I was driving Luke crazy. So, are you up for it?"

I giggle. She obviously forced Luke to make me call her.

"Absolutely. My wardrobe needs a major overhaul. I need some new stuff."

"Great. I'll pick you up tomorrow night?"

"Sounds good."

"Sweet. See you then." The conversation is so different than when I talked to Marissa. Marissa would drag on forever where Laura is sweet and to the point. Maybe Laura and I really can be friends.

After my team wins another game of basketball, Justin waits for me in the truck while I fill up my water bottle. It feels weird to be in the pool complex again. It was only a few weeks ago when Marissa's squeal and Zach's kiss changed my life forever. The pool is peaceful now and empty. I dip my toe in the water. It feels like a cool bath. I look around; the area is deserted. I slip off my shirt and shorts before I run at the pool straight on and jump in.

The water welcomes me. I surface and watch my waves ruin the pool's peaceful surface. I dip my head back into the water, smiling as the water cools my scalp. I find myself in the same corner where Marissa and Zach cheated on me. I take a deep breath, finding my breathing free. Good. I need a positive memory to fill this space.

I pull myself over the edge and get dressed. I walk back to the truck and pull out a few painting rags. I dry my face. Justin is leaning back with his feet on the dashboard as I climb in. I squish into the passenger seat. My backpack's contents are spread out over the center console. I open my backpack, searching for my essay. It's gone. I look up at Justin, who holds my crisp white essay on his lap. "Give that back." I reach over and snatch the essay from his lap. "That wasn't for you to read."

"Then why did you leave it on the seat?" He smiles. "And why are you all wet?"

"It was hot." I shrug. "And I didn't leave my essay on the seat." The white truck clanks on the way out of the association. I'm surprised they haven't complained.

Justin reaches over and touches my wet hair. "You're weird." He pulls onto the highway. "So, why the essay?"

"It's just something I wanted to fix. That's all."

"Come on, we're friends. Maybe I can help. Do you have others to do?"

I sigh, thinking about all the papers, lab reports, and math homework I'd done poorly. I don't have the time to fix those too. "No. Around Marissa I blew off my school work. Like you said, I was a total droid. I don't know when I let everything slide." I flip through my essay. "I found my original essay a few weeks ago after the whole Marissa and Zach thing. It was horrendous, a total eye opener. I knew I needed to fix it. I owed it to Mr. Taden."

"Well, this deserves an A. Your format is flawless and your content is original."

I shake my head at him. "No. I'm not getting a grade for it."

"You've been spending your summer writing an essay that you'll never get a grade on?"

"No, just last night."

Justin rubs his cheeks and smiles. "You're funny. You know that, right?"

"Why do you keep saying that?" I need to know what

exactly I'm doing that he enjoys so much. I want to do it more.

"I don't know. You just are."

"Great." I roll my eyes playfully to make him laugh. He does and my cheeks warm. I look out the window. If we're going to be friends, I have to get control.

Justin offers to drive me to school so I can drop off the essay while he checks on some basketball business. We walk into the school together. It's weird to be at his side, where I've seen Jennifer walk across this parking lot with him so often. I had no idea I'd paid such close attention to Justin Marshall back then. As Justin and I walk up the stairs to the school's entrance, it's almost creepy how much detail I remember about them together. Where he put his hand on Jennifer's waist. How his backpack always fell over his left shoulder. Seriously, I used to loath him, believing him to be such an egomaniac.

But, as the detailed memories flood me, I realize my heart knew the truth of what he would be to me, even then.

I nod toward the direction of the office, stepping away from Justin's side. He waves, before heading down toward the athletic office. He leaves a sense of loss in his place. I hate how complete I feel with him near. It's not fair. I need to suck it up, learn to feel good and whole in myself. I can't depend on Justin for that or I'll never heal. I refuse to live a half life.

It's odd walking through the school when it's empty. My footsteps echo off the bareness. The hallways look gigantic without the student posters plastering the walls. I duck into the office without notice. The administrative assistants are chatting at the copier about some barbecue. I grab a blue post-it note off the front desk and jot down a message for Mr. Taden.

Mr. Taden, I'm sorry this is late. Please don't grade it. I just want you to know that I got your note and you were right. My first try sucked. Hopefully, this one is more satisfactory. Enjoy your summer. I'll see you this fall. ~ Lucy Zwindler

Mr. Taden's mailbox is overflowing with flyers and notes. I flatten the pile and shove my rolled up essay and note into the corner. My essay will probably get lost in this mix anyway. I glare at his mailbox feeling oddly defeated. I sigh. It doesn't matter. It isn't the mailbox's fault. I should have written my essay right the first time.

I step out of the office. Time to find Justin. I glance down the corridor, past the cafeteria toward the gym. I'd avoided this route all last year. I hated how the janitor closet reminded me how much of a loser I was. Of how much the senior girls hated me for taking the most popular girl's starting position on the varsity basketball team. Of how the pain from the injuries they inflicted was easier to cope with than the pain inside.

It got to the point where being thrown into a locker was pleasant in comparison to hiding from them, with my feet up, in the bathroom stalls.

That's when I lost myself.

I pause as I pass the closet. I ate so many lunches there, with so many chemicals. I pull on the latch, it clicks and the door swings open. I wave my hand above my head in the darkness. Grasping the cord I always depended on. Light.

A red bucket is stacked meticulously in the corner. My bucket, my throne of loser-dom. There's a new open space on the shelf to the right. I lean down. Pencil markings are lightly written on the wood. *I suck. I hate this life.*

Not my handwriting.

I take a step back, alarmed that this is someone else's closet now. I notice a small pillow jammed under the box of rags. Smart, good for quick naps to save yourself from the nightmare-ish sleep the bullying from school inflicts.

I click off the light, pulling the door closed. Giving this person their space. Respect of whatever they endured last year. As the door latches shut, I make a promise. No matter what, I'll pull this kid out of this closest and be their friend next year. Not like Marissa did though. I'll help them find their way, their own feet. And I'll stick up for them. Hell, I bet with Jennifer and Justin's help, we may actually be able to change the bullying dynamics of this school. Maybe. Hopefully.

This type of world shouldn't exist.

CHAPTER TWENTY-THREE

"Lucy!" Justin's voice carries down the hall. My heart melts when he calls my name. His gorgeousness waits, smoldering and perfect. Totally out of my league. I can't help but gaze into his eyes as I walk toward him. I could live forever there.

"Ready?" he asks.

"Yup. It's dropped off."

"Great." He folds up a piece of paper and shoves it in his back pocket. We turn at the same time, accidently bumping pinkies and brushing arms as we walk toward the front door. My face heats as my pinky burns. Crap. Please don't notice my flush. Or the way my heart is galloping out of control.

This being friends thing is going to be so hard.

But it's worth it. Any part of Justin is worth this restraint. I can't have it all, but it's better than no relationship at all.

"I called your Dad," Justin says as we reach the truck. "Checking in, being polite after all the crap that went down this weekend, ya know?"

"Thanks." I climb in, thankful I don't have to make that phone call. I need a break from the constant questions.

"So," Justin says as he turns the ignition. "I kind of asked him permission to take you out …"

Out?

"As friends, of course," he rushes to clarify.

I nod with a smile, of course. Of course. "Where are we going?"

"It's a surprise."

My heart tickles, such a perfect response. He has no idea he's sweeping me off my feet. No idea what power he has.

"Of course it is." I try to sound collected, even a bit annoyed. I glance down at my running shorts and tank top. "Can we swing by my house so I can at least change?"

"Nope, what you're wearing is perfect for what I've got in mind."

I lift my eyebrows. "We're going running?"

His smile spreads and he winks back. "You'll see."

A fire ignites in my heart. I'll never be able to get enough of that smile and jaw. … He's just so freakin' hot. Everything in me burns for him. What I wouldn't do just to hold his hand. God, why can't he feel that way about me?

His phone buzzes, another text. Justin glances at the screen. "Ah, Allison," he says with a light smile.

Right. That's why.

CHAPTER TWENTY-FOUR

A white banner hangs between two trees above the entrance to the beach. *Triathlon for Champs.* A triathlon? He's got to be kidding me. There's no way I'm in good enough shape to run, swim and bike. I'd maybe be able to handle the running portion. Maybe.

Please, don't let this be his big surprise.

Justin leads toward an empty table under a blue canopy where a few older women are unloading boxes. "Kate, guess who?" Justin says as he climbs over the table, tapping her on the arm.

She squeals, taking Justin in a perfect grandma hug. Justin kisses her white curls. "I'm so happy to see you again!" He waves me over. I walk around the table with a smile. "Lucy, this is Kate, from the Children's Leukemia Research Society. Back in the day, she was our designated comforter during Jackson's battle."

I reach out to shake Kate's small hand, but she pulls me into a hug. "Any friend of Justin's is a friend of mine," she says with a grin.

"Fourteen years ago, Kate started volunteering to help families deal with the loss of a child who fought leukemia. She's held the hands of hundreds while they deal with the loss of a child to leukemia."

Kate beams at Justin, light blue eyes sparkling, full of life. "Oh hush." She squeezes my hands, "Ready to help?"

"Sure. What can I do?"

"I've got forty-five minutes before the kids show up for the beach triathlon." She hands me a three-ringed binder. "Arrange the numbers over here with the registration book. Justin," she pushes him toward the box. "Get those stakes in the water and set up two one-hundred-foot courses. One at three feet deep, the other at five. Then everyone can participate in the fun."

She busies herself, emptying t-shirts out of boxes. "Justin? When you're done, there're water bottles and certificates in the car." She shouts at him while he walks down the beach, stripping his shirt away before hitting the water.

I bite my lip, my eyes lingering over the chiseled muscles of his back. Holy crap.

Kate nudges me and laughs, "Is that what's going on here?"

"No." I flip the three-ringed binder open. "We're just friends."

She clucks to herself, "I've been throwing this triathlon with Justin since he was fifteen and he's never brought a girl along before." She starts folding blue t-shirts and placing them on the table next to me. "His guy friends, sure. They've been helping out for a few years. But a girl … This is new." She opens a box of tiny baby-sized shirts. Babies with leukemia? This world is not fair.

"I actually work with Justin, we play basketball too."

"Ah, I see."

I bite my tongue, trying to keep my face steady as I arrange the numbers in front of me.

I'm the first girl he's ever brought here. Is he letting me in?

But he brings his guy friends all the time. So, no. He's treating me like he treats his friends. Nothing special. I'm just one of the guys.

That sucks. I hate being one of the guys.

When I finish the numbers, Kate puts me to work setting up the start line as she greets the other volunteers with Justin. The families and children arrive as I place the last cone in the sand. Parents herd their children toward the beach, always having at least one child paler than the others who wears a cap or bandana to protect their bald head from the sun. Every kid runs to Kate, giving her a hug, as she pins their number to their swimsuit.

A pale girl in yellow bike shorts and a matching yellow swim suit tugs on my hand. "Can we start now?"

"Soon." I smile back. Her grin is loose, exposing a missing bottom tooth.

"I want to start with running. I'm the fastest. I swear!" She squeezes my hand tight.

"Right on! I'll be watching you."

"Will you be my bike?"

"Be your bike?"

"You know, like Justin does sometimes?"

I glance at Justin, who's swarmed with little boys. "Um, sure. Why not?"

Soon other hands are tugging at my arm. More little girls. Adorable swim suits with faces brighter than the dawn. Older girls too, gather near me. The eldest is in total tween mode. She's daring, wearing a cute bikini that shows off an athletic form. She grabs some girls for some cartwheels. A gymnast maybe? Her bandana falls off, but she doesn't care. She just shoves it into her running shorts and winks at me. "It's going to come off when I swim anyway."

"True. Smart thinking," I say as I try to hold in my real reaction. Holy crap. Brave.

A whistle blows and everyone joins us at the starting line. Kate grabs a megaphone. "Welcome to the annual Twin Cities Triathlon for Champs," she bellows. All the children cheer while the parents and volunteers holler and whoop, amping up the excitement. I cup my hands around my mouth and join the noises.

Kate begins with the rules, there will be two groups. Six plus will start first. A few minutes later, five and below will join. Designated parents and volunteers are to take their positions with the kids at the starting line. Everyone's involved here.

A hand tugs mine. "You ready for a race?" Justin steps up next to me.

"Heck yes. This is awesome."

"I know. I'll see you at the finish line." His hand still wraps around mine. My nerves tingle, an electrical current coiling in my palm. I have no power to let go. Why does it have to feel so good? The moment lasts a beat too long. He glances down at our grasping palms. As Kate blows the fog horn, he gives it one last squeeze, before darting forward and tugging me backward at the same time.

Cheat!

I dig my heels into the sand, my other hand still clutching the hand of the little girl in yellow. She hollers, "LET'S GET EM!" and we take off together. We wind our way through the beach running course, in pursuit of Justin and a little boy in a life vest, arms wrapped around Justin's neck, hitching a piggy back ride. They splash into the water mere seconds before us. Justin pulls the boy with him into the older track, on course to victory.

"The big one!" Yellow yells. "I'm seven!"

We splash into the deeper water. "You a good swimmer?" She answers with diving under the water and popping up a few feet away. "Awesome!" I'm about to dive in after her when I notice an elementary aged boy with jet-black hair standing in the waist deep water. I wave to Yellow, "You go on!" She smiles back before dipping under the water again, forging forward in the six plus race. I catch Justin's eye, who slows down, giving time for Yellow to catch up with him so he can watch her too.

I wade over to the boy standing in the water.

"What's up buddy?"

"I can't swim," he mumbles.

"That's alright. We can do it together."

"No, I can't do it. This is stupid. I didn't even want to come." He starts backing out of the water.

I reach out and take his hand. "You can do it."

"No, I can't. I have leukemia."

I nod. "I know. I'm sorry. That sucks a lot. But it doesn't mean you can't have fun. You know that, right?"

I catch a man with identical black hair nearing the

water's edge. His father. With a raise of his eyebrow, he asks me if I've got this. I nod back, I do. I've got it.

"I bet you're actually a really good swimmer, huh?" I doubt his parents would let him run out here without a life vest on if he didn't have the skills.

He smiles, "Yeah. I love it."

"Can you show me? I haven't had a swim lesson in a long time." I splash backwards, in a forced feeble backstroke, making a fool of myself. "I could use some pointers."

"You're doing it all wrong!"

"Oh? Then show me. Please?"

He rolls his eyes. "Come on." His eyebrows furrow. "But don't do the backstroke. No one does that in a real race. Not if you want to win."

"I do. I want to win."

"Then come on." He huffs as he plunges forward into the water, easily gliding into a forward dog-paddle. I join him, letting him instruct me down the course. As he pulls past other pairs of volunteers and kids, his smile grows. How long has he been letting his diagnosis stop him from having fun? I glance at his parents on the beach. It's a new diagnosis. You can see it in their creased brow. But their faces relax as the boy's smile grows in joy.

We reach the end of the swimming track and run together out of the water, up the beach to the bike line.

I give the boy a high five as he hops on his bike. "You rock! Ride on!" He pushes his pedal forward, a brilliant smile plastered to his face.

A familiar tug and flash of yellow greets me. "You said you'd be my bike."

"You don't have one?"

"Nope."

"Okay," I say through slightly labored breath. "How can I be your bike?"

"Bend down."

I do and she climbs on my back. Right, a piggy back ride.

"Go!" She yells as she points forward with a squeal.

I dash forward as I zigzag through the biking course. Dodging big wheels, parent-pulled wagons, and tricycles while making sure to stay out of the way of kids zooming by on real bikes. Pure joy and determination radiate off everyone's face. I know it's plastered to mine too. I haven't felt this great, ever. Not even the high of a basketball game competes with this feeling. Well, maybe holding Justin's hand does.

We round the final corner, "Ready?" I shout up to little Yellow.

"GO!!!"

I sprint, throwing my legs into long strides, bending forward with Yellow's light weight on my back. Justin pulls the ribbon across the finish line as they see us approach. Every kid gets the victory of breaking through the ribbon. I reach up and swing Yellow off my shoulders, determined to let her feel the rush of breaking her own ribbon. She gets it, leaping forward over the line, breaking through the loose red ribbon.

Victory!

She runs into her parents' arms and it takes everything in me not to cry. Kate nears her and swoops her into the perfect grandma-like hug, handing her the blue triathlon t-shirt and a home-printed certificate.

This is beautiful. This I love.

I step to the side, letting a boy on a bike fly through the ribbon that Justin had immediately reassembled. I duck under the course's rope as I cheer the boy on. I'll never be able to get enough of this.

Justin nudges me with his elbow, "Beat ya." He hands me the ribbon, as he slides the little guy off his back. I take up his post, re-tying the ribbon loosely and dragging it across for the next champions, while Justin brings the child back to his parents. The boy takes a few weak steps into his mother's arms before she lifts him with a hug and places him in his wheelchair.

Justin gives the kid a high five and that's when it hits me. I'm a total goner. I'm head over heels in love with Justin Marshall, and there's nothing I can do about it.

I glance away as he walks back toward me. That smile. God. Those eyes. Kill me. How will I ever survive this?

He places his hand on my back as he reaches over to untie a flag that got caught up on a pole. His touch melts me and there's nothing I can do. His palm heats through my shirt, radiating warmth over my back. My spine tingles with pleasure. Holy crap.

"So," he says with his hand still on my back, "What do you think?"

I cheer as two kids cross the finish line. "I think this is pretty amazing."

He leans in toward me. "Not as amazing as you," he says as he removes his hand from my back. He turns back toward the finish line, retying the ribbon and stringing it across.

The breeze stops with my heart. Everything slows. His dark hair's fallen into a loose curl, striking against his green eyes. Did he really just say that?

Justin waves another volunteer over, handing him the end of the ribbon with a quick exchange. He waves to the table of volunteers as he returns to my side. "I've got something to show you." His hand finds that place again on my back and for a brief moment it leads me the direction he wants us to walk. The beach.

"Alright," I say as casually as I can. I'd follow him anywhere. I know better now than to ask what he wants to show me. There's no end to Justin's depth and I'm loving each surprise.

He holds up the beach boundary rope for me to duck under. We make our way away from the celebrating triathlon champions, down to the water's edge. He sits on the beach, feet in the water. Patting the ground beside him. I join him, dipping my toes in the shallow water, still warm in the dusk's sun.

"Thank you," I say before he can show me anything. "I had so much fun."

"Good. I hoped you'd like it. It's one of my favorite days of the year." He reaches into his back pocket and pulls out his wallet. "This is what I wanted to show you." He opens the wallet, handing me a photo.

A younger version of Justin, but with blue eyes, smiles back at me.

"Jackson?" I ask.

"That was taken a few days before he was diagnosed."

"He looks just like you."

"Yeah. I used to love that about him. He was older enough for me to admire the crap out of him. Seriously, he could do anything. Best baseball player, best climber, best runner. Best brother." He smiles as he takes the picture back and secures it again in his wallet.

"He sounds wonderful."

"He was. I'm sorry he's gone. He would have loved this," he said with a nod back toward the triathlon.

"I'm sure he would've." My eyes are damp, but I don't care. It's right.

Justin opened the other part of his wallet, pulling out another piece of paper and handing it to me. "I got this from school today."

I unfold the paper, immediately recognizing the headline *Freshman leads Varsity to Victory*. Under the headline, there's a photo of me, hair in a sweaty ponytail, head between my hands, studying the floor, after the final winning shot for the state championships. My shot.

"What happened, Lucy? Why did you stop? You were great. I remember that game." He leans into me, his shoulder brushing against mine. "I remember you."

My heart pounds. "How long did it take you to recognize me?"

His lips spread into a smile. "I've always known who you were. You could never hide that behind Marissa."

"Why didn't you tell me?"

"And blow the cover you worked so hard to keep?"

"It wasn't a cover. It was more a new life. Life on that basketball team was hell."

"Why?"

"Think about it, Justin. What do you remember about that year and the freshman girl on the team?"

Justin gazes out for a moment at the water. Then a crease in his forehead appears. "Wait, those stories were true?"

"Probably."

"The beatings? The bullying? All because you took that

brat's position? I thought people were exaggerating."

I nod. "They made it impossible to endure. As the season ended, there was nothing left of me. After the season, it actually got worse. I was their sick form of daily entertainment."

Justin's hand finds mine and he gives it a squeeze. "I'm sorry. Why didn't you tell anyone?"

"Coach knew. As long as he won, he kept looking the other way. I couldn't tell my parents. I didn't know how my mom would handle it. I couldn't risk her getting too upset. I wanted to keep her stable, well."

"I wish you would have told me."

"Well, we weren't exactly friends then, huh?" I ask as Justin releases my hands.

"No. But we are now. So," he smiles, "are you going to play ball again?"

The cheers from the triathlon champions carry over the water.

"Honestly, I don't know. I always needed basketball before. Yes, I loved it, but this last year gave me a complete break. And after Marissa, I'm wary to let anything define me anymore. It's nice not to need anything to be myself."

"So, maybe?"

"Yeah. Actually," I nod back toward the kids. "This makes me want to coach. I think I'd love that."

"Good. Do what makes you happy. Whatever you decide. You deserve to be happy."

"Thanks. These kids make me happy. That event made me happy."

"Yeah. That was obvious, your smile … Wow."

I beam back at him. No one's ever made me feel so great before.

"See," he says with a wink and I think I'm going to die. The most lovely form of torture on earth. "You seemed at ease out there."

"Yeah, it's easy to be myself here." I shrug. "Around you, too."

Justin laughs. "Yeah, I know. I swear, no one believes me when I tell them about the spunk in your soul."

He tells people about me?

Justin stands up, brushing off the sand from his shorts. I follow quickly, not giving him the chance to reach down and pull me up. Too dangerous. My hand may weld itself to his if our palms touch again.

He reaches down and catches my hand anyway, pulling me up but suddenly using his weight to throw me into the water. I grasp his other arm, pulling him in after me. He falls, pinning me under him in the foot of water. I'm totally lost. I can't look away from his green eyes, somehow darker as he gazes back down at me. I know I'm crossing the friendship line, but I can't help it. I'm not going to live my life missing moments like these.

He smiles, brushing the hair from my face. His Adam's apple gulps before he rolls off of me, letting go of my palm. Disappointment washes itself over me with a wave. I welcome the water, giving me a moment to recover from his rejection. He knew, in that second, he knew that I wanted to be his. He had to.

When I've got control, I use the rejected energy to bolt from the water, making sure to splash in his face on my way out. I'm totally cool. Nothing happened. Just having fun. Friendly fun. I dash up the beach.

He doesn't miss a beat, sprinting past me. "Race you to the truck!"

CHAPTER TWENTY-FIVE

The best part of every day is my time with Justin. I thrive on his laughter. My heart aches when I crawl out of his truck in the evenings, hurting worse every day. He is my last thought of the day and my first every morning. After that moment on the beach, I have raw determination to stop thinking about him. But the more I try, the more Justin consumes my thoughts. Thankfully, or crappily, the constant flow of texts he receives from girls helps remind me just where we stand. I now love that chime of his phone. It keeps me grounded in reality.

As we pull into my driveway after a miserable, humid week of painting, Justin's phone chimes four times.

"Your following beckons," I say, handing him the phone from the console.

Justin sighs. "All in a day's work, right?" He checks the messages.

I fold my hands in my lap, remembering the way his hand grasped mine at the race. My back warms, still radiating from the heat of that touch. He hasn't touched me since. I squeeze my hands together, restraining myself from throwing the phone into the pile of fertilizer Mom has dumped on the driveway.

"It's from Jen. She's grilling out at Lake Nokomis. Want to come with me?"

My heart stops. Another evening with Justin? Yes!

Justin repeats himself, thinking I didn't hear him.

"Sure, that sounds like fun." My insides are reeling.

"Great." His broad smile accentuates his right dimple. I smile back like a fool, opening the truck door and sliding out of the seat.

"How quick can you get ready? I'm starving and they already started the grill."

"Twenty minutes?" It'll be tight but I can make it work. It's a lake so wet hair will be fine.

"Wow. You can be ready in twenty?" Justin whistles. "I can't even do that. How about I'll pick you up in forty?"

"I'll be ready."

"Sweet. See you soon." The motor sputters and a cloud of white vapor goes poof in my face. He leans out his window, "Sorry about that." I wave the cloud away, coughing.

"Sure you can make it home in that, Justin?" Dad's voice calls from the garage. I spin around. I had no idea he'd been standing there.

"She's never failed me yet, Mr. Zwindler." He laughs as he slowly pulls the truck out of the driveway.

Dad puts his hand on my shoulder. "If that boy dares to pick you up tonight in that vehicle, I'm loaning you my car."

I roll my eyes at him. "The truck's fine, Dad."

Dad shrugs. "It may be but it doesn't matter. It's the principal."

"What are you talking about?"

"A rule of thumb. Don't pick up a girl for a date in a vehicle that makes her father doubt her survival."

"It's not a date."

Dad laughs.

"No, really. We're hanging out with friends."

He lifts his right eyebrow at me.

"Jennifer will be there," I add. I'd never felt the need to tell Mom and Dad that Justin and Jennifer's relationship was over. The Jennifer card eliminated most awkward conversations whenever they brought up Justin.

Dad opens the door to the mud room. "Well, I stand corrected."

It isn't a date.

I can't think of this as a date.

"You know Mom was dating someone else when we met?" He follows me through the kitchen. "I'm just saying, it can be a date."

I spin around and glare at him. He responds with a toothy and teasing grin.

"Dad." I scowl. I sound just like Mom.

Dad throws his hands up and walks away. "Okay, okay. It's not a date."

"Thank you."

I bolt up the stairs and throw myself into the shower. Dad has stolen a few precious minutes from me. I multitask while scrubbing vigorously, choosing my outfit from memory. I'll go with my new jean shorts and the purple and white polka dot tank that I bought with Laura a few days ago. I'm so thankful I went on that shopping trip.

I pull open my makeup drawer, swooshing on a light layer of foundation and some mascara. We're going to the beach. I don't need anything more.

My heart pounds as I play with my wet hair. Is this really a date? The butterflies that have taken up permanent residence in my stomach zoom around like they're in the Daytona 500. I pull my hair to the side, braiding it down the edge of my neck. I wipe the steam off the mirror so I can see the final result. I look fresh and dewy. Perfect for a skin commercial but not exactly perfect for a date.

My reflection tells me what I know deep down.

This is not a date.

I sigh, momentarily hating Dad for planting the idea. I know better. Justin isn't the type of guy who'd spring that sort of thing on a girl. He's old fashioned. If he was asking me on a date, he would've made that clear. I urge my heart to slow. I need to relax. This is not a big deal.

I wait for Justin on the front porch. I'm not that surprised when Dad conveniently decides to mow the front lawn. I let my gaze meet his with daggers when he passes in front of me.

He's such a dad.

A tinted Cadillac Crossover pulls up the driveway. Dad looks at me and sighs in defeat. I think he was really looking forward to telling Justin and his truck off. Too bad.

Justin steps out of the Crossover and waves. "What

happened to the truck?" Dad calls over the hum of the mower

Justin's face turns sour. "It wouldn't start," he shouts back.

I cross in front of the SUV and pull open the passenger door. I don't want to give Justin the opportunity to open it for me. I have to focus—this isn't a date. Justin looks temporarily bewildered as I leave him standing alone in the driveway. He collects himself and climbs into his seat, waving goodbye to Dad.

"What's the rush, Lady?" he asks. I love it when he calls me Lady.

"I thought you were hungry?" I lie.

"Oh," he looks down at his stomach like Eric does when it growls "That I am." He pushes the SUV's power button and it softly hums alive. Justin sighs, "It just isn't the same without the sputtering or churning. Not as rugged, you know?"

"Right. Rugged is good. A quiet, purring engine is bad."

"Precisely." His laugh rolls as he pulls his fingers through his gorgeous dark hair. That's it. My heart unhinges itself from my control. I've tipped over the top hill of a rollercoaster and there is no end.

I can't live without hearing that chuckle for the rest of my life.

This is going to be a painful night.

CHAPTER TWENTY-SIX

My stomach ties into hundreds of knots as we approach Jennifer and her friends. I can't blame myself for being nervous. My history with social events is crap. But I'm not going to let Marissa and Zach ruin me. As much as it sucks, socialization is part of life. I have to learn how to do it, awkward or not. Of course, Justin senses my distress. Before we walk over the hill to the grill area, he places his hand on my back. "Don't worry about it. These people are cool."

Jennifer runs up the hill to greet us. She smiles at me and eyes Justin's hand still resting on my back. I shift, knowing exactly what she's thinking. I hope she can't tell how badly I want it to be true.

"Hey, Jen. Is the food ready?"

"On the table."

Justin runs down the hill toward the picnic table before she finishes the sentence.

Jennifer laughs. "He has an appetite of a thousand men. My dad's happy he doesn't have to feed him anymore." She grabs my hand. "Come on. You should grab something before he eats it. Seriously."

***

Justin introduces me to some guys from the basketball team. I recognize Jennifer's friends, Allison and Tiffany. They seem pretty impartial to my existence. I like it that way.

Jennifer makes me grab a hot dog before she leads me over to another group playing ultimate Frisbee. I inhale the hot dog as a tall, green-eyed brunette steps out from the game to greet us.

Jennifer blushes as she approaches. "Lucy, meet Trish."

I rub the crumbs from the hot dog against my legs. "Hey, it's great to meet you."

"Thanks. You too. Jennifer's said some awesome things about you." Trish catches my eye, letting me know that she knows I know, or something like that. She nods toward the group playing Frisbee. "My friends haven't quite clicked yet with Jennifer's." I turn around, catching Allison and Tiffany eyeing them.

I laugh. "Maybe it's the other way around?"

"Oh trust me. It's definitely the other way around," Jennifer adds. "Allison and Tiffany take some time to warm up. They're okay though. You'll see."

"Do you want to play with us?" Trish offers.

Allison and Tiffany whisper to one another. The knots

271

in my stomach tighten. I eye the ultimate Frisbee group. No expectations there. It seems like the safer bet. "Yeah, that'd be great."

I am horrible with the Frisbee. Trish tries to give me pointers but it never helps. Justin's presence, even across the lawn, is way too much of a distraction for me. My heart aches with each laugh and smile. And then it starts to burn when his attention is directed at Allison.

Allison has somehow separated Justin from the rest of the group. They are sitting on the ground and Allison is throwing grass in his face. She flips her hair and I can pick out the dimples in his cheeks. Every time he laughs is a knife through my heart. He leans in close to her and whispers something in her ear. She giggles.

I bite my lower lip. My heart has been thrown into an inferno.

I excuse myself from the game, claiming I've left my phone in Justin's car. I need a moment to recover. As I walk over the hill and back to the car, my head spins.

I close my eyes and lean against the Crossover.

My heart is breaking and it sucks.

I breathe deeply, praying for the pain to subside.

I have to get through this.

I knew this day would come. Justin was bound to find another girl after Jennifer.

He can't just stay single forever.

We're just friends. He's made that clear. I have no claim on him in any way.

I press my hand harder against my heart. I reason with it. Allison is making Justin happy. Don't I want him to be happy? He's my friend after all.

The burning eases a bit. That's the key. Justin's

happiness. I really just want Justin to be happy. I can mourn the loss of a relationship I never had later. Tonight, I will just be happy for Justin.

I open my eyes and sigh. Why did love have to be so confusing?

I walk back up the hill. Midway up, a mother plays with her baby girl on a blanket. She blows into her tummy and the baby's legs thrash wildly. I lean against a tree and continue to trespass on their mother-daughter moment. They are absolutely enchanted with one another. It's beautiful. Such simple and pure love.

I wish Mom could have done that with me.

I jump when I realize Justin stands at my side.

"Hey, what's up?"

"Nothing. I thought I forgot my cell phone in your car." My voice is lifeless.

"Yeah, that's what Jennifer said." He jingles his car keys. "I figured you needed these."

"Thanks, but I looked through the window and I didn't see it. Maybe I left it in my purse."

Justin nods up the hill, "Which is back at the picnic table."

"Right."

Justin looks at the mother and daughter. "Weird."

"Really? I think it's awesome." I study them, trying to figure out what's so weird. The mother is now rocking the baby and singing her songs. They're perfect.

"No, not them. You."

"Oh?" I take a step back from him. "What?"

"Well, don't get mad, but I was watching you before I came down. You were looking at them like you were jealous or something."

I bite my lower lip. I can't lie to Justin. My heart is too raw to try.

"I guess that's because I am." I sigh and lean back against a tree. The baby is reaching up and pulling the mother's hair.

"Why?"

"Well, my mom couldn't do that stuff with me when I was little."

"Oh?"

"She had undiagnosed post-partum depression," I explain. "She couldn't be that way with me." Justin doesn't say anything so I continue. "She sunk into a terrible, clinical depression, for years. She never rocked me to sleep or played patty cake. She'd just lie in the living room on the couch."

"Wow, that must have been hard," Justin says. "She isn't that way now though."

"No, she's better now. Once they figured out what was wrong she was able to find treatment. A pairing of medication, exercise, and gardening became her therapy. By the time Eric was born, she was better." I nod back toward the mother and daughter. "I used to watch her play with Eric that way." I sigh. "I used to hate her for it. But now I'm glad she was able to love a child like that."

Justin shortens the distance between us. "Lucy."

I tremble as he comes closer. "Do you really think she didn't love you?"

"Well, maybe somewhere inside of me, I don't know, I guess—yeah?"

Justin places his arm around my shoulder in a sideways hug. My body melts into it. "One thing about your mother that is very obvious is that she loves you more than the world itself. The way she looks at you," he nods toward the mother gazing into the daughter's eyes. "It's just like that. Trust me." He holds me a moment longer before letting go.

"I don't know why." I try to sound casual. "I've made her life horrible this past year."

"I can't say I haven't noticed tension. But lately?"

"It's getting better." I shrug. "We've been working on it."

I start walking back up the hill. Justin follows. "You know that is pretty incredible."

"What is?"

"You being so mature. You're already striving to repair your relationship with your mom. Most people don't do that until their mid-thirties, if ever."

"I got sick of acting like everyone thinks a sixteen-year-old should." I force a laugh. "It was way too much work to live up to those shallow standards."

"Only a kind and good person would find that difficult."

"Oh trust me, more like evil." I try to smile mischievously.

He laughs. "I highly doubt that." He nods down at Jennifer, "She wouldn't have told you about her and Trish if you were. Jen's got a sixth sense about people. If Jen approves of you, you're definitely awesome." His gaze moves from Jennifer to Allison. "That's why I'm thinking of asking Allison out on a date. Get to know her, she seems really smart and fun."

My heart starts to bleed.

Justin continues. "She must be a good person if she's Jen's friend, right?"

"Hmmm," I force enthusiasm into my voice. "What does Jen think?"

He sighs. "She actually refuses to tell me. She doesn't want to get caught in the middle. Wise but crappy. What do you think?"

"Well." I navigate my words carefully. "Do whatever makes you happy."

He smiles and nudges me, recognizing that same advice he gave me at the beach. "Come on, really, what do you think about Allison?"

"She seems cool. There's no harm in going on a date or two." I want to punch myself for saying it. But, it's true. As Justin's friend, I'm going to support him even if that means my heart breaking into a million pieces along the way.

Justin takes a deep breath. "Okay. I'm going to do it."

"Now?"

"Yup. Unless you can think of a reason for me not to?"

"Can you?"

"Nope." He takes a deep breath. "Here goes nothing." He turns away from me and waves to Allison. She waves back. He motions for her to join him on the hill. I sidestep away from Justin. I won't survive if I have to watch this.

"Well, I'll leave you two alone then." I nod back toward the Frisbee game. "They're getting killed down there. I better get back."

"Right." Justin rubs his stubble. He looks nervous. Does he really think there is a chance she'll say no?

I return to the Frisbee game. I pretend nothing has happened. Jen is watching Justin and Allison talk at the top of the hill. When they disappear to the other side, she smiles at me. I smile back at her. This isn't a big deal.

My heart is fine. It's just shattered, bleeding, raw.

No big deal.

The rest of the evening passes like I've drunk three espressos. Adrenaline carries me through. I play some Frisbee, make small talk, and listen to Tiffany go on and on about how perfect Allison and Justin are for one another.

As night comes, everyone starts packing stuff up and heading home. Justin and Allison still haven't returned from the other side of the hill. I won't allow myself to imagine where they are and what they're doing. I can't go there.

Eventually, only Jennifer, Trish, and I remain. Jennifer keeps looking up the hill, waiting.

"This is ridiculous," she says. "Where are they?"

"Don't worry. I'm sure they are just walking or something," Trish offers.

"But this isn't how it's supposed to be."

Trish lets out a sweet laugh. "I know he's one of your best friends, Jen. But you've got to let him live."

"Not like this." Jen grumbles. She pulls out her phone. Justin still hasn't responded to her texts. She sits across the picnic table and reaches her hand out to mine. "We can give you a ride home, Lucy. You shouldn't have to wait for him like this." Her eyes search mine.

She knows.

I watch Trish pull a strand of hair out of Jennifer's eyes. If Jennifer can trust me with her secret, I can definitely trust her with mine.

I squeeze her hand back.

"Yeah. This really sucks." My eyes fill with tears. "I'm sorry." I wipe them away.

"How long?" Jennifer asks.

"I honestly have no idea. I mean, he seriously used to irritate me to death. I dreaded talking to him. He drove me crazy. But now …"

"You're in love with him," Jennifer states.

I am in love with him. Totally gone, crazy in love with him.

But I can't have him.

"You need to tell him, Lucy."

I shake my head. "I can't now."

"Sure you can." Jennifer pats my hand.

"No really, I can't. He's happy hanging out with Allison tonight. I'm not going to disrupt that. If it doesn't work out, I'll still be here."

"Waiting."

I sigh. "Yes, waiting."

"But what if it does work?" Trish asks.

"Then I'll be happy for him. If it works that well, we weren't meant to be."

"Wow. You really do love him," Jennifer whispers.

I nod. Tears roll down my cheeks. I'm thankful for the darkness. An absurd laugh follows. Losing it.

Trish stands and extends her hand to me. "Let's get you home before you go insane, babe."

Jennifer puts her arm through mine and walks with me up the hill. Trish carries the cooler behind. Jennifer leans toward me. "I think you should tell him. You can't live like this forever. It'll destroy you."

"But what if he doesn't love me back?"

"Well," she sighs. "If he doesn't, he's an idiot. But at least then you'll know. You won't spend your life waiting for him, for a relationship that will never happen. You'd be able to move on."

Moving on sounds nice. It's better than this extreme pain.

I crawl into the backseat of Trish's car. Jennifer slides in next to me. Trish puts on some classical music as we pull out of the lot. We drive down the frontage road when Jennifer asks Trish to pull over.

"Justin," Jennifer yells out the window. Two outlines, one tall and the other petite, walk hand-in-hand toward us. The light from the headlights bounces off Justin's white shirt. Justin waves and starts jogging over to the car. Allison follows.

I grasp Jennifer's arm and squeeze. Justin can't see me like this. Jennifer shoves me down onto the seat. "You're asleep," she whispers. I close my eyes and she throws her jacket over me. I concentrate on faking long, steady breaths.

"What's up?" Justin's low voice hangs above me. I breathe in and out.

"Lucy's sleeping," Jennifer whispers. "We're taking her home."

"Oh," Justin whispers back. "I didn't realize it was so late."

"Yup," Jennifer says shortly. "Everyone else has left. Allison, Tiffany grabbed a ride home with Cole. She left you her car." She dangles a pair of keys out the window. Great, at least Justin won't be driving her home. "Cool?"

"Sure," Allison says with clear disappointment in her voice.

"Jen, can you tell Lucy I'll call her tomorrow? I need her to come with me to the Hill House again."

"Tomorrow?"

"Yup. I need her help to finish my proposal."

"Sure, I'll let her know."

"Thanks, Jen. You're the best," Allison says as she clears her throat possessively.

"Whatever. Later," Jennifer snaps back. The car creeps forward.

"Wait, Jen." Justin's feet patter against the pavement. "What's wrong?"

"Nothing."

"Just leave her alone, Justin. She's just jealous." I swear Allison hisses.

Trish sucks in a loud lungful of air. I can feel Jennifer glaring at both Justin and Allison. I want to open my eyes and see exactly what is going on but I don't dare. Justin would want to talk to me then.

"Jen," Justin says apologetically. "I'll call you later, okay?"

"Fine," Jennifer says as evenly as she can. "Have a good night." The car picks up momentum. Jennifer shakes my side. "He's such an idiot. What does he see in her?"

I sit up. "He said that if she's your friend, she must be worth knowing."

"But, not like that. We're friends only because we've known each other so long." She sighs, "Our relationship is complicated. Allison has always been there for me but she's also in unspoken competition with me. It's really sick. She just wants to use him. She thinks he'll help her become Homecoming Queen. I couldn't care less about that plastic tiara."

Jennifer continues, "You need to tell him how you feel, Lucy. Even if he doesn't reciprocate the feelings, he'll know what you feel is real. Allison is all fake."

I shake my head. I could never risk our friendship.

"Lucy, you'll save him from being used. He deserves better than that."

Her words hit me hard. The thought of Allison viewing Justin that way is disgusting. Justin is so much more than a ticket to a crown. His view of relationships and love is perfect and pure. I can't let her destroy that.

"Fine, I'll tell him." I kick the seat in front of me. "This really sucks. I spent the whole summer figuring out who I am and now I'm going to end up a broken hot mess again."

"You don't know that," Trish offers from the front seat.

I think of Justin's reaction that morning when he thought I was about to tell him I liked him. "Oh, trust me. I do."

CHAPTER TWENTY-SEVEN

I spend more time turning in bed than I do sleeping. The next morning, I wake up feeling like my heart is trying to break through my chest wall and fly away to safety. I pace around my kitchen, cell phone always in my back pocket. I am one of those girls again, desperately waiting for a guy to call.

When my cell vibrates, I start trembling. I sit down in the middle of the floor, forcing my body to be still. I take a deep breath. "Hey."

"Hey, Lady. You answered." My heart aches at the sound of his voice.

"Of course," I respond vaguely, failing at my attempt to be intriguing.

"Did Jen tell you I need help with the Hill House today?"

"Not the details. What's up?" I sound amazingly collected. I start to relax. I can hide these feelings. Maybe I'm not that bad of a liar after all.

"Mason will let us on the grounds again tonight. I just need your opinion about colors and a few problem spots. I'm kind of kicking myself for not doing the research myself."

"No problem."

"Great. I'll pick you up around five? Does that sound good?"

"That's perfect."

"Sweet. See you then, Lady." The phone clicks and he's gone. I glance at the bird clock; quarter past three. One hour and forty-five minutes to go before friendship destruction.

My heart thuds against my chest and I feel dizzy. I race to the bathroom and splash cold water on my face. My cheeks contrast bright red against my ghostly pale skin. My pupils are more dilated than when I leave the eye doctor.

This is what I look like lovesick; a complete lunatic.

I fill the bathtub. I refuse to look like this when I confess my love. I need some dignity.

I soak in the tub for almost an hour. My veins dilate and my heart rate slows. I am going to approach this as a calm and collected individual. I dry my hair and make some long, loose curls. I know I look a bit overdone but I don't care. This is my only chance. I'm not about to let my hair ruin it. Not that Justin seems to be the type of guy who cares. But still.

I grab my favorite pair of jeans, the one that Marissa told me makes my butt look fat. I pair it with an ivory lace top over a lilac racerback tank. Now to loosen up the curls;

my fingers give a gentle tug. I stand up straight and smile at my reflection. A dewy, movie-star version of me smiles back. I twirl. My reflection gives me a little hope. Maybe, just maybe, he'll be so struck that he forgets Allison all together.

I wait in my kitchen. I don't want to see him pull up. I'll be too tempted to walk out and meet him in the driveway. I need Justin's instincts to guide him to my door and ring the bell. Anything to jostle his subconscious into putting me outside of his "just friends" category.

My pacing returns as I stare down the minute hand on that stupid bird clock. I'm thankful my family isn't around. They are in Stillwater where Mom is being honored at a garden expo while Dad and Eric take a train and boat tour. There isn't any way they'd have missed my nerves or my appearance. Fate has kindly spared me that conversation.

The sound of the Canadian goose honking makes my heart flutter. Five o'clock. I stand still, taking slow, deep breaths. A few seconds later the doorbell rings. Justin, always punctual.

Okay. I can do this.

I picture Allison hanging on Justin's arm with the homecoming crown perched on her head.

I have to do this.

I throw my shoulders back and walk to the front door. My hand operates separately from my body as I reach and pull it open.

"Hey," the word sounds unusually calm. That bath really worked.

"Oh." Justin shakes his head slightly. His eyes quickly look me over. My heart leaps but somehow I remain calm. He notices me. "You ready?"

"Yup," I step out. I resist running ahead and jumping into the passenger seat. He leads me around the Crossover, pulling the door open for me. "Thanks," I say as I slide onto the seat. I feel like I'm in the final quarter of the basketball game. It's now or never. I smile at him and let my eyes linger for a full second. Terrifying.

"Uh, sure," he mumbles. I fiddle with my bracelet as he walks around the car. The guilt of my manipulation pokes at me. But I have to use what I can to my advantage. Justin climbs into the car. "What's with the new look?" he asks.

"Oh, I got bored this afternoon. Just playing around." I shrug. "It's a girl thing."

"Well," he looks me over again. My heart clunks. "It works." His lips part into a crooked smile. "Some guy will be lucky someday."

He means it as a compliment but it hits me as a rejection. I don't want it to be some guy. I want it to be him.

Justin puts the car in reverse and hands me the notebook. The notebook is nearly full with his extra notes. I page through; yellow highlighter details most of my points and his scribbling handwriting decorates the margins. "You really read this, huh?" I make myself laugh casually.

"I take my job very seriously." His tone is distant, reminding me of his cold approach just a few weeks earlier. I start feeling sick. I open my phone and check my contacts, making sure Trish's name is still listed. She'll be picking me up when this is all over.

Justin starts berating me with questions about homemade paint in the 1800's and the types of milk protein they used. My notes on the topic are sparse so I answer the best I can from memory. He hands me his iPhone to Google when I need it.

Crap. I am his research assistant. I can't be farther from where I need to be by the end of the night.

The gates to the mansion are open and Justin pulls up under the carriage entrance. Mason meets us outside and pulls the door open for me. "Wow, Lucy. You look beautiful," he says as he gives me his hand to help me step out of the SUV.

"Thanks." I act like I am told this all the time. Justin walks around to my side of the Crossover.

"Ready?" Mason asks.

"Yup. Let's show her the problems."

Mason opens the front door and I step inside. The beauty of the rich woodwork makes me stall. Mason laughs. "Yeah. She's always radiant." He places a hand on my shoulder, leading me forward. "Don't you agree, Justin?" He winks at me. At least I have one ally tonight.

"Yup. Every time I come here I discover a new woodcarving or little nook in a room. The place is full of surprises." Justin pushes past us to a small back stairway.

"Slow down, Justin. No need to rush. Or you'll miss the beauty." Justin's pace quickens down the stairs. Mason shrugs at me. "I try."

"Don't worry about it. He just really wants to get the job."

"He's going to get the job. The historical society wants more funding. They aren't going to reject the soon-to-be governor's son."

"Oh. I never thought of that."

"Well hopefully Justin hasn't either. I want him to think he deserves it when they give him the gig."

"But he does." I pull out the notebook, showing him the notes and countless drafts of proposals Justin created. "I doubt any other company has spent this much time studying Summit Avenue homes and 19th century painting techniques."

Mason whistles as he scans our notes. "Well, I'll be. He really has done his homework. I always knew that kid had class. Listen, please don't tell him what I said about him getting the job because of his dad." Mason shakes his head. "I shouldn't have said that. If he put a different name on this proposal, he'd get the job over his father's namesake." He pats me on the shoulder. "You're right. He deserves it."

I feel sorry for Justin as I follow Mason down the stairs. It never occurred to me how hard he'd have to work to prove to himself and others that he isn't just sliding by as his father's son. What I once took for his ego is actually raw determination to be the best he can be. No wonder he loves that truck— it's his own thing. Warmth spreads through my belly and I know I just fell more in love with Justin than a minute before. Crap.

"Did you say something?" Mason looks back over his shoulder at me.

"Yeah, did we see this before?" This stairway is plainer than any other area of the house.

"No. These stairs were for the hired help: cooks, maids, seamstresses, butlers." Mason cracks his back on the first landing. "But if you ask me, they deserved that grand stairway or," he laughs, "an elevator."

"I bet. I'm sure you put a lot of miles in every day around this joint."

He pulls a small box off his belt loop and hands it to

me. "I've put in nine today and I still haven't closed the place up. It's okay though," he pats his flat stomach. "I can eat all the brownies I want."

I laugh as we descend into the basement. I recognize the kitchen that we saw a few weeks ago. The room is dark and cold. Justin waits for us, tapping the wooden island impatiently. My stomach twists into a tight knot. He's probably planning on meeting Allison later.

"Over here, Lucy." He waves me to the corner of the kitchen and shows me some faded baseboards. I get down on my knees to examine the work. The trim is a dull red that I haven't seen before. A few white spots interrupt the flow of the dull color as well as a few faded brush strokes. I lightly touch the paint over the brush strokes. I can still feel the texture.

I push myself away from the baseboard and look up at Justin. "The second volume I studied featured milk-based paint. This stuff here is that original stuff. The red color looks like it was made from brick powder." I point to the white spots. "Those are water marks. They washed away the pigment." I stand up and brush off my knees.

Justin smiles at me and my head spins. I sidestep and he grabs my arm; my whole body warms at his touch. I know I'm blushing. "Are you okay?"

I force myself to step away from his touch. It's actually painful. "I'm fine," I say. "I think I just stood up too fast. That's all."

Mason walks over and bends down to examine the board. "Why is the paint still here?" he asks.

"Chances are whoever did the original painting got distracted and forgot to seal the board," I offer.

"And more modern painters were too scared to touch

it." Justin shakes his head. "I'm glad they didn't. Do you think the historical society would be interested in this?" he asks Mason.

Mason is still crouched down on the ground, touching the board lightly. "Absolutely," he says. "They can learn so much from just pulling a few isotopes." He looks up at me. "Great job, Lucy."

"Is there more?" I ask. Justin nods and leads me to a nook off the laundry room. A few shelves are painted in the same way. "Yup. Milk-based," I assess.

"This is great. Including this in my proposal will be so impressive."

"What do you propose to do with it?"

"Just seal the boards to preserve them." He shakes his head. "I can't believe no one has caught this yet." He sits down on a small step outside the furnace room. He scribbles a few more notes before shutting the notebook dramatically. "There." He smiles and I can't look away. "Now I just have to type it up tomorrow and put it on their desk on Monday."

"Is that when it's due?" I ask.

Mason rolls his eyes. "No. It's not due until December."

"I want them thinking about me now," Justin explains. He stands up, "Ready to go?"

I look around the stone laundry room. No. I want to stay here forever. My stomach ties into a giant knot and my heart is out of control. If we leave, then I'll have to tell him soon.

"Or would you like one last descent down the grand stairway?" Mason adds.

"No." The word flies from my mouth. "That's okay." I

walk past Justin and turn the corner to ascend the stairs. Adrenaline pumps through my arteries. I pace my breaths like I do pre-game.

I refuse to let my mind wage battle on my heart. I'd already made the decision to tell him. I can't reason myself out of it. My heart is in too much pain for me to care anymore. I hope Jennifer is right. Maybe by telling him, the pain will stop and I can start moving on.

I wait for Justin and Mason in the grand entryway. I trace my fingers over the curved woodwork. The carvings are delicate but strong, lasting through centuries. I will my sense of self to be as strong as the carvings. I don't want to lose myself to heartbreak. I have to be stronger than that.

I watch Justin walk toward me, explaining his proposal to Mason. He is so passionate and genuine. Butterflies zoom through me. He smiles and I ache. I can't live like this forever. I need to tell him. I need to take control of my life.

Mason opens the car door as he says goodbye. I thank him and wish him good night. He winks at me as he closes my door. Justin waves as we pull away. "I really think I'm going to get this job, Lucy." He hits the steering wheel and smiles. "Troy's going to freak out. This will change our lives forever."

He turns off of Summit onto a side road to park. "I can't go home. I'm too excited. Want to take a walk?"

I nod. Walking seems way more lending to professing my love than driving on a highway. "Want to see where I'm going to take Allison on our first date tomorrow night? It's just around the corner."

"Sure," I manage to force through my lips. My heart screams.

We walk next to one another on the narrow sidewalk so our shoulders occasionally brush. I focus on the houses, still large but not mansions. Justin nods to one with a beautiful alcove. "I want to own a house like that someday," he says. I nod back, I can't find any words. My mind races. How do I tell him? Why didn't I make a plan? Why won't fate just throw me into the conversation?

"So, I'm sorry you had to drive home with Jennifer and Trish last night," Justin says. I cringe at the memory of fake sleeping in the back seat. How pathetic. I can't live like that. I won't hide anymore.

"No big deal," I say as some old confidence surges through my blood, paired with relief. I'm not going to hide any longer.

"Yeah, I noticed." His eyes dance when he smiles. "I just want you to know that wasn't my intention. I had no idea walking around the lake with Allison would take so long."

"I bet; how'd everything go with Allison?"

"Good." His dimples pop. "I think she really likes me. I kept things casual though. I didn't really want to have the first date experience before we actually have our first date, you know?"

"Are you excited?" Why did I ask that? Shouldn't I be taking his attention away from Allison?

"I'd be crazy not to be. Allison's beautiful and really fun." My chest burns. "I think we'll get along fine." I stop walking for a second to catch my breath. He doesn't notice because he's pointing to a low cluster of white lights just ahead.

"This is where I'm bringing her, W.A. Frost's patio. It's one of my favorite places. Don't you think she'll love it?"

His warm hand suddenly rests on my back and leads me toward the fence. I peer inside, savoring the warmth of his touch. White Christmas lights are delicately strung through low tree branches. Small votives adorn each table. Waiters in white shirts dance through the narrow spaces between the tables.

It's incredibly romantic.

"It's perfect, Justin." I turn away from the restaurant and close my eyes, resting my head against the brick privacy wall that separates the patio from the parking lot. I'm in so much pain. When I breathe, it's as if knives are slicing away at my lungs.

I can't bear this any longer.

"Lucy," Justin steps close to me. His palm finds my arm. My heart hurts so much, it's already tearing apart. "Are you okay?"

"No." This is it. My heart's on fire.

"What's wrong?" Butterflies break through my stomach and zoom out of me through my legs, arms, fingers, and toes. Even they are abandoning ship.

I open my eyes. "I have to tell you something."

"What?" Worry clouds his face. He takes a step closer.

My heart screams. Agony.

"Okay." I take a deep breath and pull myself together. This is happening now. Confidence, carry me through. I can't go on.

My old confidence that used to carry me on the court finds me. Straightens my shoulders and moves me a step closer to him. Okay. "Please understand that I'm telling you this with no expectations, okay? I just have to tell you because I can't keep being your friend if I don't."

"Did I do something wrong?" He moves in closer now and I can smell him. So good.

"No. It's nothing like that."

"Then what is it?" His finger gently touches my cheek. I tremble and it's obvious. But I don't care. "You can tell me anything," he says.

His green eyes search mine. I get lost in them for the last time. I trust my instincts and abandon my last restraint. "It's just … I love you," the words slip out softly.

And the world stops.

I gaze into Justin's beautiful green eyes a bit longer. This is my last chance to be so close to him like this. I can't look away.

But Justin does.

And I'm alone, even though he's two steps away.

An intruding ring of his phone breaks the silence. He digs in his pocket for the phone and I catch Allison's name flash across the screen.

"Oh. I … I should answer this," he says. I bite my lip as he answers and walks away from me down the opposite side of the street. I bang the back of my head against the wall. Surprisingly, it doesn't hurt. I'm that numb.

Justin walks further away and turns the corner. He's gone. Maybe it's better that way? I wander across the street, grabbing a patio seat at the nearby Nina's Café. A black French bulldog sits, tied to the chair next to me. He walks over and sniffs my hand. My fingers find that spot behind his ears and he gives me a drooly grin. I focus on his soft fur and his mangled bulldog teeth. My mind shuts out the rest of the world. I can't deal with it any longer.

A warm hand pressing down on my shoulder eases me

back into reality. Justin looks down at me. "Want to walk?" he asks. I stand up, making sure to maintain a safe distance from his side.

We walk down Selby Ave. toward the St. Paul Cathedral in silence. The silence doesn't bother me because I don't have anything else to say. I like it. It puts off the final blow to my heart, allowing me to sustain this numb state a bit longer. The dusky sky reveals cool colors of lavender and green. I wander away from Justin, changing our course to walk around the cathedral. His footsteps follow.

A grassy space on top of a hill overlooks the capital. This is where it'll happen. The capital glows brilliant white against the lavender sky. I sit down. At least it'll be a beautiful break.

My heart begs, desperate for the final blow. This pain must end.

Justin sits down next to me. He picks at the grass. "Lucy," he breaks the silence. "I'm sorry." I cringe, my eyes shut with his apology. My heart goes supernova.

"I'm sorry," he says again. He places his hand on my shoulder. "I can't be friends with you anymore, Lucy."

I nod. "I know. I understand." I attempt to shrug as my heart is now dust. "It's probably best for me that way too."

"No, you don't understand." He moves his body so he is in front of me. He waits there until my eyes meet his. "I can't be friends with you anymore because now that I know—"

I put up my hand to make him stop. "You don't have to explain. It's okay."

"No, I do." His brow bends in, frustrated. My nose gives me that telling burn. I will not cry. My fingers grasp at some dirt. "I had no idea you felt that way. All summer you've acted like you only wanted to be my friend."

"That's because I did."

"Lucy, when you love someone you want to be more than friends." He sounds cross. "I'm sorry. This is just so out of the blue. You never let on."

"Well, I didn't want to be like the rest of the girls. I wasn't going to throw myself at you and risk ruining our friendship. It wasn't worth it."

"And now?" he asks.

"Loving you hurts too much. I can't live with so much heartache anymore. It's killing me." The itch turns to tears. He scoots in closer to me. Why does he have to be so nice? It just makes it harder.

"Lucy."

I interrupt him. "I know I ruined everything but it will help me move on." I nod toward the phone in Justin's lap. "If I didn't tell you, I'd be waiting forever. That thing never stops."

Justin leans in close and brushes a stray strand of hair from my forehead. I freeze with his tenderness. What? His lips part into a slight smile as he leans in closer. My world spins in confusion.

"Lucy, you didn't ruin anything." He bends down and presses his lips softly against mine. My lips tingle with his warm touch.

He pulls away from me and chuckles. "You're a funny girl."

My mouth dangles. What just happened? Justin laughs and leans in again. His lips find mine, with more passion, and he wraps his hands around my back and pulls my body close to him. I gently run my fingers through his hair.

I have no idea what I'm doing … but it feels right.

He chuckles, that beautiful chuckle. "Lucy, if you had any idea how crazy you've made me all summer …" He pulls me in close for another kiss. My heart flies and my head is a cloud. I can't process anything.

He kisses my neck and everything in me warms. "You're so beautiful." He kisses my collar bone and I can't help but sigh. "So smart." His lips find mine again. "So unique." He pulls away but I don't want him to stop. Never stop.

His forehead touches mine. "I've loved you all summer." Everything glows. My heart, my arms, feet, my whole body.

The fog slowly clears. Me? He loves me?

He loves me.

"But how?" I ask.

He brushes the strand of hair out of my eyes again. "How can I not? You're amazing. You've got spunk. When you threw that punch in the hospital, I was a goner. Right from the beginning." I open my mouth to debate. He puts his finger against it and smiles. "You are absolutely captivating." He wraps his arms around me in the perfect hug. "You always amazed me. How many times did you drag yourself off the ground all on your own and start over this summer?"

"Figuratively or literally?"

"Both," he answers. "A storm throws you off a roof and runs you down with a tornado and you jump up to check on everyone else." He kisses my forehead.

I pull away and look deep into his green eyes. "Wait, if you liked me then why did you shut me out?"

Justin shakes his head. "Not liked, Lucy. Loved." He

holds my face in his hands and gives me another kiss. "I love you." He beams and his green eyes sparkle in the moonlight. "It feels so good to finally say it."

"I love you too." I'm crying again. I never allowed myself to imagine that it would end this way.

Justin pulls me onto his lap and wipes away my tears. "I'm sorry I was so distant. I was so crazy in love with you, but I had to keep my promise to Jennifer. I had to stay away from you. I couldn't trust myself."

He entwines his fingers through mine. "The day you showed up at work wearing that skirt, I almost lost it. All I could think about was doing this," he leans in and kisses me, starting soft but swelling with so much heat and passion. Goosebumps run up and down my legs. When he stops, I gasp for air. Holy crap.

"Somehow I didn't think that would be work appropriate." He winks.

"I wouldn't have minded. Trust me." I lean into his arms again. He smells so good. "So, is that why you made me do your research? So you wouldn't have to be around me?"

"Partially, but mostly it has to do with these." He lifts my scarred hands to his lips and kisses each mark. "I can't believe I put you in so much danger." My hands are cradled in his warm, calloused palms. Man hands.

He continues, "I was an absolute fool leaving you up on the ladder in that wind. It never occurred to me to consider your weight difference. And, after that, I drove you right into the path of a tornado." His eyes fill with pain. This time I rise up and kiss his lips lightly. He sighs. "I don't deserve you."

"That's largely debatable." I kiss his perfect jaw line.

"Are you sure I didn't go comatose from heartbreak and this isn't a dream?"

Justin hugs me and I rest my head against his chest. His heart beats wildly. "Have any of your dreams ever felt like this?"

"No."

"Then you can rest assured. This isn't a dream."

Justin's phone rings and I jolt. "Allison?" He nods. Somewhere between looking into his green eyes and our kiss I forgot about her. He presses ignore on the phone. "But what about her?" I ask.

Justin sighs. "Well, before she was calling to confirm our date."

"What did you say?"

"Lucy," he covers my hands with his palms. "I told her the truth—I love you." His phone rings again. "She's pretty pissed."

"I bet." I can't help but smile. "Can I ask you something?"

"Always."

"Why did you ask her out on a date if you loved me?"

"A last ditch effort to divert myself." Justin shakes his head. "You were a big surprise in my life. I wasn't planning on meeting someone like you for a long time."

"What do you mean?"

"It's not a bad thing," he reassures. "You threw me off. I always imagined I'd date in college to find my lady." He nudges me. No wonder he always called me Lady. "And then I met you and I knew. I was so overwhelmed with my love for you. I thought taking Allison on a date or two would help me keep my feelings in check until you were ready."

"Well," I let my body melt against his. "I am."

He kisses my head. "It took you a bit though, right?" he teases with a tickle at my side.

I laugh but my arms force him to stop. Tickling is torture.

"You made me so mad." I try to tickle back. His strength holds me off effortlessly. "You drove me crazy in all the wrong ways and then somehow you drove me crazy in all the right ones."

He scrunches his eyebrows together.

"It's been a very confusing summer. That moment, in the water after the race ..."

"Was cruel." He sweeps me off his lap, onto the grass. Pinning me to the ground like he did in the shallow waves. "When you looked at me like that, I almost lost it."

I welcome his weight as he presses into me, lips finding mine. He pulls away only for a moment to say, "I'm never going to be able to stop kissing you."

"Good, don't," I say between breathes. He pushes back into me, hands in my hair while we explore each other's kiss. We make out as the sun slips away, welcoming the darkness and stars.

Justin's mouth eventually moves to my neck and collar bone. He laughs when he finally has the opportunity for air.

"Now there's only one thing left to do—tell Troy," he says as he perches himself up on his elbow, fingers against my back.

"Let's not talk about Troy. He'll be fine. Just tell him you landed the Hill House job. That should be enough of a distraction."

"Eh, maybe. He really thinks he's going to take you on

a date someday."

"Oh?"

"Did you tell him that?"

"No, I just said I needed time."

Justin's laugh bubbles and my butterflies zoom at warp speed. "Lucy," he touches his nose to mine. "A guy would wait for you forever." He brushes my cheek with his fingers and exhales. "Luckily, I don't have to."

I lean into him. "Good." I kiss him again, losing myself in his lips and embrace. I can't believe how comfortable I am in his arms. My heartbeat relaxes to a steady pace. After months of torture, I'm in the right place.

I'll stay here forever.

CHAPTER TWENTY-EIGHT

I'm as light as air when I arrive home. I float into the kitchen to grab a glass of water. Mom and Dad sit at the table, discussing Mom's speech at the gardening expo. They ask me questions about my day, but I'm not at all aware of how I'm answering. All I know is that I am incandescently happy.

Sleep is out of the question, so I wander out back into Mom's garden. A stone path, cold against my bare feet, winds through tall grasses. Small solar lights occasionally accentuate the pathways and the brilliant plant life. Everything's vivid green, an intensity I never noticed before. A grove of evergreens forges a secret garden into a natural courtyard. In the moonlight, the shadows dance between the branches and trees, as though embracing the night in the same tender perfection that I feel in Justin's arms.

I sit down, opening my palm to the sky and watching the moonlight bounce off my smooth scars. The swing creaks as I tap it into motion. How has Mom transformed an acre of suburban grass into an oasis of life?

I've missed so much.

"Lucy?" Mom's voice echoes down the path.

"Over here," I say without thinking. Only a few months ago, I would have gone to great lengths to hide from her. But as I sit here in her beautiful garden, it seems important that she be at my side. She rounds the corner and smiles at me. "It's beautiful, Mom," I say.

Her smile broadens as she holds out her hand to touch a fern's edge. "It's a work in progress." She joins me on the swing cautiously. I smile, letting her know I'm not going to bolt.

"So," Mom says gently. "How does it feel Lucy?"

"The garden feels amazing, Mom. Like I say, beautiful."

Mom laughs. "No, how does *it* feel?" she says this time with more emphasis. She takes my hand and squeezes it. "Being in love. Or, more importantly, to be loved in return?"

"How did you know?"

"The way Justin hung around here all summer, the way he looks at you, how he made you so frustrated." She winks. "It was obvious."

"Really?"

"Oh yes, he's loved you for a while." She nods up toward the house. "Your Dad and I have been wondering how long it would take."

"For?"

"For you to love him back."

I push the swing back and it lets out a loud creak. "Not that long once I figured out …" I search for words.

"Who you are?" Mom offers.

I sigh. She's right. The moment I figured out how to be myself I realized just how much Justin meant to me. She drops my hand and wraps her arm around me, pulling me close.

I don't deserve this from her.

"Mom," I begin. "I'm sorry." I point at the gate to the secret garden. "I've been absolutely horrible to you. I didn't even know this part existed. How have you put up with me?"

"I've always loved you. Lucy," she grasps my hand, "you are effortless for me to love. You always have been and you always will be." She nods toward the garden. "This garden is all about my growing love for you. Every plant, every speck of dirt, every stone and light, it all leads to the source of my love for you."

She stands up and tugs on my hand to follow past the small wooden gate into the little courtyard garden where a red, wooden box nestles among ferns. She opens the box and takes out a palm-sized stone, handing it to me.

"I love you" is written across the stone in orange painted scribbles. I gasp as the memory of sitting with Dad on the front porch surfaces. I'd had the idea to paint rocks for Mom. This was the first rock I'd made for her, hoping she'd make me an "I love Lucy" in return. I'd wanted proof; I wanted her to love me back so badly. I peer back into the box. It's filled with the rest of the rocks I made that day. There are rocks with drawings of the sun, flowers, hearts, random words, or simply stripes.

She kept them all.

I bite my lip. I really, really don't deserve this.

Mom reaches over and hugs me. "I didn't want to show you. You'd have hated me for it."

I shake my head as a tear slides down my cheek. "How can I hate you for this?"

"You must know Lucy that *you* were the reason I got better. Not this garden." I shake my head and she gives me a squeeze. "Honey, you were my reason to keep living through the darkness. My favorite part of every day was seeing your face. I lived for your smiley, goofy grin and when you used to bring me breakfast on the couch." She pauses, wiping away her tears. "The only thing I could actually feel was when you put your hand on my arm or kissed me goodnight. You were my reason to try, every day. I tried for you."

"So, it wasn't my fault?"

"You were the cure, not the cause. That fault was out of everyone's control. My father's death triggered the depression, just two weeks before you were born. Not you." She wraps her arms around me and we sway. "I'm so sorry, Lucinda. I thought you knew."

I pull away from her and look into her blue eyes. "I do now. Thank you." I hug her tightly. "I love you so much, Mom. Always have. I hope you know that too."

She nods and taps the wooden box of rocks. "I know. I've always known. I've been lucky enough to have reminders." She takes off her engagement ring and holds it out to me. It's a pearl on a band with small embedded diamonds. "Let this be your reminder, Lucy."

"No way. Dad will kill me."

"He'd love it. Trust me. Plus, he's wanted to buy me a

real rock for some time now. This will just give him an excuse." She places the ring in my palm and closes my hand around it. "Take it. I want—no—I need you to have it."

I nod and slide the ring onto my right ring finger. Its warmth hugs my finger tight.

"Thank you."

"Just promise me one thing?" She pulls me into one last hug. "Remember you are effortless to love."

She gives me a long squeeze before walking back up the pathway, somehow understanding I need time alone. I sit at the little table in her secret garden and thumb through the box of rocks. A purple asymmetrical face smiles back at me. My entire life circles back to these rocks. Once again, I'm a little girl who loves her mother. Except, this time, there is a huge difference. This time I know she loves me back.

A light smile parts my lips and a light laugh follows. How did I get here? A disastrous summer turns into the most enlightened time of my life.

I found my family again.

I found Justin.

And, more importantly, I found me.

ACKNOWLEDGEMENTS

It's impossible to begin this section of my novel without pausing to say, whoa, I've got so many people to thank!

Always first, readers, thank you for diving into my head and making it to my Acknowledgments page. I hope you love Lucy and Justin as much as I do.

To Greg, my husband, who's done so many dishes and taken our daughters out on many "Daddy and me" dates all to help make my dream come true. He's dried my tears, stood between me and the delete button, and has supported every word I've typed. He's welcomed Lucy and Justin into our family, despite how crazy I sound when I'm talking about them. And, of course, he provides endless inspiration for and proof of love. Thank you, Greg, for being my everything.

Thank you to my daughters, for inspiring me to be myself and putting up with protein bars for breakfast, probably a bit too often.

Thank you to my family, Mom, Dad, Anabel and David, for always believing in me, putting up with stupid stories about bugs and flamingos, and keeping me grounded.

Thank you to my friends, for listening to my crazy journey of publication, dragging me away from my laptop when you knew I needed a break, "liking" my pages, and putting up with my links. Your encouragement has kept me going, truly.

A huge thank you to my super-agent, Jamie Bodnar Drowley, for dealing with my crazy emails where I forget question marks, being the easiest person to talk to on the phone, and always giving me great advice. I couldn't have done this without you. So much love for my agent!

Thank you to my critique partners, Fiona McLaren and Kelley Harvey, for loving Lucy and Justin and giving priceless feedback and time that gave my novel life. Also, a huge shout out to The Off Beats, Katrina Sincek, Catherine Scully, Abby Cavenaugh, Amy Cavenaugh, Kelley Harvey, and Fiona McLaren, who have provided endless support, chats, and laughs on this road to publication. And, Nikki Urang, thank you for our happy hours, logistical conversations, and correlating freak outs. There is no other author I'd want to walk through this oddly parallel journey with.

To Rebecca Yarros and Cassie Mae, thank you for your daily encouragement, wisdom, and reality checks. Every word has meant so much to me.

To my editors, Mandy Schoen and Kate Brauning, thank you for loving my novel as much as I do and for challenging me. It definitely paid off.

To Georgia McBride and the team at Swoon Romance, thank you for all your hard work in making my dream become a reality. You've all been amazing!

Lastly, but perhaps most important, I thank God for kicking me in the butt, telling me to try, and not letting me give up.

Oh, and thank you dark chocolate and Earl Grey tea. You helped me get each word to the page. For real.

ABOUT THE AUTHOR

Lizzy Charles

When Lizzy Charles isn't scrambling to raise her two
spunky toddlers or caring for premature and sick babies as
a neonatal intensive care nurse, she's in a quiet corner
writing or snuggled up with a novel and a few squares of
dark chocolate. She married her high school sweetheart, a
heart-melting musician, so it's no surprise she's fallen in
love with writing contemporary YA romance novels.

Look for *HOW TO DATE A NERD*, *a young adult
contemporary romance, coming from Swoon Romance on
September 24, 2013*

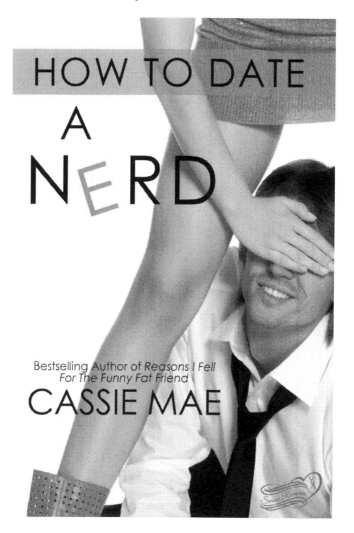

HOW TO DATE
A
NERD

Bestselling Author of *Reasons I Fell
For The Funny Fat Friend*

CASSIE MAE

CHAPTER ONE

If I say I'm sick, don't kiss me!

Rules of keeping up your popular rep:

Number one, the shorter the skirt, the better.

Number two, natural hair color is a thing of the past.

Number three, high heels are an extension of your foot. To go without them would be like losing a toe.

Number four, guys are disposable, and should never be used more than once or for an extended period of time.

And number five, never *ever* reveal you collect *Star Wars* memorabilia, you know every line to *Lord of the Rings*, and you actually know the birthdates of all the *Harry Potter* cast members.

Yeah. I'm a total closeted nerd.

I'm not cool with pity glares in the hallways, painful jabs, and social scars. No thanks. It's much easier to keep my true nature hidden beneath layers of eyeliner, skimpy outfits, and even I must admit to myself, a rockin' body. Though the push-up bras tend to do most of the work.

Welcome to high school. Where everyone tries to be someone else.

Well … everyone except Zak.

Here's the DL on my next-door neighbor. He's labeled King Dork because he wears nerdy shirts and talks in geek code. His front pocket of the plaid overshirt he wears always has at least three or four Pokémon cards in it. And if it's not that, then it's a graphing calculator he has to keep shoving down so it doesn't fall out. There's a *Star Wars* keychain always clipped to the back of his holey jeans and he sometimes carries a Wii controller in his back pocket.

And I've got it bad for the boy.

It's not just the fact he was the one to introduce me to the awesomeness of the Elvish Language, the hidden mysteries of World of Warcraft, and the magical world that lies beyond Platform 9¾, but really, he pulls off sexy geek so damn well! His dark, like super dark eyes and his matching hair that flops around his forehead when he's laughing too hard, combined with his nice height, swoon … he's like the Peter Parker of my high school.

I may be the only person who finds his nerdiness just so hecka irresistible. Everyone else treats him like some dead bug on the sidewalk. I know how it is, and I have no idea how he handles all the verbal abuse.

Middle-school Zoe—Geek Zoe, I like to call her—was made fun of and tormented so much she spent most nights crying into her pillow. High school was the break I was totally looking for. A chance to freakin' rewrite myself into someone who's socially acceptable. Summer before school started, I grabbed loads of magazines and watched all those teen movies that so aren't as awesome as *Star Trek*, but they were for my status education. And apparently, I was doing this popularity thing all wrong. I gotta be like a major bitch to people, and I'll end up getting the hottest guy in the end.

Took some work, but I think I got it down. I should win an Oscar with how awesome I am at the fake personality.

But freak, it's been two years since I was de-geek-ified, and I still find myself trying to stifle the urge to buy Comic-Con tickets, and try not to act jealous when I see Zak dressing up for the event.

Don't get me wrong, my life is pretty darn fantastic and a whole heap of a lot better than the alternative, which is getting my emotional butt kicked around. So the fake persona is definitely worth it.

There's a huge party tonight. Lots of alcohol and boys, but like every party night, I try to show off this hot bod first to my neighbor, who can see straight into my open window.

I strip down to my underwear so Zak can get a good look and turn up the music on my iPod. It's pathetic, I know. I'm trying way too hard to get his attention, but I don't care. It's not like I can flirt with him at school. Social-suicide bomb right there.

Stealing glances out my window into his, I flaunt around my room pretending like I'm getting ready for the party. But I can't get a good view of him and I don't want to be more obvious than I already am.

Nothing.

Huh, maybe he's not …

Yikes! I've reached my LOST playlist and my heart stumbles over itself as I quickly turn the music back down until I can get a more trendy song on.

"Hey, I was listening to that," a voice says from outside

my window. I *knew* he was home. Darn boy ignoring a prancing half-naked girl next door. Gosh, I thought I was doing this right. I adjust my bra to make my boobs look extra luscious, and then smoothly appear in his line of sight.

Zak is at his computer, books piled next to him. He rubs his eyes and blinks a couple times before staring back at the screen, brow furrowed. Totally not looking at me or my boobs.

"What exactly were you listening to?" I ask, using my seductive voice guys, well, *most* guys, fall over.

Looking at me—about time—he shakes his head at my revealing attire before reaching over to a cord I can't see. His blinds shut with a rejected *smack*!

Youch.

I examine my boobs, but there's nothing wrong there. Maybe I have a booger or something.

Nope. No booger, no drool, nothing.

Just me.

Great, now I'm all self-conscious. I'm not gonna even attempt a party appearance.

I throw on my pajamas—the big unflattering ones—and slouch on the bed. Stupid geek boy and the hold he has on me. I shouldn't care what he thinks.

But I do. Because I care what *everybody* thinks.

I sigh and look out the window again. The sun dips below the horizon, casting orange and yellow streaks across Zak's blinds, like something out of *Harry Potter*. Just super full of cool magic beans. I wonder if Zak's still sitting there at his computer, typing away or plunging his nose into one of his thousands of books.

I shake my head. What does it matter what he's doing? I. Should. Not. Care.

I hop off the bed, slam my own blinds shut, and whip the curtains together. My gaze flicks to the shelves lining the wall. They have been carefully constructed to conceal accusing material, with colorful doors that slide across them, revealing some things, and hiding others. Out of habit, I check over my shoulder before I slide open one of the doors, hiding the lines of lip glosses and compact mirrors and opening the section of the shelf holding several books about the X-Men.

I quickly grab the desired book and a flashlight and slam the door shut again. Some of the lip glosses topple over, but I make no attempt to straighten them. Must get under the covers stat! I curl up in the middle of my bed and throw the comforter over myself.

My sanctuary lies here as I open the book I've read thousands of times and purge my mind with paragraphs about The Dark Phoenix. Jean Grey is my idol. No one will ever know, but I base most of my wardrobe off her.

I don't know how long it's been before my phone buzzes on my nightstand. Yeah, my mind turns off to the rest of the world when I "nerd-out." I turn off the flashlight and pull the comforter off my head, keeping the book hidden as I reach over for the cell.

My stomach used to flutter whenever I read Cody's name on the caller I.D., but now I feel nothing. I really don't want to talk to my current boyfriend. He'd just call me some absurd pet name and ask where I was. So I let voicemail grab it.

I hear the text jingle a few minutes later as I am carefully placing my book back on its shelf.

Where is ur sxy ass???? U better get here b4 any more chicks hit on me.

Ugh. I think his ego can keep him company for a while. Still, I let him know who's in charge of this relationship.

Another rule that's off the record: stay in control of all the boys you let kiss you. That way they don't end up in your pants. Nasty.

I'm sick. Thx so much 4 ur concern.

There's no response, but I don't care. It won't be the first boyfriend who found someone new before breaking it off with me. I do *not* put out. Though, I don't care if they tell people I do. Helps with the rep without me actually having to do the gross part. Score!

I kinda feel bad for the girl who ends up in his arms tonight. Cody is a totally status thing. I use him and he uses me. We both know it, and neither of us really cares. It's been about three weeks, so we've pretty much hit our limit anyway. He is a good kisser though. I'll give him that one.

I look at the closed curtains, thinking of another boy with amazing kissing abilities, but I shove the thought from my mind before I lose it completely.

"Hey, I thought you were going out tonight?" My younger sister waltzes in and plops on my bed. Her dark brown hair has been curled into corkscrews and she's covered in pounds of makeup. She's wearing a blue shirtdress with a thick belt around her middle, making what little bosom she has look bigger. She's only fourteen, but in this outfit, and that hair, she could pass for my age. I raise my eyebrows at her.

"And you thought you'd tag along?"

"Mom and Dad won't know, and I'll leave you alone. I promise."

I shake my head. "I'm not going. So you can't either."

"Why not?"

6

"There's gonna be alcohol, Sierra."

She gives me a look that says "You're the biggest hypocrite." She's totally right so I play the tattletale card.

"And because I'll tell Mom and Dad you went out while they were gone."

She stands and smiles. "You know, if you're going to start tossing around threats, I'd be a little more worried about what *I'd* tell them about *you*."

I give her my best impression of Gollum on crack. "Fine, go out. See if they even let you in without me."

She tosses her hair over her shoulder and narrows her eyes. "Fine. I will." She storms out of my room and my gut tells me to go after her, but my pride blocks my exit.

I sit and catch my breath before I finally get out into the hallway.

"Sierra, wait!" I call down the stairs. Hopefully I've caught her in time. Letting my fourteen-year-old sister go to an all-night alcohol fountain party wouldn't exactly make me a responsible older sister, even though I never really fit into that category. Still seems wrong to at least not try to get her to stay.

"Sierra!" I get to the bottom of the staircase and she comes out from the formal living room, scaring the poo out of me.

"Someone's here to see you," she says bitterly as she pushes me to the side to get upstairs. Instead of socking her in the butt, like I want to, I kink my neck to see around the wall. What the hell is Cody doing here? His back is turned to me and he's holding something in his hand. I duck back upstairs to change into my sexy pajamas. No way is he seeing me in these old baggy ones.

I grab the black silk shorts and cami and hurry and slip

them on. I let my fake deep red hair down—you know, Jean Grey—so it cascades down my back and I quickly run my fingers through it. I don't worry about makeup, just slab some gloss on my lips. After all, I am "sick." But girls like me have to look good at their worst.

I throw a light blanket over my shoulders and walk back to Cody. He still has his back to the entryway.

Okay Geek Zoe, it's been fun, but Cody can't know you exist.

I take another deep breath and get ready for my act. "What are you doing here?" I ask, letting my phony anger soak into my voice.

He turns around and his eyes widen at my ensemble.

See? There's nothing wrong with *me*. It's Zak who has a problem.

"Uh …" he stutters as he clears his head. "I thought maybe since you were too sick to go out, we'd stay in." He holds up a movie, which I'm surprised to see is a total chick flick. Gross. But popular Zoe likes that crap.

"Do you feel guilty about something?" I've been through this stuff before. He's totally trying to make up for something he did that he shouldn't have done.

Oh well, time for a new boyfriend anyway.

His eyes lower to the floor and I take in a deep breath and wait for it. The inevitable "I cheated on you" or "I found someone else."

"I'm sorry about that text. I didn't mean to make you upset. I was only kidding, really."

I stare at him, not able to erase the shock from my face. "Huh?"

"I know you haven't had the best luck when it comes to your exes. I was being stupid. Forgive me?" He throws me a puppy-dog face.

Now I'm really thrown and I'm not sure how to respond. So I just mumble incoherencies.

"Um … I guess … sure … uh-huh …"

"So," he says, furrowing his brow and crossing over to me, "we're cool?"

I give him a nod, but then remember I have a part to play. I fold my arms across my waist and gaze up into his handsome face. His dark hair has been tousled across his forehead and frames his deep brown eyes perfectly. He's getting a five o'clock shadow on his cheeks and chin. Yeah … definitely a status thing with him.

"Don't treat me like that. I deserve better." I don't really mean that. In fact, right now I deserve a lot worse.

"I promise it won't happen again."

He takes me into his arms, but I keep mine folded, not responding to his hug. I do let out a fake sigh of defeat and say into his chest, "Okay."

He pulls back and tilts my face to slap a kiss on me. As usual, I remove myself from the embrace—metaphorically—and think about more pleasant company. Maybe Obi-Wan, but not like old fart Obi-Wan. Heck, I'd take Neville Longbottom before I made out with an old guy, even if he did have The Force.

A different kind of urgency pushes from behind Cody's lips and I'm snapped back into reality. I pull away, afraid of what he's thinking.

"I'm sick, remember," I say, wiping my soggy lips with the tips of my fingers. Gag.

"I don't care," he says as he tries to pull me in again. I put my hands on his chest and push back, leaning my head away from his face.

"I do." I use my stern and controlling voice, but it's not

fake this time. He better keep those pervy lips away from me.

He looks like he wants to argue, but he lets go. I almost let out the huge sigh of relief I'd been holding in my chest, but I catch it before I do. I mean, for all he knows, I'm a girl who lets just about anyone between her legs. He entwines his fingers with mine and mumbles, "So … do you want me to go?"

"Yeah. I don't want you to catch it."

"You don't sound sick." His voice is barely audible.

"Well, I am."

He pauses a moment and looks behind me, into the hallway. I crane my neck to see what he's looking at, but I'm forced back into an awkward embrace, his mouth trying to swallow me whole.

I can't move. His fingers latch into my spine and yank some of my hair. *What the hell is he doing?* I start clawing at his body, trying to break free from his strong arms.

"Holy shit, Cody!" I shout the second I get his face away from me. "What the hell was that?"

"Come on, Zoe." His hands continue to dig into my back. I wish I would've kept the baggy pajamas on because I'm sure he's drawing blood.

"Get. Off. Me." I'm wiggling around, hoping he'll let me go, but his grip tightens.

He smiles. Not one that's sexy or anything, but a very nasty and uber-creepy grin. If my legs weren't trapped, I'd knee him right in the balls. "Every guy you've been with only dated you to get in your pants." His grip tightens again and I try to keep my face as far away from his as I can. "You know it. I know it. You can't be mad at me for doing exactly what you were doing."

"Which is what?" I spit. He really needs to let go before I go bat-shit crazy on him. This is getting really scary.

"Dating each other 'til we got something out of it."

I can't find my heart anymore. My eyes fill up and the tears almost spill over. He's right.

Which sucks. I'm so stupid. I should have expected at least one of the boys I dated to be upset about not getting some, so upset they'd take it into their own hands.

"I want you to leave me alone."

"I helped you out. How many people get jealous whenever I touch you?" He reaches up and brushes my hair from my face. I'm tempted to bite his finger off. "How many clubs have you gotten into because I know someone?" His lips are near inches away from mine, his hand now locked around my jaw so I can't move. "I think since I've done my part, it's only fair you do yours."

My lips form obscenities around his as he mashes them against me. I'm wiggling like crazy, trying with every bit of strength I have to get away from him. I think I got in a good hit somewhere, but he's not letting go.

He bites down on my bottom lip, causing a yelp of pain to escape my mouth. I keep quiet after that and he moves his kisses to my cheeks, my neck, my chest, while I still try to get out of his grasp.

Oh my gosh! Is this really happening? What is he going to do to me? How far will this go? I try to detach myself—again metaphorically—but it's impossible. No one has ever attacked me like this before, and tears start to leak out the corners of my eyes.

One of his hands clasps my butt cheek as he moves me upstairs. My stomach plummets as I hope against all hope Sierra stays in her room. She cannot see this. I don't want her to see this.

We get to the top of the landing and I hear a doorknob turn, but it's not from Sierra's room. It's the front door which is in plain view from where Cody has me pinned. Cody hears it too and he shoots upright, letting go of me long enough so I can fix my top before someone walks in.

"Hello?"

I'm too relieved to be confused about Zak standing in the doorway. I jog down the stairs, coming within inches of his body, but stop myself from hugging him. My arms drop and I pretend I was going to scratch my head, looking like an idiot. His puzzled face would be comical if it weren't for the tense atmosphere. I take a small step away as Cody descends the staircase. I search deep inside my voice box for a cheery tone and blink away the water from my eyes. "Hey, uh … my dad'll be home in a minute and he can get you that book you wanted. I'm not sure where he put it. You can sit over there if you wanna wait."

I'm so glad Zak knows when to act stupid and when to play along. "Thanks, Zoe." He goes into the living room and sits down, not taking his eyes off me and my now *very* ex-boyfriend. No way will that guy ever get near me again. Cody looks like he just got attacked by fire ants with how red he is. He clears his throat and looks at me.

"I better get back to the party. You comin'?"

"No." Hell no. I don't look him in the eyes, because now they scare the crap out of me. "I'm sick, remember?"

"Your loss." He shrugs out the front door and I almost break into tears right there in the entryway. But Zak's presence shuts me off from losing it.

"Are you all right?" he asks, getting off the couch and stepping closer to me. I quickly try to erase the pain and horror from my face, putting my calm mask on.

"Yeah. I'm just not feeling well, like I told Cody. So, I'm going to go upstairs and sleep it off."

"Zoe, don't pretend like I don't know what just happened."

I feel all the color drain from my body. So much for looking calm. "I don't know what you mean."

Zak bores his eyes into mine. I fold my arms again and stare back. He's not going to get me to admit to anything. I'm not even sure what happened. It's like my mind can't catch up with the reality of it all.

"Well, next time I see him attack you like that, I'm calling the cops."

Agh! What the crap? How did he …? I gaze out the window behind him and I see he has a perfect view of the living room if he's in his kitchen.

"It's nothing to worry about," I lie. "Really, it's always like that."

"If that's the case, I'm calling the cops right now."

"Wait," I say, coming up short on excuses. I don't know why I care so much, or why I'm giving Zak the attitude, especially since he just saved me, but I find myself trying to keep up my fake persona. "Don't call the cops. I just … uh … we got in a fight, and he wanted to make up. And … uh, I wasn't exactly done being mad at him, you know?" Great, now I sound like a rambling fool.

Zak studies my face. His eyes search mine for any deception, but since what I said isn't completely untrue, he lets it go.

"Okay. Sorry I barged in. I thought it was a problem."

"No, there's no problem."

He studies my face once again before going out the

door. I hadn't realized I'd been holding my breath until the hot air escapes my nose. I jog upstairs, slam my bedroom door and put on my baggy pajamas before curling up under my sheets and crying myself to sleep.

Also look for THE FUNERAL SINGER, *a young adult contemporary romance, coming from Swoon Romance on September 24, 2013*

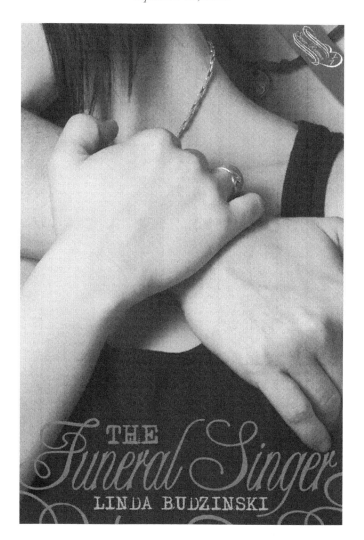

CHAPTER ONE

Normally I didn't attend my father's funerals unless I was scheduled to sing, but it wasn't every day Dad buried a rock star.

No way would I miss Mick Nolan's service. It was by far the coolest thing to ever happen at Martin's Family Mortuary. I rifled through my closet full of black dresses— eight in all, but none quite right for today. I wanted to look good, but of course, this was a funeral, not a concert, and I *was* in mourning. Mick was my second favorite member of The Grime, behind bassist Zed Logan.

Ah, bass players. Soulful, brooding, background guys.

I finally settled on a knee-length dress with long, sheer, flowing sleeves. Its neckline dipped low enough to be sexy but not, I hoped, disrespectful.

Turned out, I shouldn't have worried. Downstairs looked like the set of a music video. Girls in miniskirts, midriff tops, and strappy heels pranced around guys in torn jeans and t-shirts. A sea of tattooed arms, legs, bellies, and backs clashed against the lobby's soothing rose-and-tan striped wallpaper.

My dad walked around solemnly shaking each person's hand and intoning over and over, "Thank you for coming," and "So sorry for your loss." His dark blue suit, which usually helped him blend into the background, had the opposite effect, and he stuck out like … well, like a funeral director at a rock concert.

"There you are, Melanie." My mother thrust a wreath of red and white chrysanthemums into my arms and pointed me toward the chapel. "Set this with the other arrangements and then head out front to help Dawn hand out the programs."

The wreath was so large I could barely see around it, but I knew every inch of the chapel as well as I knew every word of "Candle in the Wind." I wound my way down the aisle and toward the front, where Mick's Grecian-style urn, hand-painted with The Grime's logo, sat on top of his keyboard. I waded through dozens of wreaths, sprays, and bouquets until I found a place to squeeze in the new addition. The sweet scent made me dizzy. Never before had I seen so many flowers. Of course, never before had we held a service for someone famous.

I stopped by the urn and said a quick prayer. Mick had overdosed on cocaine at age twenty-one. My first reaction when I'd heard the news—and I'm not proud of this—was: *What would happen to the band?* That was almost a month ago, and there had been a small, private service a few days later. Today's event, "A Celebration of Mick's Life," was open to everyone.

As I turned to leave, I spotted an older woman seated in

the front row of the chapel, fingering a delicate gold cross around her neck. I'd read somewhere that Mick's grandmother had raised him. That had to be her. I turned, hoping to escape before she noticed me, but she stood and called out. "Excuse me, sweetheart. Do you know how long it will be before the service begins?"

I glanced at the clock on the back wall. "About twenty minutes." If I were my father, I'd offer her some water or ask if she needed anything while she waited. Maybe I'd even sit down and take her hands in mine and ask how she was holding up. Instead, I turned and ran.

Avoid close family. That was my rule, and though I'd been to hundreds of funerals in the past few years, I'd somehow managed to follow it—most of the time, anyway.

The trick was to sneak up to the chapel's balcony just before the service began, perform my songs, and disappear as soon as it ended. Let my dad deal with the dearly beloved. The *bereaved.* The very word felt heavy, loaded down with a heartache and pain and emptiness I had no clue how to handle.

I made my way down the chapel aisle, through the lobby, and outside onto the porch, where Dawn, our receptionist, shot me a panicked look and handed me half of her stack of memorial programs. "Thank goodness you're here. This place is a madhouse."

The Grime hadn't had a hit in almost two years, but they still had plenty of fans here in their hometown, just across the river from Washington, D.C. The line wound all the way down and around the end of our block. "No way all these people will fit inside the chapel," I said. "Dad'll have to come out and shut the doors soon."

Dawn pointed toward a pair of cop cars parked across

the street. "That's why I called them to come out early." The police normally didn't arrive until the end of the service, so they could escort the funeral procession to the cemetery.

"You don't think we'll have any problems, do you?"

Dawn looked around. The crowd was large, but tame. "No, but better safe than sorry."

A few girls from my high school called to me from halfway back in the line. "Hi, Mel! Love your dress!"

I pretended not to hear them. They treated me like the Freaky Funeral Girl at school, and now they wanted to act as though we were best buds?

I scanned the parking lot. Only one news van—our local Channel 4. Too bad. I'd hoped TMZ would show up, or MTV, or at least Entertainment Tonight. Then again, Mick had two strikes against him: First, The Grime's second album had tanked, after which Rolling Stone had labeled them a "one-hit wonder," and second, he played keyboards. Keyboardists got no respect.

A woman with poofy blond hair rushed over, signaling a cameraman to follow. "Hey, you! Girl with the programs! Can you tell us where the band members are?"

I shook my head. "They're not here yet." The Grime's crew had come by this morning to set up their equipment and tune their guitars, but the band was nowhere to be seen.

The woman sighed and turned back to her cameraman. "Fine. Let's keep doing fan interviews. One of these idiots is bound to have something interesting to say."

They cornered a girl with pink-streaked hair and a pierced lip. "Hello, I'm Andrea Little, Channel 4 News. Mind if we ask a few questions?" About halfway through the interview, the girl started sobbing, her makeup forming two dark tracks down her cheeks. Now there was a girl who didn't go to many funerals. Should've gone easy on the mascara and made sure it was super waterproof.

My mom was big on the value of crying. She said holding back could make you sick, and that her job as a grief counselor was to get people to let it all out. That was one thing we had in common. When I was singing up in that balcony, I wanted to make people *feel* something—sadness, anger, relief—whatever it was they needed.

One thing was for certain: Pink Hair Girl didn't need help from me, my mom, or anyone else. As I watched, she fished a tissue out of her bag, wiped her cheeks, and blew her nose with a loud honk. Andrea Little backed up and grimaced, but she motioned at the cameraman to zoom in closer.

Dad came out and called over one of the cops. "We're at capacity," he told him. "We need to shut the doors."

"But, Dad …" I said.

"Fire marshal's rules, honey." He pointed to the speakers mounted at both ends of the porch. "We'll pipe the sound from the service out here. Everyone is more than welcome to stay and listen."

"But, Dad, the band members aren't here yet. We have to let them in."

Dad glanced at his watch and stepped back inside. "Right. When they show up, send them into the chapel. But no one else."

While the cops explained to the crowd what was happening, Dawn and I walked around and passed out the rest of the programs, souvenirs for people to take home even though they couldn't get in. As I handed out the last few, I spotted my best friend, Lana, making her way through the crowd. Apparently she'd gotten the memo about the miniskirts.

"This is insane," she said when she reached me. "Mom had to drop me off a block away."

I nodded toward her oversized purse. "Let me guess. Your Randy-approved outfit is in there." No way would her uber-strict stepdad have let her out of the house wearing so little.

Lana grinned and opened her bag to reveal a full-length black skirt crammed inside. "What Mr. Control Freak doesn't know won't hurt him."

"Well, you look great, as always." I led her up the stairs onto the porch. "It's standing-room only inside. Dad shut the doors, so I'll have to sneak you in."

She ran her fingers through her tight blond curls and adjusted her sweater to bare her right shoulder. "Is Bruno in there?" Lana was obsessed with The Grime's lead singer, Bruno Locke. He seemed like an arrogant, self-absorbed jerk to me, but then again, that would fit right in line with her dating record.

I shook my head. "No sign of the band yet."

Just as I opened the door for her, a limo pulled up. It was longer, sleeker, and somehow even a little blacker than my dad's limos. And unlike my dad's cars, it had shiny chrome bumpers and chrome-spoked wheels.

Lana grabbed my hand. "That must be them."

A huge guy with a shaved head stepped out from the driver's seat. Andrea and her cameraman rushed over. "Back up," he yelled at them. "The band will not do any interviews. You can film them walking in, but they won't stop to talk."

I held my breath as lead guitarist Jon Marks and drummer Ty Walker stepped out. Next came Bruno, and Lana squeezed my hand so tightly I thought my fingers might break. Bruno paused for a moment and eyed the crowd. When he noticed the camera, he tilted his head and gave his signature sneer. Oh, please. Couldn't he give it a rest, even for one day?

Finally, out stepped Zed. Shorter than he looked in their videos but otherwise even better in person. The messy dark hair, the brown eyes, the scar on the left side of his chin. So hot.

I held the door open and they filed past.

Zed shot me a half-smile. "Thank you."

"You too."

You too? Ugh. Real smooth.

16965984R00205

Made in the USA
Middletown, DE
28 November 2018